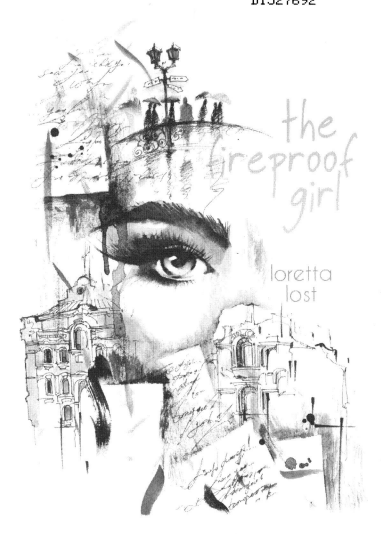

the
fireproof
girl

loretta
lost

ISBN-13: 978-1539352860
ISBN-10: 1539352862
Copyright © 2016 Loretta Lost.
Cover design by Damonza.

Table of Contents

Love is a fire.
But whether it is going to warm your
hearth or burn down your house,
you can never tell.

- *Joan Crawford*

Prologue

I knew he was going to be a powerful man from the moment I first met him. It wasn't just because the earth literally trembled when he touched my hand. We were in Southern California and that was known to happen.

It was because he smiled.

Everyone around us was alarmed, gasping and ducking under furniture as picture frames crashed to the floor. Their faces all displayed naked fear and terror. But there he was, in the middle of all that, a calm young boy, gazing at me with the gravity of an old man. His stare was so heavy that I could swear the earth was standing completely still, only under his feet.

"Do you always smile during natural disasters?" I whispered.

"Only when I survive them," he responded.

When I see him in my dreams, to this day, that is the same smile he wears. Confident, unaffected, and completely unshakable. The earth itself had no power over him. I knew then, and I never once forgot over the years to come, that Cole Hunter was something special. He was the kind of boy who could walk right *into the fire and the flood and come out unscathed.*

He would come out stronger.

I was thirteen years old at the time, and had an overly active imagination, but I couldn't shake the feeling in my gut that he was somehow responsible for the earthquakes. I know, it sounds like a load of nonsense. But if you had seen the look in his dark eyes, you would have felt the same way.

You would have known that boy was capable of anything.

Chapter One

sophie shields, 2016

Lifting the large mug to my face, I dump half its contents down my throat. As I lower the beverage back to my desk, there is a slight tremor in my fingertips, but that is to be expected when you consume enough caffeine every morning to kill a small child.

It is difficult to be awake. It is difficult to be here.

I can always tell how long I will tolerate being in a place by the number of books on the shelves. When I've read them all, it's usually time to move on. Glancing at the bookshelf in my boyfriend's bedroom, I can't help wondering why I've stayed here long enough to read all of the books multiple times. My job prohibits me from having any access to the Internet whatsoever, so books are all I have.

For the first time in my life, I feel trapped.

I'm stuck. Actually stuck. Me—the queen of running away.

Of course, I could always buy new books, but that has never been my style. Collecting sentimental possessions would anchor me to my surroundings. If I let myself get attached, when I inevitably need to leave, it will only hurt more for every item I leave behind. This is a lesson I had to learn the hard way.

Turning away from the bookshelf, my eyes fall on the dreary city outside our bedroom window. A thick, heavy fog blankets the capital, obscuring the buildings from view. Although it is gloomy, I am grateful that I don't have to look at the architecture this morning. I always remember similar buildings being sketched in pencil on sheets of white paper, by a pair of strong hands. I see superior buildings being born in a pair of stormy eyes, and the wheels spinning in a complex mind, determined to bring abstract ideas to reality.

My brother. I exhale sharply.

Every time I think of Cole, I feel like I have been punched in the gut.

When I don't think of him, it's a little better. I only have the vaguely empty sensation one might feel after losing a kidney or a lung. The body can function without a few spare chunks of meat, but there is an awkward period of adjustment before the loss becomes normal—before one stops wondering whether they really can go on with their insides mutilated.

When will this become normal for me? Five years have passed. I thought I would have made peace with his absence by now, but I am always conscious that something has been ripped away. At first, we continued to exchange letters, and that made things bearable—but when Cole stopped replying a few months ago, I started to lose my mind. Does he still care? I've written him dozens of letters, and they've all gone unanswered.

This radio silence is killing me.

"Don't be selfish, Sophie," a male voice says from behind me in the room.

I am startled from my thoughts as I turn around to see the muscular, half-naked man tangled up in the bed sheets. Zack reaches up to rub his eyes before opening them, and brushes some of his disheveled, sandy-brown hair away from his face so that he can look at me. He smiles. Lifting himself up on his elbow, he gestures to the alarm clock on our nightstand.

"Big day today," he reminds me. "I'm gonna need a cup of that good stuff, too."

If it were any other man on earth, I would toss my ceramic mug at his head for implying that I should make him coffee. But Zack recently lost a leg in Afghanistan, and some days he can't even get out of bed due to pain—and not just the physical kind. I know that the simple act of making him coffee makes his day a little easier to face.

"I think we're out of grounds," I say guiltily as I stare at the few drops remaining in my mug.

"Of course we are, you coffee-slut," he says

teasingly. "I picked up a new can. It's above the fridge."

My shoulders relax with some relief. "You're a saint. I could really use another cup." As I head to the kitchen, I try to convince myself that this is why I stick around. Zack isn't that bad. His skills as an ex-sniper might be useless in this boring civilian life, but at least he has the good sense to remember to pick up coffee. Standing on my tip-toes, I open the cupboard and retrieve the canister. I can already smell the delicious, freshly ground beans as I peel back the lid, but I am startled by a gleam of light that causes me to nearly drop the can on the floor.

In the center of the coffee can is an opened velvet box, revealing a diamond engagement ring. My eyes grow narrowed in confusion as I examine the hunk of clear rock for a long moment.

"It's all I could afford," Zack says as he stands in the doorway behind me. "I hope you like it."

Turning back to look at him over my shoulder, I try to force out some words. "This is…?"

He smiles as he limps forward to place his hands around my waist. "Yeah." His hands are large. They always startle me with their largeness when they encounter my body. "I thought you were going to run out of coffee days ago and find it sooner, but you've been living at Starbucks. So, whaddaya say, Soph? Be my wife?"

"Zack—"

"Do you want me to drop down to one knee? It's a little difficult with the prosthetic, but I will."

He grasps ahold of the kitchen counter and

begins to lower himself to one knee with a grunt, but I turn around and grab his arm to keep him standing.

"Hey," I say softly. "Let's just sit for a minute, okay?" I place the coffee canister down so I can lead Zack over to his little IKEA breakfast table. As I sink into my chair, I place my head in my hands and slowly knead my temples. This is why I should have left months ago. I knew that things were getting too serious.

There is so much that Zachary doesn't know about me. He doesn't know what I really do for a living. He doesn't know *half* the hell I've been through. He doesn't know that the reason he has trouble finding work is because my employers want me to have someone who can protect me at home, at all times. He doesn't know that I'm already married.

Although, I suppose, that was a long time ago—under a different identity.

It's funny how nostalgic I can get about a piece of paper. It was just a legal contract for the most part, done out of necessity. We had no hope of having a *real* marriage.

But deep down, it was always real to me. Too real.

"Sophie, talk to me," Zack is saying with anxiety in his voice. "I need an answer."

I shake my head slowly, unsure of how to respond. Nausea makes my stomach turn at the thought of another wedding ceremony. Who would I even invite? I have no friends. I have no family. I have no brother.

Zack reaches across the table to take my hand in

his. "I know that things aren't great right now. You're upset about Cole, aren't you? You haven't heard from him?"

My eyes widen and I pull my hand away abruptly. Am I that transparent? I guess I'm always upset about Cole, lately. Standing up, I move back to the kitchen. "Do you still want that coffee?" I ask him briskly.

"No. I never wanted any. I just wanted you to find the engagement ring," Zack explains, with hurt in his voice.

I busy myself with going through the motions of making coffee anyway, and ignore the diamond ring as I scoop grounds from the perimeter of the can.

"Sophie, will you stop for a minute!" Zack exclaims. "We need to talk about this. There's something I need to tell you, about your brother…"

If thinking about Cole is difficult, talking about him is worse.

It would be easier if I were *just* missing an internal organ; I wouldn't mind a little shortness of breath while taking the stairs. It would be easier if I were *just* an amputee, like Zack, always trying to stand on my phantom limb and crashing to the floor. It would be simple. Anything would be better than being so emotionally crippled and numb that I need to stay constantly caffeinated or intoxicated to get through the day. I haven't been happy in five years, but these last few months have been especially brutal.

"I spoke to him," Zack says finally. "I asked his permission."

"What?" I snap, turning around in horror.

"I called your brother a few days ago and asked for your hand in marriage. I know he's not your real brother, but since you don't have a father, or any other family for me to ask…"

"You asked *Cole?*" I say hoarsely. "You called *Cole?*"

"Yes. He gave me his blessing. He said he would be there at our wedding."

I can't help it. A burst of crazy laughter escapes my chest. "You called him?" I murmur, my voice incredulous. "Seriously?!" For a moment, I fear for Zack's safety. Ex-military, rifle specialist and all, he is missing a leg, and Cole is a force to be reckoned with. At the memory of the stormy anger in my brother's dark eyes, my heart begins to pound faster and my jaw clenches. I haven't heard his voice in so long, and I am jealous that Zack is permitted to use a cell phone so casually. "Did you ask him why he stopped writing to me?"

"He's been busy…" Zack begins.

"Busy!" I repeat with outrage. "He once promised that he would write to me on toilet paper, even if he didn't have time to wipe his ass."

Zack seems surprised at this, but he lowers his eyes. "People don't always keep their promises, Sophie."

"Cole does," I say with more vehemence than I intend. "The only person who has kept *every* promise he's ever made to me is my brother. And I don't understand why he's stopped now."

"He said he's not feeling well," Zack adds hesitantly.

"Not feeling well?" I ask slowly, testing the words. Cole would have to be deathly sick to stop writing me. Even if he were, he'd surely ask his assistant to send me a message. And it's been so long… No, the only real reason for the lack of contact must be that he's given up on me. He's letting go of his past and pushing me out of his life. Understandably so. I reach up to rub my forehead before sighing and moving toward the bedroom. "I'm going to get ready for work."

"What about my proposal?" Zack asks.

I had completely forgotten. Shaking my head, I shrug, trying to find the least awkward way to respond. "No. I can't. I won't—I don't want to… I'm sorry." Okay, that was still pretty awkward. With my cheeks flushed in frustration, I move to exit the room.

"Sophie!" Zack says angrily. "You can't walk out on a conversation like this. At least give me a fucking reason."

"I don't have time," I call back as I grab my keys and purse. When I turn around, I am startled to find Zack standing very close. He is looming over me, all six feet three inches of him, and blocking my path. I take a step back instinctively, wondering if he is going to hurt me.

Zack grabs my shoulders with his very large hands and looks me squarely in the face. My insides constrict in fear. Recoiling and twisting away violently, I toss my purse aside and lift my keys to defend myself.

"Sophie," Zack says in surprise, lifting his hands in a gesture of peace. "I'm not… I just want to say a few words before you leave." He pauses, looking at me in amazement. "You really think I'd hurt you?"

"I don't know," I say quietly, but I have already been glancing around the room and searching for every item within reach that could be used as a weapon.

Zack sighs and moves to sit on the bed, looking defeated. "You know, you're right to refuse. You shouldn't marry me."

Taking several deep breaths, I lower my keys. "Then why'd you ask?"

"You've been so distant. I didn't know what to do. I thought I was losing you."

He isn't totally wrong. Feeling guilty, I move to sit beside him on the bed, and we share an uncomfortable silence.

"I screwed up, Sophie," he says softly. "It's been eating me up inside, and I can't keep it to myself anymore. I've done something really terrible to you."

"Zack…"

"I lied to you," he says haltingly. "I have been lying to you."

When he turns to look at me, I realize that my stomach is doing flip-flops and my heart is beating erratically. "Zachary. Tell me. Fucking tell me what you lied about."

"Your brother—he has been writing you letters. But I kept them from you."

"What?"

Zack nods, unable to meet my eyes. "I was jealous. He's this big shot CEO and I am lucky if I get freelance work now and then to keep us afloat. I read some of the letters he sent you, the ones you kept in the nightstand… I can tell that he's in love with you. You and I never have conversations like that. I just wanted you to talk to *me* for a change. I hoped that if I kept the letters it would improve our relationship. I thought that if you kept communicating with him… you wouldn't want to be with me anymore. You would never want to get married."

My head begins to throb and I press my palms against my eyes. "Zack. God." Anger surges inside me, but I manage to just barely keep a cork on it. "Just... dammit. Did you read the recent letters? Is he okay?" I try to appear normal, but on the inside, I am paralyzed by the weight of this news. My brain hurts with the effort it takes to process this, and my emotions are going haywire. I try to breathe slowly and calmly to keep from hyperventilating.

"He… doesn't seem to be doing well. There are issues with the business," Zachary explains. "He was saying that he thought someone was trying to sabotage his work, or maybe even hurt him."

"Who?" I demand. "Did he say who?"

"He doesn't know. He was asking if you could fly to L.A. to help him out. Do you see why I didn't want to show you those letters? I had this sick feeling that if you went to California, I would lose you forever."

I clench my fists until my nails dig into my palms. "Zack, my brother's in trouble—and you *hid this* from me?"

"I can't tell you how sorry I am," he says softly.

"You asshole!" I hiss as tears of rage flood my eyes. Adrenaline courses through me, and I rise to my feet, hands twitching with the desire to punch him in the face. It takes great discipline to restrain my anger, and my whole body trembles with the effort. "Cole is the only family I have, and you *kept him from me!*"

"I know," he says with pleading eyes. "To be honest with you, Soph, I feel threatened by him. Ever since I lost my leg, I've just felt… inadequate. I feel like I'm only half a man." He places a hand on his thigh to illustrate his point, and to remind me that there is no flesh and bone under his sweatpants.

Of course. Every time Zack does something to upset me, he blames it on the fact that he is an injured vet. This one's going a little too far. I know that it does affect him, and I've seen him completely break down and cry on occasion, but I have been there for him. I have held him and reassured him, and forgiven all of his transgressions due to this overused excuse. I am starting to realize that being an amputee shouldn't mean he automatically gets to be a dick. He doesn't get to take away part of me just so he can feel more whole.

"You're just so *close* to him, Soph," Zachary says as though it gives him pain. "And you guys have so much history together! Can you forgive my jealousy? I just didn't want to lose you."

I find myself staring at him with my face twisted up in disgust. "You're a real piece of work, Zack. Cole saved my life. I don't know if I'd even be here if it weren't for him. He's the only person who ever... It doesn't matter. Do you know how miserable

I've been? You let me think that my brother had abandoned me, just like my parents did."

"I know. I've watched you getting depressed and I knew I was responsible. I just didn't know how to stop lying. I wanted you to have no one else, so that you would need me," Zachary admits. "This isn't like me, Sophie. I haven't been the same since I got home. I'm really fucked up in the head… but I do love you."

Wrapping my arms around my middle, I try to fight back my anger, shock, indignation, and above all, overwhelming relief. *He never stopped writing to me.* Unshed tears of joy replace my tears of rage, but there is no time to let them fall. Once I break the seal and let a few tears slip, I'll never be able to withhold the rest. Besides, I won't give Zachary the satisfaction of seeing me cry.

Lifting my chin proudly, I glare at him while mentally planning my trip to California. I don't care if I lose my job—Cole is all that matters now. I inwardly calculate how many of my belongings I can quickly grab before rushing out of Zachary's apartment. It's been a while since I had to abandon ship in a hurry, but I'm pretty sure I remember how it's done. I just need to stuff some clothes into a backpack, and…

"I have all the letters," Zack promises. "I always meant to give them to you, but—"

It's easy to ignore Zack as I rush around and begin packing. A pair of jeans and a few tops, some underwear, and a bra. Just the essentials. A toothbrush, a hairbrush, a razor. Everything else should already be in my purse.

"Sophie?" Zachary sounds genuinely guilty now as he clears his throat. "This might be a bad time to bring this up, but I think I saw something about your brother on the news recently."

"He's always on the news," I say in annoyance as I sling my backpack over my shoulder. There. Done. All packed, in record time.

"It was different. I think he was hospitalized."

I am halfway to the door of our apartment when I swivel around. "You didn't think it was important to tell me this sooner?"

"I thought you would have seen it. I know you've been spending time at Starbucks lately…"

The fact is, I haven't been to any coffee shops. I've been working late, and lying about my whereabouts. I frown deeply. "You know I don't watch television, Zachary."

"I didn't take it seriously at the time. You know those Hollywood types and their drugs and rehab. It's always drama with celebrities on the West Coast."

"Cole isn't a celebrity. He's an architect."

"He's a celebrity architect, Soph. But if you think something is really wrong, I will do whatever I can to help out."

Considering this for a second, I nod. "Get me your phone," I demand. Zack scrambles in his pockets for his phone, but realizes he left it in his jacket, and has to limp over to the closet.

It may have been a while since I was last in the same room with my brother, but it's been even longer since I've touched a device that could connect me to the Internet. I was banned from going online for years after I was caught hacking, but even after the ban was lifted, my employers thought it best that I do all my work with a paper and pencil. It was safer.

They wouldn't even let me have a landline.

For the longest time, I thought I needed this restriction. I thought it was healthy.

I was an addict, after all, and putting a keyboard in my hands gave me way more power than any one girl is supposed to have. It was worse than giving Zack, and all the members of his squadron, fully-loaded, high-powered assault rifles. It took me a while to detox from the thrill of my cybercrimes, but I was reformed and I had repented. Besides, I enjoyed my new job, and they certainly paid me well enough.

When Zack returns from the closet with his cell phone, he extends his hand containing the slender object toward me. I stare at it warily, like an alcoholic looking at a gorgeous, perfectly mixed cocktail. I am about to reach out and take it, but when my fingers are a few inches from the tiny piece of technology, I hesitate and withdraw.

No. There are other ways to get information. I can find out what I need to know while getting away from here. Heading to the door of our apartment, I unlock the bolt and turn the doorknob so I can march out into the hallway.

"Wait!" Zack calls, limping after me in his sweatpants.

I see it then, at our neighbor's doorstep. A newspaper. Stooping to snatch it off the floor, I quickly rifle through to the business section. I am scanning through the pages rapidly when I see Zack pointing to the newspapers in my left hand. His face is ashen and his eyes are wide.

"Soph…" he breathes.

My forehead creases as I turn back to the front page. The front page of all the sections. For a moment, the hallway spins around me as the headline grows blurry in my eyes. I stare at the letters so hard that I can see the molecules of ink staining the cream-colored newsprint. I can't seem to focus on the individual words. In a caffeinated frenzy, my eyes dart around the paper like it is an encrypted message, and each symbol and image is a clue to decipher.

I feel suddenly weightless; the sentences on the page are alive and malicious.

The words swirl around in a maelstrom of black ink, and I know that they want to drown me.

VISIONARY CEO MURDERED IN HOSPITAL HE BUILT

Cole Hunter, the prodigy architect, was known for his cutting-edge designs and is responsible for hundreds of landmark buildings all over the world. He was not even thirty years old when he was gunned down late last night…

The paper seems suddenly very heavy, as though all the little black letters are made of lead. My arms sag with the burden. *Gunned down?* Cole's name is littered throughout the article, and I can't look at it any longer. The news slowly sinks into my veins, and saps my energy. *Gunned down.* I move back to lean against the wall, and clutch the paper against my stomach as my knees grow weak. There is a deafening silence in the hallway and a ringing in my ears.

"Sophie," Zack is whispering, and his arms are reaching out for me.

I flinch at his touch. When I look at him, anger flashes through me, and I see the monster that stole my brother. But I do not have the energy to sustain my anger, and it dissipates as quickly as it comes. When I look at Zachary again, it feels like I am seeing him through thick, cloudy goggles. The air around me has grown heavy, as though we are underwater. Zack's hands are warm, and they gently rub my shoulders and pull me back to reality. I am about to push him away when I am struck by a terrible realization.

Zack is now the only person on the planet who cares about me.

He is the only person who gives a damn that I exist.

And I could really use a person right now—any person. For this reason, I let him put his arms around me, and I sink against his chest with the vile newspaper crushed between our bodies. I am alone. All my deepest fears have been brought to the surface. I feel like a child again, stripped of everything that made this world good. Stripped of any reason to wake up in the morning.

And it's my fault. I could have been there for Cole. I could have helped him.

A broken sob escapes my chest, and then I push

Zachary away.

"I need to go," I tell him as I struggle to straighten my body. Moving almost mechanically, I feel my shaky legs taking me to the elevator.

"Wait!" Zack asks, grabbing my arm. "Where are you going?"

"Airport," I mumble.

"You can't drive in this condition. Let me take you."

"I don't think I can look at you right now, Zack."

"You don't have to—I understand. I know you'll never forgive me for this, but I want to be there if you need me. I'm coming to California with you, Sophie." Zack's face is suddenly filled with determination, and his eyes are set like steel. "Whoever wanted Cole dead might also want to hurt you. I'm not going to let that happen."

I open my mouth to protest, but the truth is that I don't want to be alone right now. "Fine," I whisper, ripping my arm away from Zack's grasp. I see his cell phone sticking out of his pocket and I reach for it with sudden conviction, clutching it tightly in the palm of my hand. I can almost feel the wireless signals piercing through my skin.

It doesn't matter anymore. I don't have to try so hard to be good.

None of this would have happened if I hadn't taken this job—if I had allowed myself to use the goddamned Internet. None of this would have happened if I had stayed close to Cole. Why was I so afraid? I could have prevented this. I know I could have prevented this.

"Get dressed," I tell Zack bitterly. "I will need to see *every single one* of those letters you hid from me. And for god's sake..." My voice is so cold that the words taste like shards of ice against my tongue. "Get me a fucking computer."

Chapter Two

cole hunter, 2003

Jolting up to a seated position in bed, all my muscles are tensed to their limit. Was I dreaming, or do I really smell smoke? The air is hot. Sweat drips down my bare chest as I pant and survey my surroundings in panic. A guy my age should not be having nightmares like this. I can feel the fire entering my nostrils and making all the tiny hairs singe and curl.

But there is no fire.

My eyes are burning as I search for flames rising from the floorboards, expecting to hear them crack and splinter. I hold my breath as I listen for the sounds of the house collapsing beneath me, but the only noise is the thunderous pounding in my chest. I grasp my ribcage with both hands in an attempt to keep my heart from beating hard enough to tear my skeleton in half.

When I glance at the clock, I am annoyed to see that I have only been asleep for ten minutes.

"Ugh," I grunt at myself in disgust. These damn nightmares just won't let me be. Running both of my hands through my messy brown hair, I feel a thin film of sweat coating my scalp.

Since the night my parents died, I've had trouble sleeping.

Bottles of insomnia, anti-anxiety, depression, and ADHD medications lie on my bedside table, but I ignore the drugs. No one seems to understand that I *want* to be awake. I need to be aware of my surroundings at all times. Bad things happen, and I don't want to be numb when they do. Alertness keeps you alive.

Maybe if I had been more cognizant six years ago, instead of sleeping blissfully under the stars in our backyard, my parents would still be here. I could have warned them, or woken them up at the first sign of danger. But I had my priorities all mixed up. Once I got permission to camp outside, building an awesome castle out of tree branches was all that mattered to me. I didn't have a single care in the world.

When I was woken up by the sound of screaming sirens, I tried to rush into the house to help out, but it was too late. My whole world was burning, breaking, and literally crashing down around me; it was impossible to get upstairs where my parents were sleeping. A firefighter was able to pull me out in time, or I would have died there, too. I vowed, that day, to never sleep again. Not for real. Not until I'm dead.

A few seconds pass, and the stupid muscle in my chest finally stops thrashing about like a fish out of water. I am able to breathe and get out of bed, reaching for the baseball bat I keep close at hand. Moving to the door, I place my hand against the wooden panel, expecting to feel heat radiating through the thin material. This has become a routine for me; but like the thousands of other times I have done this, the wood is cool to the touch. Next, I turn the knob and step into the corridor, breathing deeply to try to detect any hint of smoke.

The unmistakable odor of tobacco tickles my nostrils, and I screw up my face in distaste. Professor Brown must have just walked by. That man must go through at least two packs a day, and his clothes reek with the stench of chemicals. He leaves a lingering trail behind him everywhere he goes, reminiscent of rotting flesh and decaying teeth. Sadly, it's not the worst way I've ever seen a foster parent waste the money he's receiving to help the children in his care.

The elderly "professor" has been retired for many years, and his bank account dried up a long time ago. His monthly pension and the income from fostering just aren't enough to sustain his filthy habits. I sometimes wonder if I've eaten more satisfying meals while huddled around a trash can fire or spending the night on a park bench than I have in this home. This is just one of the countless reasons I am eager to head off to college and leave this cold and unpleasant place behind.

I *had* a home. I had a loving family. This is nothing like that.

Convinced that the house isn't burning to ashes, I step back into my room. I listen closely for a moment longer, just to double-check that there are no intruders intent on murdering me in my sleep. The only sound that reaches my ears is the faint clickety-clack of my foster sister's keyboard from across the hall.

A crooked smile touches my lips. Scarlett is one of the only reasons I have remained here. Up until recently, I've made it a habit to escape from my foster homes at the first sign of trouble. I would have hightailed it out of here long ago, if not for the strange young girl who lives across the hall.

Scarlett Smith is very peculiar. She has serious lips that hardly ever smile, and a mind that's sharp as a razor blade. What really gets me is her eyes—they are pale blue, innocent, and wounded. I just don't feel comfortable leaving this house unless I know that she's going to be okay. When we're sitting across from each other at the dinner table, sometimes she studies me in a way that makes me feel like she knows me. This is ridiculous, of course, because we've only lived in the same house for a few weeks, but I still find something about her unsettling.

I was supposed to have a sister. My mother was seven months pregnant when the fire happened. I like to imagine that my sister would have been clever and capable like Scarlett. Sometimes, living in this house with her, I like to imagine that Scarlett could really be my sister. And for a moment, I feel at peace—like I haven't lost everything. For a moment, it doesn't hurt.

I never had thoughts like this before. In all my crappy foster homes, I never encountered someone that I could even stand to be around. I suppose, they did bring Scarlett to live here because they thought she could benefit from living with me, due to my impressive academic record, but it was a big surprise to actually begin to think of her as family. From what I've gathered, Scarlett has never had any family of her own, and doesn't seem to have any friends. She spends every waking moment sitting in front of her computer and typing away at mysterious projects. I think she must be the only person on the planet lonelier than I am.

The incessant clatter of keys comes to a halt, and I realize that I am staring at Scarlett's room. I quietly shut my door and head back to bed, placing my baseball bat down beside my pillow and tugging the comforter up over my legs. I am determined to try to fall asleep again when my door bursts open and a dark-haired girl fixes me with a stern look.

"I'm disappointed in you, Cole."

I blink at her in surprise. "What? What did I do?"

She marches over and dumps some papers in my lap. "You're flunking AP European History."

"Where did you get this?" I ask, reaching out to examine the papers. I fix her with a suspicious look. "Scarlett... Have you been hacking again? Are these my high school records?"

"It doesn't matter about that," she says with a dismissive wave, plopping down on the bed with a frown. "You have a paper due on the Black Death soon, but I haven't seen you working on it. You're not showing up to class. You're going to fail."

Taking a deep breath, I lean back and stretch my arms behind my head. Scarlett is wearing her thick-rimmed, black librarian glasses that she needs to view the computer screen. I should know by now that when I see her in those glasses, it means she's gotten her hands on some information she shouldn't have. "You're a year younger than me," I remind her gently. "I'm supposed to be *your* role model. You shouldn't have to keep tabs on me and show motherly concern. That's Mrs. Brown's job."

"Quit changing the subject," she says sternly. "European History! Aren't you supposed to be some kind of genius? You're doing really well in all your other classes."

I have to struggle to repress a grin. I had almost forgotten what it feels like to have someone care enough to scold me. To care about someone enough to let myself get scolded. I gaze at Scarlett for a moment, wondering if she is the reason my insomnia is getting worse. With every passing day, I grow more afraid that I will lose her, like I have lost everyone else. The impending sense of dread is keeping me up at night and forcing me to take naps during the day at school.

"Cole," she says softly, pushing my knee to get my attention. "Why aren't you going to class?"

"It's depressing," I tell her honestly. "I don't like thinking about shitty things that happened in the past."

She sends me a puzzled look. "History is in the

26

past; it can't hurt you."

"That's not true," I tell her. "The past hurts me every day."

She looks away with an unreadable expression, and I begin to feel a little guilty. The only thing worse than my past is not having any past at all. At least I knew my parents before I lost them—Scarlett has always been alone.

We sit together awkwardly for a moment before I clear my throat. "With these AP classes, it's mostly about the exam at the end, anyway. That's what determines whether I get the college credit so I can get the hell out of here faster. It's all I really care about, Scar. I'll ace that test; I promise."

"Good," she says, standing up and moving over to my desk. "If you flip through the papers I gave you, you'll find some practice questions. They may or may not be the exact questions that will be on this year's final exam."

"Are you kidding me?" I ask, flipping to the questions to scan through them. "Jesus, Scar! You're a little cyber criminal."

"No," she says, glancing back at me with an innocent smile. "I'm just a good sister."

I shake my head in disbelief, placing the papers down beside my baseball bat. "This is really impressive, but I don't need to cheat." Proudly sticking out my chest, I give her my most charming smile. "I actually *am* a genius."

"Maybe. I'm not convinced." Scarlett curiously fingers some of the sketches on my desk. "Is this what you've been working on instead of going to class?"

"Don't look at those," I warn her nervously. "They aren't finished. They are just... doodles."

She holds a sketch up to the light and squints at it. "This is a beautiful house," she says quietly, removing her glasses to study me from across the room. "Most teenage boys draw pictures of naked girls. You're a strange one, Cole Hunter."

"Most teenage girls are into makeup and shopping," I counter smoothly. "Not cyber sabotage."

"Maybe we could take over the world together," she says to me with a playful smile.

"Sure. If we survive adolescence in this house."

She looks down at her feet, and her smile abruptly disappears. "It's not so bad," she says with a shrug. "We have food and Internet access. There are plenty of books on the shelves. What more could we need?"

"Parents who give a shit," I inform her.

She gives me a sad little smile. "Well, I've never had that. The Browns are pretty great compared to some foster parents. I don't mind being here." She hesitates and places my sketches back down on the desk before looking at me shyly. "And it's kind of nice having a genius big brother."

I am unable to respond before she rushes to the door, disappearing as quickly as she arrived. "Goodnight, Cole!" she calls before slipping out into the hall and back into her own room.

A goofy smile settles on my face as I snuggle down into my blankets. Scarlett has the ability to lift my spirits so easily. Maybe I *will* take some of my medicine so that I can get a better night's rest and avoid falling asleep at school tomorrow. If I can pull off great grades while half-asleep, I am sure that I could get scholarship-worthy results with a little more effort.

Scarlett doesn't know that I have already taken the SATs and applied to colleges. I didn't want to get her hopes up if I was rejected. It's still early, but if all goes well, I could be out of this place in a few months—while I'm still fifteen. And maybe I could take her with me.

Reaching for the bottle of pills, I feel a renewed sense of determination. *Can I really do this?* When I originally planned my future, Scarlett wasn't in the picture. Could I manage to provide a good life for her, even if I am living on campus and going to school full-time? Does she even want to be around me after we leave this house? *I hope so.*

I think I can take care of her.

And I don't want to be alone anymore.

She will probably like the idea of getting away with me—anything would be better than this hellhole. Closing my eyes, I imagine how awesome it would be to get into the college of my choice. I could study architecture like I've always wanted, and start my own company as soon as I graduate. Then our real lives in the real world can finally begin.

Chapter Three

cole hunter, 2003

A muffled sound in the distance pulls me from my drugged daze. I feel like I have been sleeping deeply for several hours, and my limbs are heavy, like I have been partially turned to stone. This is strange for me as I can normally only reach a state of limbo where I am partially awake. Falling any deeper would require letting go—something I refuse to do unless I'm artificially knocked out.

When I open one eye to peer at the clock, I am surprised to see that only about thirty minutes have passed. *What the hell?* Maybe the medication isn't that effective after all. I am grabbing one of the bottles to check the expiration date when a bloodcurdling scream causes me to drop the plastic cylinder to the ground.

"No!"

Ripping the covers off my legs, I jump from the bed and rush out into the hallway. I dive for the doorknob of Scarlett's room and turn violently, but it is locked. Visions of all the horrible things that could be happening behind this door flash across my brain. I know that I heard her scream. I wasn't imagining that, was I?

"Scarlett?" I call out frantically. Imagining her bedclothes and curtains going up in flames, I place my hand on the door to check for heat. It is cool, but the temperature isn't enough to assuage my fears. "Scar!" I shout again, wrestling with the doorknob.

I hear her then, speaking softly. "How could you?" she is saying between sobs. "How could you do this?"

"I told you not to dress like that in my house!" a deep voice bellows. His speech is marred by his country drawl and the unmistakable slur of alcohol. "As long as you're living under my roof, you gotta follow my rules, y'hear? Ain't no girl o' mine gonna go around town looking like a slut!"

"Professor Brown!" Scarlett begs with a gasp. "Stop. Please—dammit. *Don't!*"

"You filthy orphans are all the same!" Mr. Brown spits with an angry hiss. Something crashes to the ground and the volume of his voice escalates. "We took you in to save you, but we should have let you rot. You don't belong among civilized folk with good breeding. You're just dirty little animals. Dirty, disgusting animals!"

There is another crashing sound, and I hear Scarlett sob.

I feel like I am going to be sick. "Hang on, Scar!" I shout, running back to my room. My mind is racing, and fear is pumping through my veins as I quickly grab the baseball bat. On second thought, I pause and reach under my mattress to grab a switchblade I have tucked away there and shove it into my pocket, just in case. I rush back to the door and slam my foot into the wooden panel near the doorknob.

"Leave her alone!" I yell as I kick the door until it splinters. When it is starting to open, I shove my baseball bat into the opening and use it like a crowbar. I am startled when the baseball bat is ripped out of my grip, and the partially broken door swings open to the inside.

I am assailed with the scent of Jack Daniels and cigarette smoke. These two substances seem to seep out of Mr. Brown's pores. I reach for the knife in my pocket, but the large man is already slamming my baseball bat into the side of my head. I find myself crashing into the wall. Dizzily, I stumble backward, and Mr. Brown looms over me with a sneer.

"You ungrateful little shit," he says slowly, advancing on me.

His eyes are full of hatred and drunken rage. My own anger grows as I wonder about Scarlett. What has he done to her? Is she okay? My heart beats in my throat and I try to pull myself off the floor, but Mr. Brown plants his heavy boot in my shoulder to kick me back down. He clenches his fingers tightly around my baseball bat, and I tense up, ready to defend myself from the swing.

"I give you everything," he says. "I work my fingers to the bone to keep you fed and clothed, and this is how you repay me? By damaging my property? By ruining the house that shelters you? Worthless pig." He sneers at me hatefully for a few seconds, as though he is considering smashing my head in until my brains spill out on the floor. I would like to see him try. He may weigh around two hundred and fifty pounds, but I'm fast and I know I can take him.

My fingers hover over the switchblade in my pocket.

Glaring at the old man, I almost challenge him to act, but he seems to change his mind. He spits on me, tosses the baseball bat to the floor beside my arm, and then walks away.

As quickly as I can, I push myself off the ground and run into Scarlett's room. I am relieved when I see that she isn't unconscious or lying in a pool of blood. She is kneeling on the floor near her bed and staring at her smashed laptop, which lies on the floor before her in several pieces. A lump forms in my throat, for I know how much that little machine meant to her.

She looks up at me with tear-stained cheeks. "He broke it. He broke my computer."

I move to her side and crouch down so that I can give her a hug. I can feel her small body shaking in my arms.

"Damn him," she mutters. She turns into my chest and buries her face against my shirt. "I hate him!"

"It's okay," I tell her, holding her close against

my chest. It occurs to me that I don't remember the last time I hugged someone like this. It may have been back when my mother was alive. I am in the middle of thinking that I might need this hug even more than she does, when I notice that her black-rimmed glasses are also broken and lying near her laptop. "Scar," I ask her urgently. "Did he hurt you?"

"It doesn't matter," she says in a shaky voice. "My whole life was on that laptop. What am I going to do now, Cole? I'm useless."

"The computer is replaceable," I tell her reassuringly, trying to soothe her by running my hand over her hair. "Don't worry. I can try landscaping again to make some extra cash. I'll get you a new one soon. I promise."

"You don't have to do that," she tells me. "You need to save up for a car, and college…"

"Scar," I say suddenly, noticing the way she is clutching her side. "Did he hit you?"

She turns away from me, trying to conceal her body. "It doesn't matter."

Reaching forward to grab the hem of her t-shirt, I pull the fabric up to expose her abdomen. My eyes widen at the sight of her skin. "Shit," I whisper, staring at the scars in disbelief. My fingers reach out to examine her wounds, and it takes a moment for me to be able to speak. "How long?" I finally manage to blurt out.

She shakes her head in response.

Little circular lesions are littered all over her side like ugly, unnatural freckles. They can only be one thing: cigarette burns. One of the wounds looks fresh, like it was made tonight, but several of the other marks look older and faded. I lift her shirt a little more, and I see blue and purple bruises on her skin, like she was punched repeatedly. Some of the bruises are turning yellow, so I know they are relics of past injuries. Unfortunately, it looks like there have been new bruises added to her pre-existing ones.

How did I not know this was happening?

I gulp down a bit of bile that has been gathering at the back of my throat. The muscles in my jaw tighten until it hurts. I suppress my urge to unleash a cavalcade of curses inappropriate for the ears of a young girl. "How long has he been doing this?"

"A while, I suppose."

My blood is simmering to a boil beneath my skin. "You suppose?"

She shrugs and brushes her hands over her middle as if she could remove the pain as easily as pieces of lint. "It doesn't bother me that much. I can easily block it out."

"But..." I say slowly, trying to keep calm, "but I barely sleep. I would have woken up. I would have heard you scream before now."

Scarlett shakes her head. "I don't scream, Cole. I'm not weak. I mean... I guess I screamed tonight, but that was only because of my laptop. Not because of pain."

"This ends now," I say finally, rising to my feet. "The professor is right about me. I'm a useless piece of shit. I could have stopped this sooner. I had a feeling something was wrong, but I never came into your room to check on you..."

"It's okay," she says softly.

"I'm going to kill him."

"No, no, Cole. Please don't." Scarlett grabs my hand with both of hers to keep me from leaving the room. "This isn't a big deal. I swear. I'm happy here. Relatively. I'm happy-ish."

"You're happy?" I ask her incredulously.

"Yeah. You don't know what my life has been like." She gives me a small smile. It's rare to see her smile, and it catches me off guard. Her voice grows softer when she speaks. "This is easy."

"Easy?"

"Just sit down," she says, tugging on my hand. "Relax. A few burns aren't the end of the world."

"Burns killed my whole family," I remind her gravely.

She sighs and uses all her strength to pull me back down beside her. "Just sit with me for a minute. I'm glad you're here."

"I should call the police," I say suddenly. "He should go to jail for this."

"No!" Scarlett says sharply, fear flashing across her eyes. "We'll be separated. They'll take us out of this home and move us god knows where."

I pause. "You—don't want to be separated?"

She looks down and shakes her head. "No. I really just need some stability. It's driving me crazy, moving around all the time. A new school, a new town, a new family. I'm so sick of it."

"I understand," I tell her softly. She's right. If I call the cops, we will probably never see each other again. I'm not going to risk that. "Just let me get my baseball bat. What if he comes back?"

"He won't. Professor Brown gets tired quickly when he's this drunk. He will barely remember any of this in the morning." Scarlett pauses and studies me carefully. "Cole... did I ever tell you why I ran away from my last home?"

"No. But you said you were adopted by a really rich guy who was paying for you to go to private school. I thought that sounded like a sweet deal."

"It was," she says, with lowered eyes. "It was great. Until I got my first period."

I look at her in confusion. Fear grows in me as I study her expressionless lips. Is she saying what I think...?

"He was molesting me," Scarlett explains.

My jaw muscles grow slack. A wave of heat washes over me, and I feel sick to my stomach. She speaks so calmly that it gives me chills.

"No one believed me," she says as she stares at her broken computer. "My adoptive father was a well-respected member of the community, and anyone would take his word over some troubled orphan kid. He was a politician, you see. Everyone I tried to tell called me ungrateful for not valuing his kindness more. The local police were all his buddies—and the social workers considered him a hero. These were the people who were supposed to protect me."

"Scarlett... that's terrible."

"Yeah, but I started to realize they were right. In my situation, I couldn't afford to be choosy and I needed to try to see the bright side of things. It didn't matter if Benjamin—that was his name—came into my room at night; I had a good life, a good school, many comforts I'd never experienced before. He wasn't really hurting me that much; he was gentle. Most of the time, I just had to lie there and focus on something else, and it would be over quickly."

"How old were you?" I ask her hoarsely, almost afraid to hear the answer.

She hesitates. "Nine. I was nine when it started," she responds.

I feel like I'm going to be sick. I am caught between a violent surge of rage that makes me want to grab my baseball bat and break everything, and just wanting to cry into Scarlett's shoulder and tell her how sorry I am. Her body is so delicate and small, even though she is now fourteen. Her wrists and ankles are paper-thin. The thought of someone abusing her like that—for so many years—when she was even smaller and more delicate than she is now…

It's unimaginable. It breaks my heart.

It's wrong. It's completely *wrong* that she had to suffer this.

I briefly close my eyes. *Nine.* She was only nine.

That number again. That stupid number. Nine is how old I was when the fire happened. My thoughts drift back to the person I was then, who is so clearly immortalized in my mind. I hardly remember who I was when I was eight, or seven, but I remember every second of every thought and feeling I had when I was nine. All I know is that it was an awful age for awful things to happen—or is every age that awful? I can imagine a younger Scarlett, just as young as I was, going through pain similar to what I experienced.

But maybe hers was worse.

I had lived in pure blissful ignorance until I was nine, in a real home that was filled with love and laughter. Scarlett never had that. Her life was just one awful experience after another. Her life was just a series of getting her hopes up that she would find a placement with a good family and then being disappointed. I wonder if she remembers all her years as clearly as I remember the one when I was nine? And as clearly as I remember all of the miserable years since?

"It wasn't so bad," Scarlett says with a shrug, in a voice that I am starting to realize she uses when she lies. "I would have stayed there until now, but I started freaking out when I knew I could get pregnant. If I stayed in that house, I probably would have. I was twelve at the time, when I ran away." She turns to fix me with a serious look. "I can take anything, Cole—I can tolerate any kind of abuse. But the idea of bringing a child into this world, and not being able to take care of it, and letting it grow up scared and alone like I was…" Her eyes fill with tears, and they flash like daggers when she shakes her head violently. "No. That is one line I will not cross. Never."

"That… was brave of you," I tell her haltingly. "I'm glad… you got away." It's hard to find the words. Scarlett's mouth is set in a hard line, but I notice something I never saw before: her lips quiver slightly at the corners, revealing how fragile she is under this falsely tough exterior. I swallow, wishing I could have somehow been there to help her. "I'm glad you're here, now," I say in an awkward whisper. "No matter what the circumstances were that led you here… I'm so thankful I met you."

"I didn't mean to tell you all this," she says suddenly, looking up at me with surprise. "I don't know why I'm telling you any of this."

"It means a lot," I tell her quietly. "I want to know everything. I want to know you."

She reaches out to place her fingers on my hand and squeezes it gently. Is *she* comforting *me?* I swallow. I hope it's not causing her pain to share this. I hope it's healthy for her to talk about it and get it off her chest.

"What ended up happening with Benjamin?" I ask, encouraging her to speak more.

"It wasn't easy to leave," she says, looking over to the window. "He threatened to kill me. He said that if I ran, he would find me. But more importantly… I was attached to my home, and I didn't *want* to leave. For the first time in my life, I had my own desktop computer in my bedroom. I was comfortable, never hungry. I always had nice, new clothes that fit me. I was winning trophies in school for both sports and academics. I could really imagine staying in that home until adulthood."

"Even with… everything he did?" I ask her, really trying to wrap my head around this.

She gives me a self-deprecating smile. "You know, it's almost better to be touched at all, in any way, than to be left entirely cold and alone for years. I managed to convince myself that he really cared. I started to convince myself that I cared about him. It was the only way I could get through each day—by pretending it was normal. He was an attractive enough man. I know that in some countries, and cultures…" Her voice trails off.

I shake my head, unsure of what to say.

She reaches out to touch the keyboard of her destroyed laptop. "It was just my stupid period that messed everything up. I went to Planned Parenthood to get birth control, but he found it in my room and tossed it out. He was very religious, and he said that he had plenty of money to take care of any kids I might have. He said that he could just blame a boy my own age, and spin it into a heroic deed about taking care of a pregnant teenager's baby. He said it would make a great story for his pro-life supporters."

"What the hell?" I whisper. "That's so messed up."

"Yeah," Scarlett mutters. "He did a lot of good things for the community while there were cameras on him, but behind closed doors… he thought that those good deeds gave him license to do whatever bad things he wanted."

"This guy is insane," I tell her matter-of-factly. "He should be in prison."

"I left a suicide note so that he wouldn't look for me," she says as she fingers her computer's smashed circuitry. "I stole money to take bus rides all the way out here. I lived on the streets for a while because I was still scared that he would find me if I went back into the system. But that's okay—it's easier to live on the streets in California than New York."

"Scarlett… God. I had no idea."

"Yeah." She places her hand on her injured abdomen and gives me a crooked smile, as if to relieve the tension caused by her brutal honesty. "The stuff Professor Brown is doing? The cigarette burns and mild violence—it's not that bad. It only hurts me, and only temporarily. It doesn't put my future at risk, and it doesn't put any possible children in danger. I can live with the kind of abuse that doesn't hurt anyone else."

"It hurts me," I tell her. "You shouldn't have to choose between being raped and being hit."

"What are the alternatives? Choosing to starve. Choosing to sleep in abandoned warehouses with drug addicts."

"Some group homes aren't that bad," I tell her—but that hasn't really been my experience.

She rolls her eyes. "Really? Choosing to be completely ignored. Choosing to have a shitty education. Choosing to be treated like crap by the other teenagers who are really messed up, and worse than the professor. Choosing to be locked in a box."

"I guess… for now, maybe this isn't the worst place for us," I admit, but I hate the possibility that it could be true. I don't want to be so defeated that I believe that this is an acceptable situation. I want to hold on to my memories of better times, and work hard to somehow make them real again.

Scarlett nods, glancing at me. "Trust me, Cole. It really isn't that bad. Besides, you're here, aren't you? I thought that it was bullshit when my social worker decided to place me in a home with a Mensa kid, and I expected you to be an annoying, arrogant nerd. But… I like talking to you. You're kind of… a sweet boy." Her cheeks darken a little and she tilts her head to the side teasingly. "Besides, I've never had a role model before."

I scoff at this. "There's nothing I can teach you, Scar. You're doing so well in school, and you're tough as nails. Compared to you, I'm a spoiled brat, and I should take a page out of your book. How the hell did you get so smart?"

"Libraries are free to the public," she explains with a shrug. "I just read a lot, as much as I can."

Shaking my head in amazement, I stare at her. "How do you manage to impress me a little more every single day?"

"I do?" she asks, in surprise.

I nod. "My parents spent a lot of money homeschooling me with the best tutors, and I grew up pampered with tons of attention. I took it all for granted, and I never knew what I had until I lost it. If you had grown up with the opportunities I had—you would probably be working at NASA or something by now."

"You're just saying nice stuff to make me feel better," she says shyly. "Maybe I have a little skill with computers, but… that doesn't really matter if my computer is smashed, does it?"

"I will replace it," I tell her. "I promise."

"Please don't make promises to me, Cole." She lets her face sag forward into her hands with a heavy sigh. "Everyone always breaks their promises. I can't bear to hear any more empty words."

"I always mean what I say," I tell her earnestly. "Cross my heart and hope to die. You'll see, someday soon. But in the meantime, I believe it is my duty to teach you a very important lesson—something I learned from my parents while they were still around. When it comes to abuse, the only policy you should have is a zero tolerance policy. When you overlook these things, and let them continue for too long… it takes a toll on you. It changes who you are."

"I know that," she says softly. "But what can I do? A zero tolerance policy for abuse sounds like a fairy tale. Come on, Cole. If I walked away from everyone who hurt me, I would be living on a deserted island somewhere, foraging for fruits and nuts."

"We can still change this," I tell her, rising to my feet and offering her my hand. "We need to do something about Mr. Brown, and make him stop hurting you. Let's go confront him."

"Cole," she says hesitantly, "that will just make it worse. I'm fine with the way things are."

"I'm not," I tell her firmly. "And I'm not going to let him get away with this. He's just an insecure jackass and a bully, picking on someone much smaller than he is so that he can feel like more of a man. If we stand up to him, I guarantee he'll back down."

She shakes her head in refusal. "You can't talk to him now, when he's drunk out of his mind like this. You'll only make things worse. Go back to bed, Cole."

"No way in hell. I can't just go back to bed like nothing happened."

"You're very heroic," she tells me slowly, "but heroes often fail."

"I already failed to save my parents. You're the closest thing to family I have had in years—I couldn't live with myself if I just sit around and do nothing while you get hurt. What if Mr. Brown goes too far one night? What if he breaks something more important than your laptop?"

Scarlett looks at me as if I am insane. "There is nothing more important than my laptop."

"*You* are more important than your laptop."

"Whatever," she says stubbornly.

I study her face and see that she is genuinely upset by everything that has happened to her, and not just on this night. If I rock the boat, we could end up getting removed from this home and separated, and that wouldn't do either of us any good. I take a deep breath. "All right," I tell her, grabbing a pillow from her bed. "I will take some time to think about how to approach him, and I'll deal with him in the morning. But for now, I'm going to sleep here."

"What?" she says in surprise.

I place the pillow on the floor, halfway between her bed and the door. I quickly pop outside to grab my baseball bat before returning and lowering myself to the pillow. I place my bat beside me and link my hands together over my chest resolutely. "It's the least I can do. After all, I broke your bedroom door," I tell her with a grin. "So now I've got to be your personal bodyguard."

"Fine," she says quietly as she rises to her feet. With one last, forlorn glance at her smashed laptop, the dark-haired girl moves to turn off the light that illuminates her room. She turns on a smaller reading lamp before crawling into bed and adjusting her remaining pillow. Positioning herself close to the edge of the bed, she looks down on me from above.

For a long time, she gazes at me, and there is a strange look in her glassy eyes. Their blue is so pale and almost transparent, like I could see right through and read her secret, innermost thoughts as they dance across her brain. I try. Carefully and methodically, I search her eyes to better understand the mind of this mysterious girl whose life is becoming closely entangled with mine.

All I see is pain. Pain and scars that are so overwhelming they almost consume her existence. Pain and despair that so many people have abandoned and harmed her in her short lifetime, which doesn't feel quite so short. Pain and tiredness for it to all be over, and for things to finally be calm and better.

I keep searching until I find something else. Rebellion. A tiny glint of rebellion against everything that has ever given her pain. Rebellion against misfortune and all the failings of humanity that have led her here and everywhere else she should have never been. Strength. Impossible strength and dogged determination to survive anything life throws at her—and everything life takes away.

She can't even help it. She doesn't even try. She just needs to survive.

Am I really seeing all this in her, or is it just my imagination running wild? Do her strangely clear eyes have the effect of a mirror, and am I just seeing bits of my own soul reflected back at me? Can a person ever look at someone else and see anything other than the qualities and feelings they recognize as their own? I am mesmerized and puzzled by her, and held completely spellbound.

Until she blinks. The spell is lifted, and I am free.

"Thanks," she whispers as she turns to look at the ceiling. "I feel better that you're here."

Warmth washes over me at her words. A tiny bit of pride swells in my chest to know that I'm helping at all. I wish I could help more and take away all of her pain. Maybe over time, if I stay beside her and try to lift some of her burden, she will start to feel like she isn't so alone.

I won't give her any empty words and promises. I will only show her that I am here, by consistently being here. I will make sure that I am close whenever she needs me, until she knows that no matter what, I always will be. She needs someone like that in her life—someone consistent and reliable, who cares unconditionally. I know because *I* need someone like that. Everyone needs someone like that.

For starters, your mother or father is supposed to be the person who cares about you. Ideally, both. Maybe, if you're really lucky, an aunt or an uncle, too. Grandparents. Siblings. Eventually, friends.

But we haven't been so lucky.

Lying here on the floor, I can see the silhouette of Scarlett's face in the dark. She has a sharp, beaklike nose that is both regal and predatory. The curve of her chin is soft and feminine, yet it juts out proudly with stubbornness, even as she rests. It suddenly occurs to me that she knows how special she is. She knows her own worth, and she values her own intelligence. She has healthy self-esteem, and a strong sense of her own identity, but she is unsure of her place in the world.

Looking up at her like this makes me feel like she is a princess, and I am her loyal knight, standing guard over her. This thought gives me a bittersweet smile. I wish I had a younger sister to play games like that with. But it's too late now. Scarlett and I are no longer children. The time for make believe and building castles in the sand is gone.

When children are born into good families, with good parents, they can afford to stay children for as long as possible, well into adulthood. They rarely learn the meaning of hard work and independence. But when children have no parents, or have shitty parents, they quickly learn to fend for themselves. They are forced to grow up sooner, and be adults while the actual adults are absent or uncaring.

In some ways, I wonder if losing my parents improved me as a person. I might have been an eternal child if they were still around. But now, I know that I cannot afford to build castles in the sand that will be washed away with the tides. I cannot afford to build forts out of sheets and pillows. I cannot afford to waste time.

I need to build something that lasts. I need to build towers that stretch to the sky. I need to build houses that won't burn down. I need to build a life for myself, because I don't have someone else's life to piggyback on.

Staring at Scarlett, I wonder if she feels this way, too. I wonder if she can understand the drive and desperation inside me to establish a foothold here. I think she does.

We barely know each other, but somehow, we need each other.

"Cole!" Scarlett says softly. "Can you keep it down?"

"I didn't say anything," I tell her with confusion.

"You're thinking loud enough to wake up the neighborhood. Why don't you try to get some sleep? It sounds like there's a whole construction crew in your brain and they are all drilling and jackhammering and bulldozing."

"Wow. That's exactly what it feels like inside my head," I say in awe. "How can you tell?"

"I am connected. Wirelessly."

Her voice is cryptic in the darkened room and it gives me a shiver. "What are you talking about?" I ask her with a nervous laugh, wondering if she somehow hacked into my head. But she does not respond. She is already asleep.

"Goodnight, Scar," I tell her softly.

Chapter Four

sophie shields, 2016

By the time we arrive at the airport, I have hacked into the police files containing the ongoing investigation into Cole's death. I have also downloaded footage from the hospital's security cameras on the night that he was murdered. I need to keep finding details to focus on so I can occupy my mind. I need to stay distracted. As soon as we get past security and arrive at our gate, I pull the laptop out again and proceed to continue my work.

"Jesus," Zack says as he glances over at my fingers flying across the keyboard. "Those are some mad skills."

I ignore him and continue to gather information. I need to get as much as I can before we board the plane, because I'm not sure if there will be reliable

Internet access in the sky.

"I thought you just didn't *like* having electronics around in the home," Zack muses. "I thought maybe you weren't tech-savvy…"

Glancing at him with a raised eyebrow, I quickly turn back to accessing Cole's email account. I then copy his cellphone notes and calendar, his car's GPS detailing all his recent locations, his home security system…

"Who the hell are you?" Zack asks in amazement.

"Aren't you supposed to know the answer to that question before you propose to someone?" I snap at him hotly.

"You never really gave me a chance to know you, Sophie."

I suppose he's right. Out of curiosity, I proceed to play the hospital security footage on fast forward, covering half of my screen with the feeds from three different cameras, and the other half of my screen with Cole's recent text messages. I scan through them both simultaneously, my eyes darting around the screen and barely blinking with the effort of multitasking.

"How did you gain access to the hospital tapes?" Zack asks as he leans over to study my screen.

For a few seconds, I continue what I'm doing and do not respond, but then I start to feel like I'm being rude. "That was the easy part," I explain to Zack. "I designed all the security systems that Cole uses in his buildings, so I know how to access the servers. They haven't updated the system that much since I left."

"You can design software? Why the hell are you working as a librarian in Arlington?"

"I'm not." I stare at him and shake my head in amazement. "It's a cover. I thought you would have been able to figure that out."

Zack leans back in surprise. He looks around to make sure no one is nearby before speaking in a lowered voice. "You mean to say that you work for…"

"An agency. I figure I can tell you now that I've probably lost my job."

His face displays hurt, but also fascination. "What do you do, exactly?"

"I'm a cryptanalyst," I tell him. "A code breaker."

"I know what a cryptanalyst is," he tells me. Then he frowns and gestures to my laptop. "But it seems like a step down from what you did before. Being the person who designs the codes."

Glancing at the laptop, I give him a tiny nod. "They recruited me because they needed help with a puzzle their other code breakers couldn't crack. They needed me to hack into some foreign satellites." A small smile touches my lips. "I designed some of the most impenetrable security systems in the country, so they figured that if anyone could do it, it would be me. And I did." I pause, turning to look at Zack. "I do sometimes consult about the software used for our own national security, but not very often."

For a few seconds, Zack is quiet. Then he leans back and exhales with a low chuckle. "I'm proud of you, Sophie. That's pretty amazing. I had no idea you were so smart."

I make a face at him before returning to my task of searching Cole's files. Still, I am impressed. I always thought Zack would have a strongly negative reaction if he ever found out I'd been lying to him all along. I'm pleasantly surprised that he understands.

"Could have used someone like you in the field in Afghanistan," he muses. "Maybe I'd still have a leg. But a mind like yours is too valuable to put at risk."

With a small shrug, I continue to look through Cole's text messages and the hospital footage.

"And Sophie isn't your real name," Zack says slowly. "I was wondering about that, when I saw the letters your brother sent you. He kept calling you Scar. I thought it was a nickname, like maybe something to do with those scars on your stomach and legs, or how you got them."

I look up in annoyance. "There are no scars on my stomach."

"You did a really good job of covering them up with those little orange circle tattoos, but a man who's lost a leg can always see scars beneath ink."

Turning away with a frown, I study the computer. "They aren't circles," I whisper stubbornly, to no one in particular. "They are dragonballs. They grant wishes."

"So what's your real name?" Zack asks. "Is it Scarlett? That's a pretty name."

"No. Zack, can you please stop asking questions? I'm trying to figure out what happened to my brother. If I had gotten his letters, and gotten to him sooner, maybe none of this would have happened. So please, just shut the hell up."

"I want to help," Zack says, "and I want to know you. Maybe if I had known more about you, I wouldn't have been so insecure and hidden the letters. At least tell me your name. Should I call you Scarlett?"

"Sophie is fine. Scarlett wasn't my real name, either. It was just the name I used as a teenager, when Cole met me. I was on the run from someone at the time."

Zack leans forward. "Could that person be after you now? Could he be the one that killed Cole?"

I close my eyes. A little shudder jostles my shoulders at the reminder that Cole was killed. It feels so unreal. I try to push past the emotions.

"Probably not," I tell Zack softly. "I don't know. Let me look."

Going to Cole's recent emails, I search for the word *Benjamin*. When it gets a few hundred results, I am alarmed, but then I see that the emails are sent to an accountant in his firm named Benjamin. His name is Benjamin Carver, not Benjamin Powell. A bit of relief touches my stomach, until I keep scrolling down and see the word I am so afraid to see.

Powell.

There are dozens of emails about a new building commissioned by my ex-father, and Cole responding and being helpful to him. Heat floods my chest, and I am instantly enraged. I see red, and my hands tighten on the laptop.

"No. *No!* Why would he do this? Why would he work with this man?"

"Senator Powell?" Zack asks. "You were on the run from a Senator?"

"He wasn't a Senator back then. He was just your average neighborhood child molester."

Zack pauses before speaking. "Did Cole not know—"

"He knew!" I say, fuming as I open the emails. "He knew everything. And he accepted money from this man! He designed a building for him. How could he do this to me? How could he *help* someone I consider an enemy?"

It takes Zack a minute to respond. "Sophie, I hate to say it. But you're going to have to look at Cole's letters to better understand what's been happening these last few months."

I glance at my backpack, where I placed the stack of letters Zack gave me before we left. The mere thought of holding those letters in my hands and seeing Cole's familiar handwriting makes me want to break down and cry. They are all I have left of him, now, and it doesn't even matter what he wrote.

Every word is a reminder that I put distance between us, when I could have had more time with him. Every word is a reminder that he loved me with all his heart, and that his heart is no longer beating. I am not ready. I will turn into an ugly, sopping mess of tears, and the airport people will decide I am too mentally unstable to board the plane.

"Sophie?"

"Not now," I tell him hoarsely. "Not yet. Maybe

when we're in the air."

Besides, there's plenty of additional electronic information I can access until then. My eyes are growing tired from rapidly scanning the computer screen, and I reach into my purse to pull out my black-rimmed glasses. I place them on my face and adjust them on my nose as I continue to hack into every aspect of Cole's life that left any sort of record. The next step is to examine his financials, bank accounts, and credit card statements.

I continue this for half an hour, while Zachary sits beside me and looks over my shoulder. It usually drives me crazy when people watch me work, but I am way past the point of caring. Besides, we are in an airport.

I fiercely hate airports.

At some point while I was working, our plane must have arrived at the gate, for the previous passengers are all filing out of the plane. I watch them disembark as memories prick the insides of my skull, threatening to take me back to a dark place.

When I was homeless at age twelve, I spent a lot of time in airports. People would treat me nicely as long as I managed to shower often, clean my clothes, and present myself well. No one could ever tell that I was homeless. All I needed was a nice piece of luggage, and I could sleep in an airport without being bothered. It just looked like I was going somewhere important soon, like everyone else. There was security all around, and bright lights—it was one of the safer places to spend the night.

I liked to imagine that I actually *was* going

somewhere soon. Somewhere better. I would pretend I had a ticket in my pocket that led to anywhere I could imagine, in this world, or even somewhere fictional. Sometimes, I was headed to an exotic land that I'd read about in the library, where adventures awaited me. Or to the colorful worlds of the children's television shows I'd seen, and Japanese anime. I was sure that everything would be better if I could only fly to a place where the seven dragonballs would grant me wishes.

I would wish for a family.

Most of the time, I would just pretend that I was going home. That I *had* a home somewhere on the planet, and that people who loved me were there waiting. I would pretend they were worried sick about me, and my whole life was all just one great big misunderstanding.

Once they found me, they would open their arms to accept me with the warmest, tightest hugs and never let me go again. I would be their cherished daughter, returned at last. We would be normal and happy, and celebrate Christmas together, just like the families on television.

Obviously, that never happened.

What really ripped my heart to shreds was when I had the poor judgment of wandering over to the arrivals section of the airport. A few times, I thought I would stand and wait, or sit and read a book while pretending that my family was coming to see me. I had no idea that it would be so excruciating. To be in that room for even a few minutes—to witness all the naked love and emotion so plainly visible on the faces of the families reuniting all around me. It was unbearable.

In normal settings, families do not display much affection to each other. They spend most of their days together, and they grow numb to the presence of their loved ones. But after a short absence? After a long journey? After being reminded of what your life is like without the people closest to you?

Everything is visible—everything comes rushing out.

Tiny children would sprint and bounce into the arms of their mothers or fathers when they returned from a business trip and cover their faces with kisses. The professional façades of the stiff, suit-wearing parents would instantly dissipate as they became soft human beings embracing their little ones. My heart would ache until it might burst.

The reverse would also happen. College-aged kids would come home to their parents, acting cool and aloof while sporting their sweatpants or piercings and wild hair. They would pretend that their parents calling out their names was embarrassing, and try to act unaffected as their mothers and fathers rushed up to them with excitement.

But once their parents hugged them, their tough exteriors would fade, if only for a moment—and their faces would reveal that those tiny, loving children still existed somewhere inside their fully grown, indifferent bodies.

I would stand among them all, watching the tender displays of humanity as an outsider.

Would I always be excluded from this? Would I

ever have someone to wait for? Someone to come home to? It seemed unlikely. Would anyone ever be happy to see me? No one had ever cared much, so far.

Where in the world was my mother, if she was even still alive? I bet she didn't even remember my existence. Was it her choice to abandon me, or was it something she was forced to do? Did she have some kind of postpartum depression that led her to ditch me? And why on the side of the interstate and not a dumpster or a church doorstep like a respectable infant-abandoner? I might never find out.

Would *I* ever have children who loved me? How could I, when I had never seen an example of good parenting? I might not even be healthy enough. I have no parental medical records to know what I might expect out of my future health. Would I experience the same postpartum depression as my mother, and possibly go crazy and abandon my baby, and then kill myself?

No one cares about me. No one even knows where I am. Why shouldn't I just kill myself right now? Right here, in this airport?

These were the thoughts that used to plague me, until I was left sitting in a bathroom stall with tears streaming down my face and seriously considering slitting my wrists. Sometimes, I would cut them a little, as practice, just so I would be tough enough to go through with it someday, when I really decided there was no other choice. For the longest time, I wondered if that day would be tomorrow.

I used to carry a pocketknife and carve that word into the bathroom stalls. Tomorrow.

Tomorrow.

Maybe I'll die tomorrow.

Embarrassingly, I sometimes misspelled the word. It happens when you're twelve.

After Cole came into my life, things started to change and get better. I finally had someone to wait for at the airport. I had someone to leave, and someone to come home to. Wherever he was, that was my place in the world. Wherever I was, I kept a mental map of his location and how far apart we were. That's how far away I was from home.

And now Cole is gone.

That old familiar ache starts seeping back into my heart as I watch the people leaving the plane, and I imagine that many of them are headed to greet their waiting families. The ones that aren't are probably texting their families back home and saying that they arrived safely, miss them already, and will be home soon.

I'm on the outside again.

For a few years, I knew what it was like to be a human being, and to be loved. To feel love. To feel sad about being away from someone and longing to be close. Now, I'm all alone. Now, I've lost the only person who ever gave a damn about me. As I study the weary faces of the plane's passengers, I know that some of them must also feel unhappy and unloved.

Maybe I'm not alone. Maybe loss is a more common human experience than love. It certainly seems more common to lose love than it is to keep it, once obtained.

I feel the weight of a heavy hand on my

shoulder, and I am startled.

Zachary is staring down at me with concern. "Are you okay? You look like you're a million miles away."

He does know me quite well. I forgot he was here for a few minutes, but knowing that he is gives me some comfort. As much as I can't stand Zack right now, and feel upset at myself for letting him come with me, I suppose it's better than being here by myself. I hate sitting and waiting in airports. It gives me way too much time to think. I don't like to be reminded of those hard times when I was young, before Cole. I don't like being reminded that I am now about to enter more hard times, after Cole.

"How did you get so good at hacking?" Zack asks me, trying to distract me from my thoughts.

Shutting the laptop's lid with a sigh, I look up at the clock. "We'll be boarding in a few minutes, Zack. We don't have to make small talk."

"I have found out more about you in the last hour than I have from months of living with you and sleeping beside you. It's not small talk to discover that I don't know my girlfriend's real name, real job, or real… anything."

"It doesn't excuse what you did. Also, I'm your ex-girlfriend."

"I am not making excuses, Soph. I'm just trying to take advantage of this rare opportunity to get to know you. So talk to me."

The second hand moves slowly on the airport clock. I watch it closely, as though I can will it to move faster.

Tick.

Tick.

Tick.

Sadly, telekinesis is still not one of my talents. Trust me—I've tried.

Zachary nudges my knee with his own. "Why hacking?"

My shoulders lift ever so slightly in a shrug. "I just wanted to find my parents."

"Ah. You searched on the Internet a lot?"

"Yeah. I was obsessed with trying to find them, from my earliest childhood. I tried everything. When I first discovered the Internet, my mind was blown with the idea that I could reach any part of the world in seconds. I thought that I would be able to find them for sure, wherever they were, if I just looked hard enough."

"Did you ever get close?"

I shake my head. "No."

"I'm so sorry, Sophie."

"No biggie." I give him a little self-deprecating smile. "I can crack almost any code, shut all the lights off in entire cities, hijack satellites to do my bidding, rob banks in my pajamas while eating ice cream—but I can't find my own goddamned parents."

Zack leans over to place his arms around me again, and I don't stop him. I just stare at the clock.

Tick.

Tick.

Tick.

"Now boarding first-class passengers for flight 7033 to Los Angeles."

"That's us," I say, stuffing the laptop into my backpack and standing up. I feel a little bit of nausea in my stomach, because I know that once I'm seated on that plane, it will be time to read Cole's letters.

I'm not ready.

Once I finish reading them, I will never receive another letter from my brother again. I wish they could remain unopened forever, so I could keep myself in anticipation. I could keep him alive. At least in my mind. It would be like knowing I was going to receive a phone call from him, or have him show up on my doorstep for a visit. It would be like knowing he was going to reach out to me and share something personal again.

It would be pretending. Like I always did when I was younger. Pretending things aren't as bad as they really are so that I can get through the day and make it to tomorrow.

As we move to stand in line to board the plane, I place my hand on the side of my abdomen, where my scars are sitting beneath my shirt, covered in little orange tattoos.

I could really use a wish right now.

Chapter Five

cole hunter, 2003

Scarlett didn't come home today.

I've just discovered that when your teenaged sister's whereabouts are unknown, it is impossible to keep from freaking out. It's almost midnight. 11:57 PM. On a school night. The Browns haven't noticed, or they fail to care.

Scarlett said she was staying at school late to work on a project, but I expected her home hours ago. *Where is she?* I have been unable to study. Unable to relax or watch TV. Unable to draw. I have been compulsively pacing the halls, checking her room, and running downstairs to see if she's approaching the house.

My worst fear is that she has run away.
What if I never see her again?

It's almost too painful to think about. Would she do that? Without telling me? Why? I've been sleeping in her room every night, and Mr. Brown hasn't harmed her again—not since he broke her laptop. We spoke to the Browns and threatened to report them if it happened again, or to leave. Mr. Brown agreed to watch his drinking, and he apologized for destroying the computer. He said he couldn't afford to replace it, but that he would try to spend less money on cigarettes and booze and more on things we actually need.

There has been some mild improvement in the state of affairs around the house. Not a huge change, but we've mostly been left alone, and it has been tolerable. At least, I thought it was tolerable. I have no idea how Scarlett really feels, as she is very guarded and quiet most of the time.

What if Benjamin found her? Part of me wants to call the police and report her missing, but if the Browns get accused of neglect, then we could be separated. That would defeat the purpose of trying to make this work.

What could be keeping her so late? She doesn't have any friends—at least, none that she has ever mentioned to me. She could be hanging out with some guy. The thought makes me a little sick. She's only fourteen, but she is very mature for her age. She is quite beautiful and probably gets a lot of male attention. I feel a surge of anger that some punk could be keeping her out until midnight. I am not sure if it is brotherly instinct, but I am mentally rolling up my sleeves in preparation to kick his hypothetical ass.

The truth is that a boyfriend would be the least of my worries. Scarlett had been homeless for quite some time. She could be getting into trouble with some of the street kids she used to know. Thugs. Thieves. Drug dealers. Could she be doing drugs? Scarlett wouldn't do that, would she? She is way too smart.

Images rush to my mind of the skin on her pale arms and the tiny scars on the insides of her elbow and her wrists. I grind my teeth together tightly. The scars looked self-inflicted, but I never asked her about them. I didn't want to bring up something that might make her sad or upset. What if those scars are connected to drug use? Track marks from needles? I swallow a painful lump in my throat. What if she has a contact who can supply her with meth or cocaine? She never mentioned any of this to me, but I can imagine how rough her life was after she escaped from Benjamin Powell.

I briefly lived on the streets, too, and I know how this works. I know how kids with shit lives are often desperate to escape their pain. It's easy for a girl to acquire drugs, even if she has no money. All she needs is her body, to trade for them. After Scarlett's experiences with Benjamin, it might not seem like such a painful price to pay. She was willing to let Mr. Brown keep hurting her just so she wouldn't have to change schools and start over. She must be used to sacrificing her dignity in exchange for comfort and security. But drugs aren't comfort—they are pleasure.

I think she would make sacrifices for necessities, or for her future, but not for pleasure. Not for escape. Right? I'm not thinking straight. Her absence is making me go out of my mind with worry.

She wouldn't do this. I barely know her, but I need to believe she wouldn't do this.

She is too smart to get involved with drugs. She is too strong.

I can't lose her.

If she goes down this path, she will be lost. Like so many kids who grow up without parents, she will end up getting into trouble with the law, or worse…

Scarlett has such a fascinating mind, and vast potential. Every time I'm near her, I can sense that she will accomplish great things. All of that could be destroyed by a few bad decisions in a few weak moments. She is so fragile right now. She is so delicate, like brittle glass in cold weather.

My chest begins to hurt as all these thoughts ricochet within my mind. It feels like the anxiety is firing bullets throughout my nervous system, making my limbs move as frantically as my thoughts. I find myself putting on my shoes and moving out into the street and scanning the neighborhood with panic.

Would she really run away? *No.* I tried to make things better for her. Things were getting better. Does she not want to be here with me? Is she running *from* me?

Come on, Cole. You need to think like Scar. What does she want? What does she need? What drives her?

"My laptop. I am useless without my laptop."

Yes. She's been pining for the Internet for weeks. What if she decided to get involved with drugs to get the money for a laptop? My heart skips a beat. This makes the most sense, so far. I shouldn't have let this happen. I have been making a little money from landscaping, but I should have worked harder to save her from having to put herself at risk. If I can find her, I vow that I will get her that computer quickly, no matter what it takes.

My feet begin moving before my brain, and I find myself headed in the direction of the school. It's a safe bet to check there first, since it was the last place she said she would be. Terrible images spin through my mind like a film reel. I picture her doing cocaine. I picture her being fondled by some boy. I picture her depressed and hurting herself. *God, anything but that.* I need to find her and know that she's safe. *Please let her be safe.*

I find myself walking faster and faster until I am running down the sidewalk in the direction of our high school. It takes only a few minutes before I arrive at the building. The doors are all locked for the night, but I know a side entrance that I can break into. I quickly jog around the building, until I come to a door with a basic lock near the cafeteria. I reach into my pocket for my switchblade, and slide it into the space between the door and the doorframe to jimmy the lock open.

It's fairly easy. I am able to get it open within a few seconds, and I carefully move through the darkened halls to the computer lab. If she is still in the school, then that's probably where she would be. Either there or the library.

When I reach the lab, the door is locked. I

glance inside through the windows, and there is no sign of Scarlett. The chairs are neatly placed and all the computers are off—there is no evidence that she was ever here. I continue moving toward the library. There are a few computers there as well, and Scarlett has a voracious appetite for books. In the week or so that I've been sleeping in her room, I feel like she has read at least one novel of considerable size every single day. That's in addition to studying and doing her homework.

She never has fun. She is a serious girl, and she always does the right thing.

I shouldn't be so worried about her getting into trouble.

It was an impossible task to even get her to watch television. I made it my mission to make her relax for even half an hour a day, so I introduced her to my favorite Japanese anime, *Dragonball Z*. At first, she seemed a little confused by it, and raised her eyebrows at all the explosions. She was determined to keep her face buried in a book while we watched, but I coaxed her to give it a chance. After a while, she started to warm up to all the danger and the romance. The real charm of the show is the way the characters will do anything to protect their family and friends.

For years, many of the boys my age—and a few tough girls—have adored these epic adventures and grand battles where the fate of the universe is often at stake. How could anyone with a heart resist this show? Scarlett eventually put her book away and really got into the story, and it has become our daily ritual to watch an episode together. She said she would be home in time to watch an episode with me today, but when she never showed up... I started to imagine the worst.

When I walk into the library, I immediately see a chair that is slightly ajar. I rush over and find three books lying beside the computer. *Great Expectations, Jane Eyre*, and *Anne of Green Gables*. I am a little puzzled by this strange combination, but then it dawns on me. They are all books about orphans. Leaning over the keyboard, I enter my school ID to log in. I know that Scarlett is careful, so when I go to check the browsing history, I am expecting to see that it has been cleared.

But it hasn't.

My heart aches at what I find. News articles on abandoned infants from the late 1980s and early 1990s. Scarlett was definitely here. But where is she now? Moving away from the computer and scanning the darkened library, I don't see any shadows. I briskly walk through the room and scan between the aisles, but it feels empty. On a hunch, I move to exit the building and walk out into the football field.

It's a clear night, so the field is eerily lit by the crescent moon. I move forward, listening carefully to the silence that is punctuated by the chirping of the crickets. This field is normally so noisy and bright in the day, and I did not expect it to feel this peaceful when it isn't swarming with obnoxious teenagers.

I find myself moving over to the bleachers to sit, and when I grow closer, I see a dark shape huddled beneath them. For a moment, I am nervous, and I place my hand in my pocket to grasp my switchblade. But then the figure moves, and I hear my name being called softly.

"Cole?"

I exhale in relief, and my shoulders sag as I walk around the bleachers and collapse in the grass beside her. I note the sad way she is sitting, curled up in a ball in a dark corner and hugging her knees.

"You're going to be the death of me, Scar. I was worried sick."

"Worried?" she asks in surprise. "About me?"

"Yes. Do you know what time it is? You were supposed to be home hours ago."

"I'm sorry," she says softly. "I didn't think you'd notice."

"What the hell does that mean? Of course I noticed! I was freaking out." Reaching up, I run my hands through my hair. The freshly cut grass around us smells good, and it is starting to calm me down. "Do you know how many crazy things I was imagining? I thought something happened to you. I nearly called the cops. I thought you ran away…"

"I was thinking about it," Scarlett admits.

"What? Why!"

"Because things are all screwed up, Cole. The Browns hate me. I'm a burden on you. You have been sleeping on the floor because of me, and…"

"Stop!" I nearly shout, grabbing her hand and squeezing it. "You are not a burden. Actually, I think you're the one doing me a favor. I don't get any nightmares when I'm close to you. I may be on the floor, but at least I'm actually resting and not just thinking about people burning to death. You take my mind off the things that drag me down."

"You really mean that? You aren't sick of me?"

"No," I tell her. "I could never be sick of you. Don't you dare think of running away unless we do it together."

"Well," she says softly. "I was thinking of a slightly different kind of running away."

I pause and stare at her hard in the dark. "What are you talking about?" I demand.

She shrugs a little in dismissal. "I don't know. I'm just so tired. I promised myself that if life didn't get better this year, I wouldn't waste more time trying. I don't think I can survive much more of this."

"Did something happen?" I ask her. "Did Mr. Brown do something?"

"No." She sighs and carefully lowers herself backwards to the grass. "It's just taking forever to grow up. I don't know how I can get through it, to the other side, and remain in one piece. I can't be patient anymore. I feel so powerless, and I feel so small. Why should others have dominion over my life because of a number? I can do more than they can. I can make better decisions. But being young, and homeless—it makes me so dependent, like I'm not even a person. I have to take so much crap. I don't want to be anyone's possession anymore. I want to belong to myself and be… free."

"You are free," I tell her, lying back on the grass beside her. I look up at the slivers of sky that are visible through the bleachers. I breathe deeply, and everything feels fresh and clear. It's a beautiful night, and I feel like I haven't looked at the sky like this in a long time. It's so healing that I wonder why I don't do it more often.

"It's my birthday," she says in a whisper. "I am fourteen now. Today is the day that the old lady found me on the side of the road."

My forehead wrinkles. "I thought your birthday was in August? I thought you were already fourteen."

She shakes her head. "That's Scarlett's birthday. She was fourteen when she died."

A chill prickles the hairs at the back of my neck. "Aren't you Scarlett?"

"No. She overdosed on heroin a few months ago. I buried her body and stole her identification. She was around my age, and looked fairly similar to me. She had no family. It's the only way I could make sure that Benjamin wouldn't find me."

"Wow. That's hardcore." I reach out and touch the tender inside of her elbow questioningly. "So you did drugs, too? With her?"

"Yes. Kind of. I pretended to shoot up, just to get close to her. I knew that she was going to die, from the moment I first met her. It was just a matter of time. She was too delicate for this world." Scarlett pauses, staring down at the scars on her arm. "She was a sweet girl. Sometimes, I wonder if she made the smart decision, to permanently escape all of this."

"No. Don't say that," I tell her, sitting up a little and placing my hands on both of her knees. "Don't even think that. Promise me you're never going to consider that shit again."

Scarlett shrugs. "I've run away so many times, Cole. It never works. Every time I thought I could find somewhere better, I didn't. What if I messed up? What if I should have stayed with Benjamin? What if there is nowhere better? What if it only gets worse from now on? Why should I bother living a life like that?"

"Do you trust me?" I ask her, gently squeezing her knees. "Life is going to get better. I'm going to make it better. Just give me a chance to try."

"Please don't say things like that," she says with a sigh as she pulls away and falls back onto the grass. Her dark hair spills out all around her. "I've never trusted anyone, Cole. It's terrifying."

"I'm going to make things better," I tell her softly. "I won't let you down."

"Damn you," she says slowly, through gritted teeth. "You make me feel… good." She speaks bitterly, like it's an insult. "You make me feel like there's a chance that things might be okay. You're so strong. And positive." She clenches her fists, and I see tears brimming in her eyes. "Dammit, Cole! You give me *hope.* I can't bear it. It hurts like hell. Don't you understand? It's killing me. I can't let myself feel hope if it's going to end up being false."

I move to lie on my side near her in the grass, supporting myself on my elbow so I can look down at her carefully. I study her clear blue eyes in the dark. "I'm not going to give up on you, Scar. I know you have one foot out the door—but if it hurts, it means that you don't really want to go. Something in you is still willing to fight, and I'm right here, ready to fight beside you. I can't do this on my own. You need to give yourself over to hope, and abandon all your fears.

Because I'll never lie to you, and from now on, we're in this together."

"Oh, I hate you," she says miserably. "It would have been so easy to die, thinking there was no one like you in this world. I hate that you ask about my day and seem to actually care. I hate that you came all the way out here to find me in the middle of the night. I hate that you protect me from an abusive alcoholic, and most of all, I hate that you show me stupid, beautiful TV shows. Just *go!* I'm used to it, Cole— I'm used to getting hurt. So why don't you just walk away, and leave me alone, like everyone else? Why don't you just hit me, or rape me, or murder me, so I can maintain a realistic view of this world? A realistic view of people."

Tears begin sliding out of her eyes relentlessly.

"Go away," she whispers, "because I don't want to die so much when I'm around you. You can't protect me, Cole. The only way to be safe in this world is to be dead."

My heart breaks for her as I watch her lips tremble with emotion. I lean forward to press my forehead against hers, and I shut my eyes tightly to fight back my own tears. "Scar," I say gruffly, "or whatever your name is. Shut up. Okay? Shut the hell up, now."

When she grows very still, I open my eyes and look down into her blue ones. We are only inches apart. I feel like there is fire burning in my irises, and I hope she can see how serious I am. I grasp her elbow firmly to punctuate my words. "You are never to speak about killing yourself again. Do you hear me?

You will never think about suicide again. I won't allow it. Those days are over."

"Why?" she demands to know, jutting her chin out defiantly. "Why on earth shouldn't I die? Give me a reason. Give me one good fucking reason."

Those eyes of hers. Heaven help me. My hand lifts from her elbow to rest on her cheek, and I hold my palm there for a second before letting my fingers drift down to get tangled up in her hair. I brush my thumb over her ear as I stare down into her angry, but innocent eyes. They pierce directly into me, seeking. They pull me closer. Her lips part slightly and soften, and my pulse quickens. My heart begins to pound so loudly that I can feel it in my ears. Every part of my body feels awake and alive and tingling with sensation.

She wants me to kiss her.

She is so close that our breath mingles. I can already taste her. She is challenging me, daring me, and asking me all at the same time. It's impossible to refuse.

Our lips barely brush, so barely that it might not even have happened. But I summon a bit of inhuman strength so that I can pull away.

"Because," I tell her through my heavy breathing. "Because things are going to get better now."

"Cole," she whispers brokenly, gripping a handful of my shirt to pull me closer.

She arches her body a little to press against mine, and I groan at the sensation of her softness and warmth against me. My head falls a little, until our noses are touching.

I need to kiss her. I nearly do.

Her eyelids flutter closed halfway in anticipation, and I grow dizzy with how much I want this. I want to kiss her until she knows how I feel— how much I care. I want to wrap my arms around her body and hold her close, and promise her everything. I want to promise her the world. I want to promise her forever.

But then I see it all going up in flames. I see the whirlwind romance. I see us making love, and I see how passionately and desperately we would cling to each other. I see me getting lost inside her. I see me growing addicted to her. I see her begging me for more, until I become her escape, and I become her death.

She did not seem to care much for heroin, but no one is immune to the simultaneous opiate, narcotic, and stimulant that is love.

I see us bleeding each other dry. I see us both sacrificing our goals for one more moment together. One more mind-numbing and soul-crushing moment of bliss. We will erase each other. We will blend into each other until we forget who we used to be. Who we could have been.

I see how broken she is, how afraid and insecure, and I see me wanting to do anything to make her whole. I see my own brokenness, and the way I would use her body to try and forget my own pain and loss. I see me expecting her to nurture me enough to replace my mother and father; I see me endlessly asking her for more, and more, and more. I see me leaning on her a little too much every time it becomes difficult to stand on my own two feet and become a man out there in the real world.

I see us drowning in a love of overwhelming power, and both of us unable to breathe or come up for air. I see us being consumed, and eventually incinerated.

This love is a dangerous one. I can feel it now, as I teeter on the edge of falling in. It is a flame that burns so white-hot it could only destroy everything it touches. It would destroy us.

We're not strong enough yet.

We are just two frightened kids who have nothing, and no one. If we had each other, we would tear each other to shreds. We would devour each other, looking for all the things that we're missing, and all the things that we were supposed to find in ourselves first.

I see it all so clearly, and it gives me the courage to pull away from her—even though it feels like I am ripping off my own flesh. It gives me the courage to stop before I can kiss her—because once I do, there's no going back.

"Scarlett," I say as tenderly as I can. "No."

Chapter Six

cole hunter, 2003

"No?" she repeats in disbelief. Her eyebrows are lifted in surprise, but I can see the hurt building.

"We were in the middle of a serious discussion," I tell her, trying my best to appear resolute. "And you wanted a good reason."

"Cole…" Her voice is both asking and warning. Even at her tender age, she knows the power that she holds over men, and over me. This is something I wish she had yet to learn. I can tell she is used to getting what she wants, whenever she wants it. But I need to be stronger than this. I need to show her that I am not governed by my urges, and I am capable of thinking.

So think, Cole.

Scarlett is frighteningly beautiful here in the

night. But how can I let myself get swept away in her beauty now, when there is a chance she could throw it all away? I take a deep breath to collect my scattered thoughts, and try to find a way to communicate clearly. "I know how this works," I say, and my voice grows more confident with each word, even if I'm not exactly sure what I'm saying yet. "You change the subject now, and I think things are fine, and one day I find you with your wrists slit in a bathtub. No. Do you hear me, Scar? Absolutely not."

She sits up, looking a little baffled as she wraps her arms around her middle.

"I'm not going to let you sabotage us," I tell her. "I'm not going to do something unforgiveable, so you can actually hate me. I don't want you to ever put me in the same category with everyone else who has hurt you."

"I wouldn't do that," she says in confusion.

"I'm not going to get distracted from this. I'm not going to be a distraction. Please," I tell her firmly, "please promise me that you'll never think about suicide again."

"I can't."

"Scar, I need you—to be *here*. I can't lose another person. I need you to be my family. I need you to be my friend. You need me to be your brother. That's what we both need right now."

She shakes her head slowly. "No. I'm only still here because I'm a coward. I keep deciding that I'll give it one more day, to see if things change. They never do, but I keep trying and hoping anyway. I keep on living, out of sheer habit, when I've already decided that it's not worthwhile. That makes me insane, doesn't it?"

"No. It makes you persistent. And wise. Because things are about to change."

"How do you know?"

Determination pulses through me, causing me to rise to my feet. "Can't you feel it? You've had so much bad luck in your life that things need to turn around, sooner or later. Why don't we make it sooner? We can make it happen. I know that I can help, if I really try. I can take care of you the way a brother should."

"I've had so many brothers, Cole. I can't even remember all their names. You know how the foster system is. People come and people go—a revolving door of strangers. The best ones were those who never noticed me, and the worst ones were those who noticed me a little too well. Brothers are like mailmen; all I have to do is switch houses and I get a new one."

"That's exactly why I need to show you that I can be different. You're remarkable, Scar. You shouldn't let assholes like your parents, or Mr. Brown, or Benjamin Powell make you lose the will to live. You shouldn't ever let anyone make you feel like you are less than you are."

"It wasn't just them," she says softly, lifting her shoulders a little. "It's just… everything."

"Then I'm going to change everything," I tell her seriously. "Do you believe me? It doesn't matter. I'm going to do it anyway. I'll show you. Just say that you'll let me." I smile and lean down to take both of her hands. "Promise me that you'll live. That's all you need to do. Because nothing can get better if you don't live."

"Cole," she says, and her voice wavers. "Even if you manage to make things better temporarily, I'm going to lose you. You're going to go off to college. Professor Brown will go back to using me as an ashtray, and I'll get sick of it and end up on the streets again. Please—please, can we be realistic? We're getting older and things will change. We'll be separated."

"Not if I can take you to college with me. Not if I can become emancipated, live on my own as an adult, and gain access to my inheritance early. Maybe I could be your guardian."

Scarlett stares at me in puzzlement. "Emancipated?"

"It's something I've been thinking about. But if this doesn't work, I'll find another way. I'm not going to leave you behind. Just put your life in my hands," I tell her as I squeeze hers for emphasis. "If it's not safe in yours, you have to trust someone else. I will take care of you, and I am not a mailman."

"You're crazy," she says softly.

I suddenly grin, tugging gently on her hands. "Come with me!"

She follows with a skeptical look on her face until we have exited from underneath the bleachers and moved out into the open football field.

"There's your reason!" I say, pointing a finger into the endless expanse of darkened sky. "How can you look at all those billions of stars and not feel humbled? Every problem we face is so small and insignificant that it's foolish to let it weigh us down. We are free, and we are perfect. We are part of something greater than ourselves, and something great is in each of us. We're connected. It's easy to forget that when you've mired in all the crap people have done to you. But you're so much more than your past, and your pain. You need to rise above it all. You're part of *this*, Scarlett. You're part of eternity. That's the truth."

"Cole, are you high?" Scarlett asks me, but she is smiling.

"Yes. Isn't it crazy, when you really think about it?" I stare up into the sky until I get chills running through my body. "It's easy to forget when you've got your nose stuck in a book or a computer all day, but we are organic, spiritual beings. You're not an orphan, because there is no such thing as an orphan. Two people don't create a life. Your parents were just a vehicle for your existence. They were part of a long line of ancestry—thousands of human beings who met by random coincidence, and had children for any number of strange reasons, or by pure accident—all culminating in the person that is *you*. You're a child of nature. We all are. And it's just amazing and mind-blowing, everything that has led to us standing right here, right now."

Scarlett does not respond, but she simply stares at me. I cannot read the expression on her face. I feel suddenly very embarrassed, because here I am, rambling on like an idiot. The excitement and energy rushing through me is overpowering, and I'm not sure where it came from. I hope she'll forgive my madness, and I hope she'll feel that I'm right.

"You're too special to even consider ending your life," I tell her firmly. "We're made up of stuff that's billions of years old. Stuff that's grown and changed and been ripped apart and put back together in millions of different ways. What's a year more? What's four years more, until you're eighteen and legally an adult? It's all nothing. It's an infinitesimal speck of time for your soul. You think you want to die, because it hurts, but you can handle so much more than you think you can."

I step forward and smile at her as she looks at me quizzically. I can see a little spark of interest in her eyes, and it encourages me to keep going. "Right here, right now? This is precious. This is life. You're *alive.* Somehow, all of the genetic material of all those thousands of ancestors came together in the perfect combination to make you, exactly as you are. That's magical—it's the greatest kind of magic I know. Our very existence."

My fingers slide over her hair, which is blacker than the night. "I know that you're suffering. That's what life means. It means suffering to survive. And we have to keep doing it, because it'll all be over in the blink of an eye, anyway. Even if you live eighty more years, or ninety more years, it's nothing at all. It's just this tiny bit of life you get to experience, before we return to dust, so why waste it? Suffer with me, and experience life with me, while we're lucky enough to be here, together. We might never get another chance."

Scarlett shakes her head, and puts her hands up in surrender. "Okay. You've convinced me. For the time being, I will not speak of killing myself, and I'll try to stop thinking of it as an option. Unless something goes horribly wrong, I'm going to try to tough it out." She looks up at me, and a tiny smile touches her lips. "I promise that I will live, but just so you know: if it sucks, I'm blaming everything on you."

"I will happily take the blame," I tell her, leaning forward to crush her against me in a zealous hug. "But if it's great, then you better blame me for that, too."

She hugs me back tightly, resting her forehead against my shoulder. "How are you so strong? If I had lost what you've lost, I couldn't be so strong."

My shoulders stiffen slightly, and my lips pull into a frown. But I glance back up at the sky and exhale. "It might be *because* of what I lost that I can be strong. I watched my parents get lowered six feet deep, and I know we'll all be returning to dirt someday. When that day comes, we can't feel any more pain. I don't know about you, but I'm not in any rush to put myself in an early grave. I'm going to fight, and struggle, and treasure every moment of life I've got. I want to feel it—all the pain I can possibly feel. I'm going to make a mark on this world, and I'm going to do all I can while I'm here. You just watch and see, Scarlett."

"I will," she says, pulling away slightly to look at me. Her eyes are hard, like she's starting to believe me, and starting to focus on her own future.

My heart soars. Is this really working? Have I really changed her mind? *No.* I need to spend every day changing her mind. Maybe I've lit a fire under her, but that fire will go out if I don't keep feeding it. I need to be loyal, and good, unshakable and fierce.

"Life is going to be great," I say, giving her an earnest smile. "Life should be great. Why not? We can do anything. I have all these goals, and I can't wait to really get started on achieving them. Nothing's going to stop me from getting what I want. Nothing is going to stand in my way. No one can hurt me or bring me down. Never again."

Scarlett nods slowly, but I can see that she is still having doubts.

"And no one," I add softly, "is ever going to keep me away from you."

She looks up sharply, and her eyes flash with emotion. "I don't get you, Cole. What do you really want?"

"What do you mean?"

"I don't know," she says, but her gaze is piercing. "Are you trying to make me fall in love with you or something?"

My eyes widen. "Are you? Hey. Because… I—I don't mind."

"What if I don't want you to be my brother?" she asks, stepping closer. "What if I want more than that from you?"

God. She is so direct. I'd be lying if I didn't say I wanted to jump at the opportunity. Or jump her. I take a deep breath. "Right now, I think it's all I can give safely." My voice falters and I hesitate.

Am I making a huge mistake? Will *right now* be the only chance we ever have to be together? Is this the only moment I will ever get to decide this? Am I about to waste years of my life keeping her at an arm's length for stupid reasons? I speak the words I know I should speak, instead of the ones that are ready to springboard off my tongue:

"I think it would be wrong to ask more of you, when you're in such a vulnerable state."

"This is because I told you about Benjamin," she says, lowering her eyes to her sneakers. "That's why you think I can't handle a relationship."

"No. It's because we're not established enough right now," I tell her. "And you're not emotionally healthy. From what I hear, rape isn't something you get over easily. You ran away at age twelve? And you just turned fourteen? That's not a lot of time to heal."

"You think I'm a child," she responds stubbornly. "I'm only one year younger than you."

"Almost two years," I correct, but then I grow sober. "Seriously, Scar. You might be smarter than me in a lot of ways, and more mature—but I need to be the adult here, and act in your best interests. I think I know best, in this particular way. I wish… things could be different. But just trust me, and be patient."

She glowers at me. "I suck at patience. If life is so short, and so precious, why should we waste any of it?"

"I think we could end up wasting a lot more time if we do the wrong thing at the wrong moment. I think people have taken a lot from you, and I need to show you that someone can give, and not take."

"Fine," she says. "I'll accept this for right now. But what about someday?"

"Someday, I'm hoping that you won't need a big brother quite so much. Then, maybe… I can be something more." I smile at her. "Let's put a pin in it?"

"A pin? What does that mean?" she frowns. "Like stick it up on a wall with a thumbtack and address it later?"

"Kind of. But I think it actually comes from grenades. We need to keep a pin in it so that it doesn't explode all over our lives."

"We're going to need a really big pin, Cole." She crosses her arms over her chest. "You know, if you don't like me, you can just say that."

"I like you, Scar. Trust me, I like you very, very much." I grin at her madly, because she looks so damned cute when she's annoyed. "How about this? Someday, when I think we're both ready, we'll come back here to discuss it. Then, if we're both confident that we are strong enough, we'll take the pin out of the grenade. Look, this goalpost right here, this will be our pin."

Moving over to the large goalpost, I get out my switchblade and begin to carve some letters in the paint. The paint is already fading and chipped in some places, and I wonder how long the letters will last.

2003
CS
PIN

"How's that?" I ask her as I wipe my blade off on my jeans.

"You're crazy," she says. "I bet you're going to forget all about that in a few days."

But I don't forget. Scarlett doesn't know that I have a mind like a steel trap, and I'm already hatching my master plan. It starts with a letter. I'll write her a letter tonight, as soon as she goes to bed. I already know the first two sentences. It will be the first letter I ever write her—but I doubt it will be the last. What I do hope, is that it will be the last letter of mine that she ever needs to read.

The road ahead is going to be rough. I wonder if I can be half as strong as she's going to need me to be? It doesn't matter. I have no choice. I will dig deep inside myself and find a way. We could really help each other through all this. We could be the family that we both need so badly—the pillars of support that were ripped out from under us way too early. We could be everything to each other—everything that's been missing for so long. We could be together.

It's hard not to imagine that day, in the distant future, when everything is finally safe. I can see it now, the older, better versions of ourselves and how happy and successful they will be. They will have everything. They will own the world.

"Come on, Cole," Scarlett says softly, grabbing my shirt and tugging me gently away from the goalpost where I am staring at the letters. "We better go home. We have school in the morning."

Snapped out of my fantasy, I turn to her and nod.

We begin walking through the wet grass in the direction of home. Our temporary home, until I can find us a better place. I can't help glancing at her sideways. I know that her life has been wretched until now, but she is still so sweet and capable of love. I want to do everything I can to protect her and keep her safe. I want to be so amazing that I'm her first choice; so trustworthy and reliable and caring that she simply can't imagine anyone else.

I don't want to be a reckless, bad decision. I don't want to be a Band-Aid or a quick fix, or a diversion. I don't want to be a temporary source of recreation. I don't want to be a reminder of a time in her life she can't bear to remember. I don't want to be used.

I want to be her endgame. I want to be the only one.

I don't care how long it takes, or how many years I have to wait.

And maybe when she's finally ready, I will be, too.

Chapter Seven

sophie shields, 2016

"Vodka," I tell the stewardess. "Two of them. And some whiskey, for my coffee."

She complies quickly, with a professional smile. I'm glad that we got first class seats for the complimentary drinks and quick service. The extra room is also helpful, although Zack's laptop is taking up most of the space on my pull-down tray, and I am using his tray to store my liquor.

"Whoa," Zack says as he looks at the little airplane bottles judgmentally. "Don't you think you should slow it down? I've never seen you drink so much."

"Well, there's a first time for everything. Like finding out your brother was murdered."

"Sophie, I don't think this is helping." Zack

reaches out to take the vodka bottles away while I pour the whiskey into my coffee, but I grab his wrist.

"Don't you dare touch my alcohol," I tell him in a deathly whisper. "I am not in the mood for this right now."

He drops the bottles and lifts his hands in surrender. "Where are you even putting it all? You're a tank, Soph. Like, do you even have working kidneys?"

My bladder is decidedly full, but I am too focused on my task to pay attention to the screaming organ below my bellybutton. The security footage from the hospital was incomplete, and I was not able to see the person who shot Cole. I may have downloaded videos from the wrong timeframe, but there is nothing that I can do right now to access the feed—not without the Internet. It is also possible, but unlikely, that someone might have altered the footage to protect the shooter. That would mean that either someone on Cole's own security team did it—or someone hacked into my system.

There's no use worrying about that now, so I've been focusing my attention on other details.

It has taken me a while to comb through the information on the laptop to get a good picture of the last few days and weeks of Cole's life. All I know so far is that he was under a lot of pressure, with an impossible workload. He had doctor's appointments woven into his schedule regularly, along with massages and sessions with a psychiatrist.

This last one bothers me a little. Cole *hated* therapy. After losing his parents, he was forced to go through grief counseling, and he also had mandated therapy several times as a teenager. He complained that it only made things worse. After being diagnosed with various disorders and pumped full of medications that made him feel like a zombie, he grew stubbornly independent and decided he didn't need any more professional advice.

Cole thought he could do anything, all by himself. He thought that the only medicine anyone ever needed, for any ailment, was just simple, good ol' fashioned hard work. And he did work hard. He healed himself by making forward progress and never losing that momentum. No matter what went wrong, physically or otherwise, he cured himself of everything with a positive attitude and proactive measures. I wonder if he could somehow cure himself of death?

"What's this about?" Zack asks, pointing at the screen where I have some of Cole's emails open.

Distracted from my thoughts, I look back at the work I've been doing. At the start of this flight, I began examining all the correspondence with Benjamin, but I eventually started to drift toward some of Cole's more personal emails. Maybe I was sick of seeing Benjamin's name, or maybe I was curious about what Cole's life has been like lately, but I feel a little guilty when I see that I have opened several emails and text messages from one particular woman.

"I don't know who she is," I explain quietly.

"Annabelle Nelson," Zack says, squinting and looking closer. "Is she one of his employees? It sounds like they were close. They are talking about going for drinks, dinner… a weekend trip. Oh. Do you think they were… together?"

For a moment, my anger is blinding. The laptop screen explodes into various colors and shapes that hurt my brain. My head swivels sharply toward Zack. "How the hell do you expect me to know that?"

"Sophie," he says gently. "You need to look at the letters. We only have about an hour left until we land in California. You can't really understand his life from scanning security camera footage and emails—all of that could be a lie. The face he showed to the world. You need to look deeper than the surface. You need to see what was inside his head."

I find myself scowling. "If everything I've found about his whole life is a lie, why do you think his letters to me were truth? Everything you've been saying to me for months has been a lie. Why would the other men in my life be honest? And how are you even able to *imagine* someone being honest?"

Zack clears his throat. "Partially because I read some of those letters, and they felt raw. They felt real. And partially because I trust you, and you say that he's never lied to you."

"He hasn't," I say softly. My hand hesitates for a moment before I begin closing Annabelle's emails to Cole. I shouldn't be prying into his personal life like this. If he was romantically involved with this woman, it is none of my business. I should be focusing on Benjamin. I haven't found anything so far, but the senator always was a sneaky bastard.

I am upset at myself for letting jealousy distract

me from my task. There are dozens of emails from the legal department about various lawsuits against Cole's company, and I have begun to compile a list of people who have made threats against him. I know of at least two major competitors who despise him for stealing their business.

"The girl could be helpful," Zack suggests. "She could know details of his life that we can't find otherwise. Maybe we could talk to her when we get to Los Angeles?"

"Maybe."

"Or you could see if he wrote to you about her. Or Benjamin. Or anything," Zack says. "Come on, Sophie. If you keep putting it off, you'll never read them."

I feel sick. "Maybe you shouldn't have hidden them in the first place, if you wanted me to read them so badly."

"Do not get distracted and focus on your anger at me when we have more important things to do." Zack grabs my backpack and unzips it, pulling out the letters. "Come on, Sophie. Read."

He hands me the first letter on the top of the pile.

My fingers shake as they close around the envelope. I see my name written in Cole's careful, masculine penmanship. I can imagine his hand holding the pen as he addressed this letter to me, so clearly that I could almost reach out and trace the olive veins on the back of his hands, running down to his wrists and forearms. I can imagine feeling his heartbeat in those veins, as they pulsate with his blood, with his energy. His life force. I see him so clearly that it causes everything in me to ache.

Turning the envelope over mechanically, I lift the flap and withdraw a few lined pages that are folded over twice. When I move to unfold the pages, I feel like I can almost detect the scent of Cole's skin. Just in case I'm imagining it, I hug the letter against me and inhale deeply, until the faint musk pervades my senses. His scent is comforting. I feel like he could be right beside me, smiling and reaching for my hand. I can feel him close and hear his breathing.

I can feel him all around me.

He once tried to tell me that life was short, and I didn't believe him. As usual, he was right.

It's funny how death makes every morsel of a person precious. Every strand of hair, every skin cell, is a treasure. He won't be making any more. There must be something of him on this letter, more than just the thoughts on the page. He touched it, when he wrote it. Some of the oils from his body were surely transferred, or a few droplets of moisture from his breath when he sighed. Maybe, if I'm really lucky, he scratched his head while writing, and there are a few infinitesimal flakes of dandruff sprinkled somewhere around here.

Cole's hands were always in his hair when he was thinking, and he was always thinking.

The paper might be infused with his feelings and fears, but it also holds remnants of his physical body, and it's all that I currently possess of him. It might be all I ever possess.

I don't want to open any more envelopes, for

fear of letting these relics escape.

"Sophie," Zack says, leaning over. "Look, he mentions Annabelle there, several times."

My hands tighten around the pages. Oh, god. Do I have to read about how he's found someone else and he's happy? I don't think I can bear it right now. But what right do I have to be sad or upset? I told him to move on. I told him I had a boyfriend. I told him when I started dating Zack.

I started dating Zack specifically for the purpose of creating a barrier. I can't be upset if I succeeded.

If you put up enough walls, and tear down enough bridges, eventually it's going to stick. People will give up on you. All relationships, no matter how solid, can be burnt to ashes and destroyed.

What am I really afraid of? What is the worst thing that could be in these letters?

Cole telling me that he is done with me. He's exhausted with waiting, and he doesn't have the strength to hold on any longer. He wants me to sign a few documents so he can move on with his life, and separate me from his business and his heart. He wants to be done.

Does that mean I wanted him to keep waiting for me?

Yes, of course I did. I'm just a liar. I'm just a petulant child. I've just been throwing a five-year temper tantrum. It was all a test. A test to see if he really meant all those ridiculous things he always said about forever. No one ever means those things, right?

But Cole did. He meant every word.

I could never really let go of the one person who

makes this world good for me. The person who renews my faith that people can be true. The person I dream about every night, and try my best not to think about every day.

I also couldn't hold on to him.

I wonder if it would have been easier to go through life if I had never met Cole. Growing up with him and spending every day with him for so many years allowed him to get deep under my skin. Getting him out of my system would require draining my own blood, until I was completely dry.

That's how I feel right now. Empty.

It's too late. There is nothing left to let go of, or to hold on to.

"Here," Zack says gently, taking the letter from my fingers. "Let me read it to you."

Only when the letter is removed from my hands do I realize that I have been staring vacantly into space for several minutes.

"Dear Scar," Zachary begins. "Where the hell are you? I miss you so much that I'm going insane."

"No," I hiss, ripping the papers out of his hands. "Don't ever call me that. And don't look at my letters. Just don't…" I want to curl up into a little ball. I want to lift my knees so I can push my forehead against them, but the laptop is on the tray in front of me, blocking my ability to move.

I suddenly feel very cramped in this plane. It's such a small cabin to stuff so many souls into, but more importantly, their bodies. There are so many people all around, in front of me, behind me. If the plane were to crash, we'd all be smashed up together into a little people sandwich.

To calm my racing mind, or possibly make it worse, I reach out and grab my Styrofoam coffee cup. I put it to my lips and chug the contents greedily, hoping that it will give me serenity, or at the very least, superpowers.

Finishing it off and putting it down, I look at the damn letter.

Dear Scar,

Where the hell are you? I miss you so much that I'm going insane.

Are you even getting my letters? I refuse to believe that after all these years, you'd stop replying to me. This can only mean one thing: something terrible has happened. Or the letters just aren't reaching you. God, I hope that's all it is. You know how my mind always goes to the worst possibility first.

I am so close to just hopping on a plane and flying over there right now, even though I promised you not to. Is someone intercepting these letters? If you're reading this, and you're not Scar, I don't care who the fuck you are. I'm going to find you someday, and fuck you up. You don't think I'm serious? Check my criminal record.

These letters had better reach their intended recipient, if you value your mediocre life.

I glance over at Zachary with a raised eyebrow.

"Did you just want to show me these letters to save your mediocre life?"

"Kind of," Zack says with a weak smile. "It has been weighing on my conscience. By the way, what's his criminal record all about?"

"He… went to prison for a while."

"For what?"

"He saved my life."

"From who? It could be important."

"No. It's ancient history. I don't want to talk about it."

I turn back to the paper in my hands.

So if you're not Scar, why am I even still writing this? I guess I'm just desperate. I guess it's just habit. I guess I just need to try—if there's any chance at all that I could reach her, I have to try.

I need you, Scar. As pathetic as it sounds, I don't know how to live without telling you every little detail of my day. Everything is a mess. I've made so many bad decisions lately and gotten in over my head. You're the only one who can help me now. When I started this company, you were by my side, and you saw me through every bump in the road. Things were just so much easier when we were together. Now, it's all spiraling out of control, and I don't know what to do.

I want to tell you more about Annabelle, who I mentioned in a previous letter. We've been spending a lot of time together lately, and she's become very important to me. She reminds me of you, in many

*ways—mainly her intelligence. She's beautiful, in an
innocent, simple sort of way, like the sort of girl who
doesn't even brush her hair or look in the mirror most
days. She doesn't need to. She's very wise,
fascinating, and kind. I don't know why I feel so
drawn to her, but I've just needed someone to talk to
when everything's been falling apart, and she's really
been there for me. She's an amazing listener, and I
feel like her advice has been invaluable.*

*Don't get upset, but there is something comforting
about being able to pick up the phone and call
someone in the middle of the night, when I can't
sleep. I would give anything to be able to call you. The
nightmares have been coming back lately, and some
nights, I need you so much that it hurts. I just wish I
could hold you...*

I quickly fold the letter closed and put it down
on the laptop. I feel like I'm going to be sick. There is
no way I can deal with reading this here, in front of
Zack, and on an airplane filled with people. I need a
soundproof room, so that I can scream and cry and
beat my fists into the walls.

Reaching for one of the vodka bottles, I unscrew
the little metal cap. The material is so flimsy that it
gets crushed between my fingers as soon as I manage
to rip it from the plastic bottle. I lift the little serving
to my lips and pour the clear liquid into my mouth,
letting it burn my insides as it trickles into my empty
stomach.

"Sophie," Zack says, moving to stand up and

grabbing the laptop from my tray. "You should probably use the facilities. It's been hours and you are obviously in pain. All that coffee and liquor needs to go somewhere, and I think you're just ignoring your body."

I look down at my bladder in dismay, wishing that I were a machine. Computers and technology are so efficient, while the design of living beings is often flawed. That must be why I constantly abuse my system in small ways, out of sheer annoyance at its failings and the inconvenience of its functions. I like to prove to myself that I can conquer the petty whims of my body by choosing mind over matter.

Besides, no one likes to use airplane bathrooms. They are gross.

"Go," Zack tells me, pointing firmly. "I see you clenching your thighs together and hunching over in discomfort. You need to pee."

Wow. Have I been doing those things? I examine my posture and see that he's right. I guess Zack is rather perceptive, and once again, I think to myself that it's not so terrible that he came along on this trip. I'm obviously too messed up to even be able to tell that I need to go to the bathroom. I might need reminders to sleep and eat, as well. Thank heavens for autonomous functions, like blinking and breathing. Maybe the body isn't as useless as I thought.

But I am. It just occurs to me that I should have been able to figure out that Zack was hiding these letters. I'm a code breaker, for fuck's sake! Why couldn't I see the signs of him lying to me? And why did I automatically assume that Cole didn't want to talk to me?

I guess my abandonment issues run pretty deep and leave me blinded to the truth about people. I might be able to create or decipher complex cryptograms, but god help me, I'm a complete dunce when it comes to human emotions. Or urination.

When I try to stand, I realize that I do really need to go and it is painful to move. I went from thinking about almost everything but peeing to only being able to think about peeing.

And for a few minutes, I feel peaceful. I am distracted from all the other, emotional pain.

I move into the aisle and past Zachary. "Thanks," I tell him softly, heading toward the bathroom at the front of the plane.

When I reach the door, I stop. Staring warily at the "vacant" sign for several seconds, an eerie feeling of dread washes over me. A small shiver jostles my shoulders and causes the hairs on the back of my neck to stand up like needles. I am not sure why, but I have the unshakable sense that airplane bathrooms are among the worst places on the planet. Something dreadful must have happened to me in one, in a past life.

Once I'm in the tiny room, I lock the door behind me and look at myself in the mirror. I'm a mess and pale as a ghost. I guess I haven't been hiding my heartache as well as I initially thought. A sudden feeling of claustrophobia seizes me, and the walls of the tiny bathroom seem to move inward by a few inches. I stare at them very hard, until they move again by another few inches. They are definitely closing in on me. I reach up with both hands to hold the bathroom walls open as I gasp for breath.

I'm not usually afraid of small spaces. I don't really care. But this airplane bathroom feels like the smallest space I have ever been in. It's so small that there is hardly any air, and it is difficult to breathe.

It's the first time I've been alone since I found out that Cole died.

There is a strange kind of pain behind my eyes, and I realize that I want to cry. But I'm not ready for this. I clench my fists and continue to hold the walls as I gasp for breath, and struggle not to cry. The effort causes my stomach to lurch.

The worst part is, I don't know if I'm emotional or upset because he's gone, or because he might have been happy with another woman. Someone else got to spend time with him and receive his phone calls in the middle of the night. Someone else got to hold him after his nightmares.

Annabelle didn't take him from me. I basically threw him at her.

It should comfort me that he wasn't alone, and that he had someone to take care of him. He was a sensitive boy, and he never liked to be alone. Clutching my stomach, I tell myself that he deserved to be happy, and I am happy for him.

Leaning over, I vomit into the bathroom sink. See, this is a prime example of the human body malfunctioning. I think I've been holding back my tears so hard that they came out in the form of vomit.

Chapter Eight

sophie shields, 2016

As our car drives along a sunny avenue lined
with palm trees, it seems bizarre that we are heading
to a morgue filled with dead bodies. But that's just
California for you. The perfect temperatures and the
cheerful sunlight are almost insulting in a bleak
situation. Couldn't the sky show a little decency and
muster up a few clouds at least? A bit of rain, even
just a drizzle? *Nope.* Even misery, death, and grief
need to be felt while being bombarded with pure
paradise.

I must admit that I miss living on this side of the
continent, on the shores of this gentler ocean. Back
home, I barely spend any amount of time outside. I
enter my car and drive to work, and exit my car to
enter work. That's about the extent of my exposure to

the sun. And even in those few minutes, I manage to get sweaty and burned, or frozen stiff, and it has led me to developing a great annoyance for the brutal elements.

But isn't it just as brutal out here? Isn't it far more brutal, being closer to the equator? Why does the sunlight feel so kind out here, when it's beating down on you just as much, or even more than it does up north? It's all an illusion. Our bodies deceive us with their feelings of comfort and complacency. But this world is just as violent and harsh as my world, or my brother wouldn't be lying motionless in a morgue.

When we arrive, Zack thanks the Uber driver and puts a hand on my knee to alert me to the fact that we are at the hospital. I have been staring angrily at the palm trees, and the clear blue sky, and everything deceivingly beautiful about this place.

"Do you want me to carry your backpack?" Zack asks.

I roll my eyes. He asked me this several times at the airport as well. The backpack contains Cole's letters, in addition to everything I need to live, and I am not parting with it. Zack suggested we check into a hotel first and drop off our belongings, but I wanted to head straight to the hospital.

Grabbing the door handle and stepping out, I swing my backpack over my shoulder. I take the long strap of my purse and pull it over my head, letting it sit across my body as I begin moving toward the building.

The building is the worst sight of all. The stunning modern architecture of the hospital has

Cole's fingerprints all over it. I can see him biting his lips as he sketched those windows and the elegant slope of the towers. I remember discussing this design with him. I remember the effort he put into creating a meticulous floorplan that would allow fast transportation between the emergency room and the various departments of specialization and surgery. It's a masterpiece. At least he was murdered in one of his masterpieces. That would make him happy. Right?

No.

I feel so surly and crass that I want to run through the streets, stomping like Godzilla. I want to smash everything in sight. I want to reach out and break off one of the hospital's peripheral towers and use it to stab myself in the gut. The building is already stabbing me in the gut by simply standing there and looking beautiful. A testament to Cole's greatness and how much he achieved in his short life. A testament to his mastery of the art and science that he loved. A testament to what I've lost. What the world has lost.

There are not many minds capable of fusing science and art in such a cohesive and efficient structure. Simple, yet elaborate. When you enter one of Cole's buildings, you always experience a sense of having your every need fulfilled. He thinks ahead and plans for these things. If you need an elevator, or a bathroom, or a large window to illuminate a dark day, all you have to do was turn to your left, or your right, or reach out a few inches, and the amenity you desired is right there, waiting for you.

His buildings are welcoming, and they envelop you when you enter, embracing you with their perfectly placed walls. It was clear that hospitality and kindness to each visitor was his primary concern.

It wasn't a lie. It wasn't a deception.

Part of me feels incredibly grateful that these buildings will persist long after Cole is gone. That's what he always wanted. I often told him that walking inside one of his buildings felt like walking into his mind, or his heart. The complexity of the structure was hidden under the guise of simplicity and function. Effortless function. Reliable, impossibly resilient function.

Maybe that's why it's difficult to enter now. Zack touches my back gently, encouraging me to walk forward with him.

"Come on, Sophie," he says softly.

Oh, how I'm sick of his falsely gentle touches and falsely soft words. I glare daggers at him before taking a deep breath and stepping forward. Fine then. To the morgue. We might as well.

I don't need to look at the signs on the walls as we walk through the hospital halls. I have memorized the floorplans.

This strikes me as unusual. I have read so many thousands of books over the years, and I hardly ever remember any precise quotes from their pages. I only recall the feelings and impressions that I got from the experience of reading and the time spent with the characters. Why, then, having worked closely with Cole on dozens of his buildings, should I remember the specific design of one floorplan so clearly? Do I remember all his floorplans this well?

I couldn't say. I generally try to avoid his

buildings, so that I can avoid these feelings and thoughts. It's just a reminder of my own failure and inadequacy. It's a reminder of how emotionally stunted I am, and unable to appreciate all the good things I've had in my life.

"Have you been to this hospital before?" Zack asks as we turn around a corner.

"No," I answer succinctly.

I don't want to bother explaining any more. As we continue, I see a crowd gathered around the doors leading to the morgue. I begin to feel the anxiety building in my chest when I notice members of the press holding large cameras and microphones.

Oh, god. What if Benjamin finds me?

What if this is all a plot to smoke me out, like a trapped animal?

I reach up and pull some of my dark hair down in front of my face. I double check my hair quickly to make sure that it is, in fact, black. It's funny how the mere sight of a camera can transport me fifteen years back in time, and make me feel instantly like a frightened little girl again. Gazing through the small gap in my hair carefully, with my head tilted downward, I notice police officers conversing with doctors. I am suddenly concerned that I will not be allowed to see Cole's body.

God help me, no one else better keep me away from him today.

I reach for my purse, thinking about what I can say to be let into the room. I need to carefully choose what I say around the press and police. What if they take me in for questioning? They will almost certainly take me in for questioning, and I've had enough of that in my lifetime. The anxiety mounts in my chest, and it starts to feel like a small boulder is sitting on my breastbone. Since I was young, I've learned not to trust law enforcement very much.

It's difficult to expand my lungs as I approach the closed doors and all the people standing around them. But I keep walking forward, because I know that Cole is in the room.

"Keep your mouth shut," I tell Zack quietly, with a sideways glance.

He looks surprised, but he nods.

Marching past the policemen, I move directly to the security guard standing outside the morgue doors. "I'm here to see Cole Hunter," I tell him simply.

An imposing officer is instantly beside me. "Excuse me, miss. This area is closed off due to an ongoing homicide investigation. I'm afraid I can't let you enter."

I lift my chin defiantly. "You need a family member to identify the body."

The police officer looks confused when the doors open behind him and a small bald man steps out, holding a briefcase. My heart instantly soars at the sight of the tiny, elderly fellow, wearing a Jewish yarmulke.

"My word!" he says, moving over to me and grasping my arm. His face is tired and wrinkled, but his compassion is genuine. "Scarlett, my sweet girl. You are a sight for sore eyes. I am so sorry for your loss."

I nod, trying to force some gratitude onto my

face. "Thank you, Mr. Bishop."

"Let her pass," says Mr. Bishop says to the officer. "It could be helpful to have her in there."

"What the hell?" says a female voice from the sidelines. "You are letting *her* in there, but not me?"

"No. I'm afraid I can't let her in," says the police officer. "It's family only, Mr. Bishop."

"She is family," Mr. Bishop says, looking at me expectantly.

"Yeah?" says the woman who spoke before, stepping closer. I see that her hair is striped with harsh blonde highlights, and her eyes are caked heavily with shimmering eye shadow. "Cole doesn't *have* any family. He never mentioned anyone. Who the hell is she?"

Reaching into my purse, I withdraw an old wallet that I haven't used in many years. I hope the worn leather doesn't give me away. It makes my chest ache as I undo the buckle, and only partially because I wonder if all the identification is up to date. I withdraw my old driver's license, like I do it every day at a bar, and lift it for the police officer to examine it.

"My name is Scarlett Hunter. I'm his wife."

Chapter Nine

sophie shields, 2016

"His wife?" the brunette repeats. "That can't be right. He isn't married."

"But he is, Miss Nelson. I was there at their ceremony, thirteen years ago," Mr. Bishop says with a smile.

"B-but," the brunette sputters. "That's impossible. Cole would have been what? Sixteen years old?"

"That's correct," says the lawyer, taking my arm. "We have been trying to notify his next of kin for a few hours now. Thank god you're finally here, Scarlett."

"Why has he never mentioned you?" the woman barks, her entire face going very red.

So, this is Annabelle Nelson. I don't want to look at her. I don't want to be that cliché jealous bitch. But my feminine curiosity wins out, and I turn to my side and give her a quick glance-over. Bad idea. She is clad in a classy designer pantsuit that nearly makes me flinch, and wearing one of those alligator-skin purses. *Wow*. You can always tell which girls played with a lot of Barbie dolls growing up and continued to play with them well into their teens.

Her makeup looks like it came directly from an Instagram tutorial, for she has the perfect winged eyeliner that I have never been able to achieve. Not once. I immediately feel inferior, in my old jeans, wrinkled t-shirt, and unkempt state after a five-hour flight. Plus, my purse is nearly worn to tatters, and I am carrying my whole life on my shoulders in a backpack that makes it look like I am still in high school.

I pull my lips together tightly at the uncomfortable situation, but I shouldn't feel too bad about betraying some emotion: the expression on her face is horrified and disgusted. She is pointing at me as though I am a creature with three heads and a spiky tail. From her betrayed reaction, I imagine that she was very intimate with Cole. I am a little surprised, as she doesn't seem like his type. But it has been a while, so what do I know?

"I travel a lot for work," I explain to her with a little shrug. "Cole probably didn't mention me because he was annoyed that I wasn't at home more often."

Annabelle's eyes flash at me with rage. "He probably didn't mention you because he was ashamed of making such a huge error in his youth." She looks down her nose at my ratty jeans. "How horrifying this all is. I am shocked, simply shocked."

I feel a hand on the back of my arm, squeezing just above my elbow. A man clears his throat.

Turning around, I see the look of hurt on Zack's face. Oh, shit. I totally forgot about him.

I suppose he must feel the same way Annabelle does.

"Well, Mrs. Hunter, you may enter the morgue," the policeman says. "My apologies. Detective Rodriguez will want to speak to you."

"Thank you," I say, stepping forward.

Zack tries to follow me, but the policeman stops him. "You can't go in there, sir."

"It's fine," Zack tells the police officer, leaning forward as if they are friends, and speaking in a low voice. "I need to be with her. I'm her bodyguard," he explains. "Until we know who was responsible for Mr. Hunter's death, we can't assume that Mrs. Hunter is safe."

Whoa. That was such a good lie that I almost believed him. His height and build make the statement more credible.

"Oh, certainly, sir. I understand. Please go right in."

"Thank you, Officer."

I look at Zack suspiciously, impressed by his ability to think on his feet and adapt to the situation. He only found out that Cole and I were married a second ago, and he was able to go along with this Mrs. Hunter thing quite easily. Even I haven't been Mrs. Hunter in so long that it feels like I am play acting a character. Maybe it always felt like I was play acting a character.

As we step past the officer and into the morgue, I hear Annabelle mumble something under her breath. I turn to glance at her perfectly applied, matte nude lipstick to better understand what she's saying, and I immediately frown.

"Bitch. You're the reason he's gone."

I am not sure if I read her lips right, but I don't have time to ponder this as I step forward and the doors close behind me. The stress of the identity change and marriage situation quickly leaves me as I remember that Cole is lying in here, dead. I stop still for a moment, staring at all the silver drawers containing bodies. My breathing begins to come in short, shallow gasps.

I feel Zachary's hands on my shoulders.

"Mrs. Hunter," he says to me, just in case anyone is listening. "It looks like the body is over there."

I can't look. Why the hell did I come to this place? Why did I even fly to California? What is wrong with me? I should have flown to the opposite end of the planet. I shouldn't be here. I abandoned Cole in life. How can I show up now, claiming to be his wife, pretending to fulfill wifely duties, when he's lying in the fucking morgue?

I am about to turn and run out of the room, but Zack holds me fast. A woman's voice calls out to me, and I turn to my left to see her standing beside a body covered in a sheet.

"Scarlett!" she exclaims with recognition. Her

voice breaks in a sob. "Oh, sweetie."

"Miranda," I murmur with pleasant surprise, suddenly finding the courage to take a step forward.

She smiles sadly and rushes over to me, throwing her arms around me tightly. "My dear, it's such a terrible thing. Such a terrible thing. But don't you worry, I am here for you. We'll take care of each other and get through this."

I exhale slowly, reciprocating the hug.

Miranda Walters is a brilliant scientist, and Cole and I worked closely with her for many years. In fact, she is a huge part of the reason that his company was so successful and Cole's buildings were so special and innovative. Most people don't think of synthetic biology being connected to architecture, but Miranda and Cole worked together to create buildings that were almost alive, and able to heal themselves.

Of course, my security systems also made the buildings special, but it took many skilled professionals, from various disciplines, to work together and create Cole's masterpieces. This hospital isn't even close to being the best of them. The developer's budget was low, and they wanted a more basic building.

In the repertoire of Cole's work, this hospital is nowhere near the caliber of his greatest hits. It's a filler song on one of his albums that went unnoticed, and never would have been noticed if he hadn't been killed here. His true masterpieces are the experimental and eclectic pieces that are scattered across the globe. Japan, Russia, Brazil, Dubai, Australia, Sweden.

Those iconic pieces of work are what made him

a world famous architect; buildings that could withstand almost anything.

And now he's lying on that table over there.

"Oh, don't worry," Miranda says with a sniffle, waving her hand in dismissal as she glances at the table. "He's not in here. They already performed the autopsy this morning, and the body has been sent to the funeral home. I hope you don't mind, honey. I started on the funeral arrangements without you, because I didn't know when or if you'd get here."

I exhale again, in relief. "That's okay, Miranda. I just—I did want to see him, but..."

"Honey, I would rather shoot myself in the knee than force to look at that. Cole was just..." She shakes her head, unable to continue. She bites on her lip to keep them from trembling, and I can see that she is close to falling apart. "Cole was so..."

"It's okay," I tell her softly, reaching out to touch her arm. I can see new wrinkles around her eyes and mouth that were not there before. Miranda must be in her mid-forties now, but she still looks fit and well maintained. When I left, she had three small children whom I used to babysit occasionally. With Cole.

Miranda was one of the few adults in our life that we could really trust and look up to. She was almost motherly to us when we first started our business and began working together.

I had blocked it all out; how much I cared for her. How much I liked my life, before I ran away. How many good people were around us, rooting for us. How hard it was to find those people.

"How are Darla and Dane doing?" I ask her. "And Max?"

"Max is starting college this year," she says with a sad smile. "Can you believe it? The twins are a handful, as always. They just got matching tattoos, and cartilage piercings. They play in a garage band," Miranda says with a chuckle.

That finally brings a genuine smile to my face. I remember those kids banging pots and pans all night long. I remember doing karaoke with them at their home.

"Excuse me, ladies," says a man in a police uniform, approaching us. "I hate to interrupt this reunion, but did you say you were Scarlett Hunter? Cole's wife?"

"That's correct," I tell him quietly.

"My name is Detective Rodriguez. I will need to ask you a few questions, ma'am."

"Sure, Detective," I say weakly. "But do you mind if we do this another time? I just got off a five-hour flight, and this is all still a bit... much."

"Of course, I understand." He reaches into his blazer to pull out a business card, which he hands to me. "You can come by the station anytime, or we could just meet up for a cup of coffee after the funeral tomorrow."

"Coffee is good," I tell the detective in response.

"It will help with the jet lag. I'm always so tired after a long flight," he responds in a friendly way.

Is he trying to butter me up for information? He wouldn't be stupid enough to actually flirt with a vulnerable widow at a time like this, right? Zack is still standing behind me too, and I think I hear him step a little closer, protectively.

"We should let the poor girl get some rest," Miranda says, putting an arm around me.

"So what are you all still doing in here, if Cole isn't here?" I ask with a knotted forehead.

"It's kind of a meeting, honey," Miranda explains. "We don't know who would have wanted to harm Cole, and whether the offices are bugged, or anything. We don't know if they'll come after us next. Detective Rodriguez has been giving me some tips to stay safe, and we've been trying to sort out some kind of plan, going forward. Maybe you can help us, dear."

At that moment, Mr. Bishop enters the room and clears his throat. "All right, Scarlett and Miranda. We need to discuss his will and the future of the company. Both of you are beneficiaries, so I will have copies given to you after the funeral tomorrow." He pauses to look at Zack. "Scarlett, do you mind me speaking in front of your bodyguard? Or the detective?"

"No," I say softly. "Go ahead."

"All right, well I just want to give you a heads up about the will, because as the executor, it's going to be a lot of work. Of course, as his wife, you will receive almost everything, and you now possess controlling shares in the company. Cole stipulated in his will that he wanted you to take over as CEO if anything ever happened to him."

"No way," I say with a little gasp. "I have a job. I can't be the CEO of Snowfire. I'm a software engineer. Miranda, you need to take over."

"I'm a biologist, sweetie. Cole wanted *you*."

I put my head in my hands. I feel like my forehead is creased so tightly that I am creating permanent lines there and changing the very structure of my anatomy.

Mr. Bishop clears his throat again. "There's also the very sensitive matter of his… er, semen sample."

I rip my hands away from my face and look at the lawyer as my cheeks flush a deeper red than my name. "Oh, dear god! What does his will stipulate I do with that?"

"Nothing," Mr. Bishop says, "but it belongs to you, and Annabelle Nelson is requesting that you give it to her."

I blink slowly. It suddenly occurs to me that I had a lot to drink, and not very much to eat. That must be the reason that the room is spinning. "I need to sit down," I tell Zachary, and he reaches for a stool and helps me collapse on it. Without his help, I might have toppled over—my backpack is heavy and it feels impossible to find my balance. "Why are we here?" I ask them again. "Why are we here talking about this in a morgue?"

It might be my imagination, but I feel like I see the three of them exchange secretive looks. They were discussing something important before I got here, and they don't trust me. Why would they? I'm an outsider. I've been gone for years.

"Scarlett, honey… it's been a difficult day," Miranda says softly, moving to my side. She combs her hand over my hair in a maternal fashion, the way she might have done to her daughter when she was young. "You should get some rest. Tomorrow, or sometime soon, I'm going to need to ask you to help tighten up our security systems a little. And maybe you could work with Detective Rodriguez a little, and tell him about... you know."

I don't know. My mind draws a fuzzy blank.

Miranda is still speaking, and I try to follow what she's saying. "Detective, Scarlett is a master cryptanalyst, and technological expert. Combined with her personal knowledge of the victim, she could probably help you find out who would want to hurt Cole quite quickly, and make your job a lot easier."

"I will keep that in mind, Mrs. Walters. I know this is difficult, and I don't want to be disrespectful to your mourning by asking too much of you all while you're still coping with this loss. But we do need to move quickly to find the killer, in case he or she is not finished."

Miranda sighs. "Our primary goal is to make sure that all of us are safe. Especially you, Scarlett. We will need to discuss where you're staying tonight, because Cole's house might not be safe."

"I can check into a hotel," I tell her.

"That's great. Maybe have your bodyguard get an adjoining room," Miranda suggests. "Will you make it to the funeral, honey, to say a few words?"

I suddenly remember, and I hesitate. "I don't know, Miranda. I don't like crowds very much, or public speaking. Especially with all these cameras..."

"Gentlemen," Miranda says to the three other men in the room. "I would appreciate if you all gave us some space and let us speak in private."

Zack seems reluctant, but the men all nod and filter out of the room.

"Honey," Miranda says finally. "I think you should tell the detective about Benjamin."

I stiffen. "What is that going to accomplish? They are going to bring him in for questioning and ask if he raped a nine-year-old girl. He'll know that I'm alive, if he doesn't already. He'll lie, and cover it up, and get away with it, like he always did before."

"Cole worked with Benjamin on the new business towers downtown," Miranda says softly. "I find it an odd coincidence that Cole was killed shortly after the ribbon-cutting ceremony."

"Here?" I say in surprise. "But I thought his business was focused in New York."

"Not anymore, dear. They've expanded—quite significantly." Miranda fishes into her purse for an item, and pulls out an old keychain. "You will need the keys to Cole's house, in case you want to stay there at some point. I know you love that house." She pauses. "Your car is still sitting there, in the garage. He had it serviced and maintained regularly. He knew you loved that little car, and he always thought you were coming back. I wish… you had come back a little sooner." Miranda lifts a tissue to the corner of her eye. "I'm sorry. I'm so sorry, dear. Look at me, making this all worse."

"It's okay," I tell her. "You're right."

Miranda fumbles in her pockets to hand me a business card. "Get some rest, sweetie. Send me a text, and I'll get you the details of the funeral tomorrow."

"All right," I say quietly, clutching the keys in the palm of my hand. She doesn't know that I still have my old keys, nestled neatly on my keychain in my purse, just in case I ever got over my issues and decided to come home and surprise Cole.

It was going to be a happy day. He would be sleeping, and I would sneak into his bedroom and tackle him, and he would freak out and wake up in a panic and start defending himself. We would wrestle for a few seconds until he realized it was only me, and then we would laugh. We would laugh so hard, and he would hug me and tousle my hair like when I was a child. Then he would kiss me. He would kiss me so hard, and angrily, to punish me for leaving. Then he would push me down on the bed and tear off my clothing.

Okay, he probably wouldn't do that. But it's called a fantasy, people.

I look around at the morgue and all the stark metal beds, some of them covered in sheets. The giant freezer contains dozens of pull-out drawers of bodies, stacked closer than beds in the youth hostels where Cole and I used to stay—but with much more privacy. I am lucky that Cole is no longer in this morgue, because I would want to climb into that freezer with him and cuddle his corpse, and talk to him for hours like a madwoman until I also inevitably froze to death.

That might make me feel better about all this.
Instead, I still feel empty.
This isn't exactly the homecoming I imagined.

Chapter Ten

cole hunter, 2003

Scarlett fell asleep reading a textbook again.

I walk into the library barefoot, my feet soundless against the carpet laid out over the hardwood floor. This library is the best part of the Browns' home, and surely the reason that we were placed here at all. There are hundreds of books and a magnificent stone fireplace with a mantle. Their home looks like a place where decent people live, so whenever the foster agency comes to check it out, they always pass the inspections with flying colors.

Mrs. Brown is an old fashioned housewife. She does nothing but clean all day and seems obsessed with making the house spotless. This goes a long way to maintain the illusion of decency. People judge quickly, and it is commonplace to assume that a nicely put together home is a sign of comfort, happiness, and stability. This isn't always true. Sometimes, it's a sign of OCD and placing more value on material possessions and superficial appearances than the actual well-being of the other people in the home.

It takes a lot of time to clean an entire house to the point of spotlessness. Every single day. Mrs. Brown would much rather do this than have a conversation with anyone, smile, or prepare a decent meal. It is possible she picked up the habit early in their marriage, as a way of avoiding Mr. Brown and his temper. The Browns have two children of their own, a son and a daughter, but both have long since moved out.

I would move out of this home, too, at my earliest opportunity, if I were their children.

They probably started fostering a bit because of empty nest syndrome. I hear it's really difficult on older adults when their kids leave the home. It can get very lonely, not having anyone around to abuse and berate all day.

Trying to ignore my surroundings, and my distaste for this house, I look down at the package I'm holding proudly. A grin settles on my face as I move closer to the sofa where Scarlett is sleeping, and crouch down to my knees. Her black glasses are sitting askew on her nose. I am excited to surprise her with my gift, but she looks so adorable that I can't resist the urge to bother her.

Isn't that what big brothers are supposed to do?

Placing my rectangular cardboard box down on

the carpet beside me, I slide it slightly under the couch to keep it out of sight. I gaze at her innocent form mischievously and try to keep from laughing out loud. Scarlett's shirt is lifted a little, exposing her bellybutton. Before I can stop myself, I find myself leaning forward and putting my lips against her stomach.

I blow a very loud raspberry.

Scarlett shrieks and flails as she awakens abruptly, shoving my head away and clutching her stomach defensively. Her book goes crashing to the floor, and I erupt into laugher. She reaches out to smack me, but I dodge her blows and roll backwards on the carpet, laughing my ass off.

"Cole!" she exclaims, between deep, shuddering breaths. "Ugh, gross! What have you done to me? I'm going to kill you."

I don't expect her to leap off the sofa and tackle me, putting me in a surprisingly strong headlock for a girl of her small size. This only makes me laugh harder as I wrestle with her for several seconds until I have her pinned on the carpet beneath me.

"You need to be more aware of your surroundings when you're sleeping," I advise her, still grinning. "You never know what could happen. Creeps could sneak up on you and blow raspberries on your stomach."

She makes a face of disgust. "I hate you! You're the worst."

"I'm just being a good big brother," I tell her teasingly, repeating a line she often says to me. "Besides! I am pretty sure I have a present that will make you forget all about this raspberry incident, and make you want to call a truce."

"No way. You better watch yourself when you fall asleep, because you might wake up with a moustache painted on your face with permanent marker. I will never forgive you for this."

"You're going to forgive me in a few seconds," I assure her.

"Bet you fifty bucks I won't."

"Scar, you don't even have fifty bucks."

"Neither do you," she says stubbornly. "It's a hypothetical fifty bucks."

"You're on."

Reaching out to grasp the cardboard box, I slide it over until it rests beside her head.

She turns to glance over at it, and her eyes grow wide. "Cole... what did you do?"

I watch the expressions on her face carefully as she scrambles out from underneath me to sit up and grab the cardboard box. Her eyes grow serious when she studies the writing on the sides. "Oh my god. This is the one I wanted. How the hell did you afford this?"

With a shrug, I smile. "Told you I'd pick up some extra landscaping jobs. Turns out I really have a knack for designing gardens, and people are willing to pay a lot for it."

Scarlett looks at me suspiciously. "Cole. I know you're amazing, but this laptop costs over a thousand dollars, and you didn't have lunch money a week ago. You have also spent several days studying and not working at all. How did you get this computer? Did you steal it?"

I fidget a little under her harsh gaze. "Gee, Scar. I thought you'd be happy."

She glares at me. "I just want to know the truth. Be honest with me."

"Okay. Promise you won't hate me?"

"Never," she says quietly.

"I—well. I did a little bit more than landscaping."

"Cole. You're scaring me."

"A housewife. At one of the houses where..."

"Oh my *god!*" she exclaims.

"It was nothing," I tell her quickly. "We didn't have sex. I just..."

"*No!* No, no, spare me the details."

"She said she liked the way I trimmed her bushes," I explain, blushing red hot. "And that if I needed some extra money, she would love to have me come inside and work on another bush..."

"Ewww!" Scarlett says, making a face. "Dammit, Cole. You expect me to use a laptop that you prostituted yourself to get for me?"

"I… I understand if you don't want to."

She moves forward to throw her arms around my neck and kiss me on the lips. I am taken aback by her enthusiasm and too stunned to return the kiss. My lips soften for a millisecond, just before she pulls away.

"I love you," she says when she picks up the laptop box, hugging it tightly against her chest. "Please don't make yourself uncomfortable like this again on my account, but this means the world to me."

Frozen in shock, I try to recall my command of

a human language. "Scar, that wasn't very sisterly of you."

"I was just trying to help. Give you a little something to help forget whatever you did with those lips before." Her smile is wicked.

"Seriously? You're not upset?"

"You didn't hurt anyone. You didn't sell drugs or mug some old woman in an alley. You didn't shoplift like an idiot and risk a criminal record. You just gave up a little bit of your dignity, for me. I think that makes you a freaking hero. Thank you, Cole." She touches my knee and smiles. "Now, if you'll excuse me, I have to go and find an AOL disc with a free trial so that I can use the Internet."

"Okay," I tell her happily, grateful that she didn't judge my actions. When she's about to leave the room, the grin returns to my face, and I call out, "Hey, Scar?"

"Yeah?"

"You should see the way I trim bushes. I'm getting really good at it."

"Ewwwww!" she exclaims, before running away. But not before I saw the deep red blush in her cheeks, redder than her name.

Chapter Eleven

cole hunter, 2003

How did we ever survive without a computer in the house?

Scarlett has been sharing her laptop with me, and I feel like it was the best purchase I ever made. For one thing, it makes her happy. But I have also begun to really look forward to the few hours that I get to use it when she's sleeping, or otherwise busy. Like right now.

I have retreated to my room to surf the Internet tonight so that I don't bother Scarlett, but I always leave my bedroom door open so that I can keep an eye on her. Of course, my use of the computer is pathetic and childish compared to hers. I haven't been doing anything really important. My main activity has been obsessively checking the status of my college applications, but I have also done a bit of reading about how to improve my architectural drawings. Scarlett's time with the laptop always takes priority, because in her hands, it becomes a magical machine that can cast spells and grant wishes.

I'm not even kidding.

Now that I've been staying in her room, I get a chance to peek at her sometimes when she uses the Internet. I often find myself staring with a slack jaw. The way her fingers fly across the keyboard is mesmerizing, and she bites her lip with such concentration as she works, reminiscent of an Olympic athlete training for a competition. I can understand why Scarlett was so depressed after Mr. Brown smashed her laptop.

Taking away her technology is the equivalent of breaking a wizard's wand. The power doesn't come from the wand—it comes from the wizard. But the wand is the key to releasing that pent-up energy, and without it, a really powerful wizard might go insane. Having a gift, and having unlimited potential to use that gift, is a great burden to bear. Being banned from using that gift must feel like only being half-alive.

At least, this is what I imagine it feels like. I don't totally understand Scarlett, but I'm trying to.

I would never want to do that to her—take away the thing she loves most. She doesn't love very much in this world, and her hacking skills are all she has. It seems mostly harmless, and extremely useful. In fact, I often find myself wanting to ask her to find some information for me, or even to change some information for me. It's been difficult to resist.

Watching her has taught me a lot, and inspired by her investigation skills, I am trying some investigating of my own. But the only thing in my life worth investigating is *her*. I feel a little nervous and guilty about what I'm looking up, and I'm worried she'll be able to find out even if I clear the browsing history, but I can't resist. As I spend more and more time with Scarlett, my curiosity builds, but I don't want to ask her certain questions outright and remind her of events and people she would rather forget.

It takes me a while to find a politician named "Benjamin" who had previously adopted an orphan. I keep finding articles about orphans named Benjamin instead, or politicians working with orphanages. Scarlett probably could have found this way faster—not that she would have needed to, since she lived it. I just want to see his face. I want to see the face of the person who hurt her. My searches are amateurish, and I open a dozen tabs before I find one that strikes me as odd.

It's a recent article, published in the New York Times on the day that I found Scarlett huddled under the bleachers. Her birthday. I wonder if she saw this? It would explain her depression that day.

I grit my teeth as I look over this article, and a feeling in my gut tells me that this is the guy. Mayor Benjamin Powell made headlines for his charitable work with *children,* and there are pictures of the man surrounded by dozens of smiling kids. My face contorts in anger as I scan the article.

He sounds like a nice guy. At least, he does an excellent job of appearing that way. The article speaks about how he adopted a young girl who went missing and how he has never gotten over that loss. It says that the mayor was throwing an event to provide at-risk youth with access to computers and free educational programs to promote computer literacy. He was doing it in honor of his lost daughter, and sponsoring a scholarship to the Computer Engineering program at Columbia University.

"The Serena Powell award," I read out loud. There is a photograph in the paper: a headshot from a school picture. I peer a little closer and I am surprised to see that the girl has lighter hair, but the same facial structure as Scarlett. Is her natural hair color not really black? I should have known. I have never seen hair that black, and her skin is so pale that it seems unlikely.

"Are you having fun?" asks an annoyed voice from behind me.

I jump a little in my chair, and shut the laptop guiltily. "Uh… Hi, Scar."

She makes angry eye contact with me, but then sighs. "I think he might know that I'm alive," she says, moving over to open the laptop back to the article. She stares at it for a long moment, crossing her arms over her chest. "He threw me a birthday party."

I turn to my side to study Scarlett. She is wearing an old-fashioned white nightgown that I believe was a hand-me-down from Mrs. Brown's daughter. It's weird to see her in a dress, because all her clothes are normally so tomboyish, but I think her pajamas are in the laundry. Peering closely at her, I reach out and touch her hair to examine the roots.

Sure enough, there is a light brown color near her scalp. How did I never notice this before?

She swats my hand away. "I started dyeing it to look different. I don't want him to find me."

"Your name was Serena? Like Sailor Moon?"

"You watch too much anime, Cole. Yeah, that was my name." She hesitates. "Well, technically it was 'Serenity' on my birth certificate, but no one ever called me that. A bunch of cops chose that name at a police station, when I was brought in by the old woman who found me in the snow. But it was mostly shortened to Serena when I was in school. The only person who ever called me Serenity was Benjamin." Her voice grows very soft. "I grew to hate that stupid name. He would always say it over and over. That's what he used to call me… in bed."

My entire body quakes with rage, and I can feel the bile rising in my throat.

Someday, I'm going to make it my personal mission to ruin this man. I'm not sure how, exactly, yet, but I will take revenge for Scarlett, and all the harm that was done to her. I will take revenge for her lost innocence. If I told her this, she would probably say that she wasn't innocent, to try to downplay what happened to her and shrug it off, but I know better.

It's still eating her alive every day.

I can see it behind her pale eyes, which she hasn't yet begun to shield with contact lenses. I am sure she will, soon, once she can afford them. She's running and hiding away from the world. She's burrowing deep inside herself, and trying to avoid letting anyone see who she really is. I'm lucky that she lets me have a glimpse of the truth.

"Do you think he knows I'm alive?" Scarlett asks, moving over to sit on my bed. She stares out the window, at the darkening sky. She has made it a habit to stay up all night and sleep immediately after coming home from school, so it's currently her morning. "I wanted to go to Columbia University," she tells me. "Maybe he thinks I will apply for the scholarship, and that's how he'll find me? Maybe it's an invitation—an olive branch. Maybe he's guaranteeing me acceptance and a full ride."

"Screw him and his stinking scholarship," I tell her. "You can get any scholarship you want! You don't need his money."

"Maybe," she says softly. "But also, maybe not. I found a job at the mall, Cole. I want to give you some money for the laptop. But even if I work every day after school, it will take months to pay you back completely for the computer."

"Hey," I say, getting up to move over to sit near her. "It was a gift. There's no reason to pay me back. Besides, I'm using it too, aren't I? Don't take the job at the mall. You need to focus on your studies so that you can get those *other* scholarships."

"I need money," she tells me with determination. "We need to get a car."

"Don't worry," I assure her. "I can get us all the money we need."

She looks at me with narrowed eyes. "The way that you earn money isn't exactly safe, Cole. There are risks, and it's beneath you. I don't want you doing that. I mean, I appreciate that you did. But I could always… access some money using the Internet."

"Isn't that risky?" I ask her. "You could get caught. You could get in big trouble."

"Everything is a risk. But if you promise not to do anything dangerous or illicit for money, then I promise to do the same," she offers.

"Deal," I tell her softly. "We'll keep each other good."

She smiles, and leans over to place her head on my shoulder for a second. A large yawn escapes her lips. "Hey, Cole? Do you need to use the computer any more tonight? For anything other than stalking me?"

"Nope! Not really. I finished all my homework."

"And you don't want to watch any anime porn about Sailor Moon before bed?" she teases.

I grin. "It's called *hentai*, but no. I have better things to do than watch porn. Besides, I have this amazing thing called my imagination. It's way better."

"I think I've heard of that website," she says playfully. "Can I take the laptop down to the library?"

"Of course. Just promise me you won't do anything illegal?"

"I won't," she says with a sleepy smile. "I'm a good girl."

I resist the urge to chuckle at this as I stand up and move to close the laptop. "Here you go," I tell her, lifting it and handing it to her before moving to grab the plug. "It's all yours."

"Thanks," she tells me, rising to her feet. She turns to leave, but hesitates to look back at me. "Will you try to get some rest while I study?"

"I will. I just need to brush my teeth and I'll move to your room."

"Good. Sleep tight, Cole," she tells me, heading for my bedroom door with the laptop clutched tightly under her arm. "I'll see you in the morning."

Chapter Twelve

cole hunter, 2003

I am harshly awoken from my sleep by… nothing at all.

There is dead silence in the room—not even the sound of Scarlett's breathing. I blink and look around in confusion. "Scar?" I mumble sleepily. Squinting at the bed, I seek out her sleeping form. Panic begins to spread through my chest when I don't find her there. I place my palm on the floor to push myself to my feet as I stumble toward the door in search of her.

Then I hear it: a male voice, shouting. It's coming from downstairs.

The library. I remember she was studying in the library.

Dammit.

Reaching for my baseball bat, I bolt out of the

room and run down the stairs, taking them two or three at a time. The sight that greets me is one that instantly makes my blood boil.

Mr. Brown is holding Scarlett by the throat, with her back up against the blazing fireplace, as if he intends to push her in.

"Answer me!" he bellows. "You thieving little bitch! Where did you get it? Where the hell did you get it?"

She can't respond, because his hands are crushing her windpipe, so her voice comes out in a muffled croak. Moving forward, I slam my baseball bat into the professor's back to distract him, but he barely even flinches. I expected him to him focus his attention on me, but he only momentarily grunts and shoves his elbow into my stomach, sending me hurtling backwards.

I land on the floor and my bat goes clattering away. He is such a bulky, heavyset man, and he hits surprisingly hard. I am angry with myself for letting him get the upper hand again.

"Where did you get the money for that computer?" the professor demands, close to hysterics. He shakes her viciously. "Did you swipe my credit card? Did you steal from my safe? Where the fuck did you get that money?"

Lifting her off the floor by her neck, he shoves her closer to the fire, until the flames are dancing around her ankles. Her toes curl as the flames lick at the sensitive bottoms of her feet.

I was about to rip myself off the floor and dive at him again, but I have to pause, mid-motion.

The sight of the fire makes me frozen.

Pieces of ash and sparks of fire are drifting up into Scarlett's hair, and a few tendrils are glowing as they begin to catch fire. No small amount of terror courses through me at this sight. I have seen such flames before. I still see those flames every single night, when I close my eyes. I feel like they have been searching for me. All this time, the fire had unfinished business, and it was seeking me out, to completely burn everything I love. I see Scarlett tightening her small hands around Mr. Brown's wrists. I see her legs kicking wildly as she tries to break free. I see my house burning. I see the rafters falling. I can smell the smoke, and Scarlett's burning hair.

I am rooted to the spot and unable to move. But then she screams for me.

"Coh—co—*oole!*" is Scarlett's muffled moan of pain as she struggles to free herself. Both of her hands are clawing at Mr. Brown's larger ones, trying to tear them away from her throat. But he is continuing to throttle her. He is going to kill her. If I don't stop him, he's going to kill her tonight. My heart palpitates in my chest when I see that the flames have caught onto her nightgown and have started making their way up her dress.

I am not entirely thinking when I reach into my pocket, pull out the switchblade, and walk forward. Before I realize what is happening, I have plunged my blade between two of the professor's ribs, and into his kidney. I jerk the knife back and forth and twist it. The man hollers, like a cow being slaughtered.

"Don't touch her," I tell him coarsely. "Don't

you fucking lay a hand on her again!"

In the middle of roaring in pain, the man releases Scarlett and she falls to the floor in front of the fireplace. I am so focused on her, and afraid of the flames that are traveling up her dress, that I don't notice when Mr. Brown twists around, putting his hand on the switchblade and tearing it out of his back.

"You little piece of shit!" he screams as he advances on me and slashes out with the blade. He hacks into my chest, cutting a large gash across my lungs.

I grunt and step back, hoping that I am quick enough to keep the cut from going too deep. The pain makes me see double. When blood starts pouring from my chest, I place my hand over my wound in shock.

"Little boy with dead parents," Mr. Brown says with a drunken cackle. "Do you ever think maybe your pops wanted to die? Better than slaving away to raise a wretch like you. You're just a waste of space. Eating my food, shitting in my toilets, sleeping under my roof. You can burn, the both of you. I'll just tell the agency you ran away. Good riddance!"

Mr. Brown comes at me again, hacking at me with the knife. I stumble backwards awkwardly, clutching my chest and trying to dodge his blows. When he strikes out with the blade and stabs me in the stomach, I double over with a sharp intake of breath. My head spins, and I try to remember what organs are located in the area that he stabbed. Is it something vital? My liver? My pancreas?

He withdraws the blade and I fall to my knees,

coughing out blood. He immediately goes to hack at me again, and I am in too much pain to move away. I awkwardly turn to protect my middle, and he cuts a deep gash into my arm instead, but not before I hear a sound that I will never forget:

It is a sound like death.

It is a scream so shrill and demented that it makes my blood run cold.

I see a flash of flame and cinders, the crash of an impact.

"Get *away* from him!"

I realize that Scarlett has reached into the fire with her bare hands, grabbed one of the burning logs, and smashed it against the side of Mr. Brown's face. He stumbles and falls at the force of the blow, and the log rolls to the carpet.

Scarlett doesn't stop there. Climbing on top of the man, she pummels her fists into his already busted face, over and over. Her hands are small, but they are knotted up tightly into little balls that might as well be made of steel. When her fists connect with his cheekbones and nose, I hear the cracking of bones, and I know that some of them are hers.

She doesn't seem to notice. She doesn't even notice that her hands are badly burned from the fire. She doesn't even notice that her skirt is being consumed by flames that are twisting around her legs. She screams as she hammers her fists into his face, filled with a fury that is almost feral.

I have never seen a creature more beautiful and wild.

My jaw hangs open, and I forget that there is

blood pouring out of three gashes in my body. "Scar," I whisper hoarsely. "Scarlett, stop! Scarlett? *Serena!*"

She turns to face me suddenly, and there is fire in her eyes. I thought I had seen fire before. I thought that the blaze that burnt my family to ashes had been really something. I thought that I had developed a healthy fear of fire and respect for its destructive nature.

But that was before I saw her eyes.

All of a sudden, I realize that I don't know her at all.

"Shhhh," she says softly, putting her index finger over her lips. "Serena doesn't know. Serena doesn't like hurting people."

Her voice sounds different. The strange intonation sends chills down my spine. Her eyes are crazed, and she is way too calm.

"Scar, what's wrong with you?" I gasp out as I try to crawl toward her. "You're on fire! *Scarlett!*"

"I am not Scarlett," she says as a small giggle escapes her throat. "Scarlett was a stupid little whore. I'm the one who killed Scarlett."

"What?" I say in horror.

"Serena doesn't know," she says again, rising to her feet and stepping over Mr. Brown's body. A savage smile transforms her features as she steps toward me. "Serena is soft. Soft and sweet, like a tender little marshmallow. That's exactly what she tastes like. Do you like marshmallows, Cole?" She lifts her fingers to her lips and licks them, as though removing the sticky residue after a campfire.

My body is frozen with fear and shock. How

can she joke like this when she is on fire?

"Poor girl," she continues. "But I did it all for her. I killed that little whore, so that she could live. And now I've killed the professor *for you*, brother." She holds out her hands to me, palms upturned like a goddess from an Eastern painting. "Can you keep a secret, Cole? Let this be our little secret."

I don't understand how she is just standing there. There's something wrong with her. "The fire," I whisper, clutching my chest. "You're burning alive."

"No, I'm not," she tells me, while the flames reach her midsection. She steps closer to me, with a smile still on her face and the flames reflecting in her glassy eyes. There is something angelic about her, standing there in her white dress, and something demonic about the look on her face. Who the hell is she? "I don't feel the fire, Cole," she says softly. "I don't feel any pain at all. I'm fireproof. So you will never lose me."

She's gone insane.

I can smell her burning flesh.

And I doubt she tastes like marshmallows.

I crawl forward, bleeding and hurting, but desperate to reach her. When I get close, I try to use my hands to put out the flames on her dress. It's too hot. I reach up and grab her by the waist and throw her down on the carpet, grunting with pain as I roll her body back and forth to quell the flames. It's too much. Reaching for the front of the dress, I rip it open and peel it off her before rolling her away. I don't care that she is mostly naked under the dress. There are a few pieces of burning fabric stuck to her thighs, and I quickly use my hands to pat them down to cinders and peel them away.

It's done. It's over. She is safe. My own hands are burned, and my lungs are smoky, but she is safe. This taste of ash and cinders is one I remember all too well. I collapse beside Scarlett's body and place my head on her naked chest, hugging her midsection to assure myself that she is okay.

I can feel her chest heaving with rapid breaths, and hear her heart beating beneath my ear.

She's alive. She hasn't burned to death. For real.

It takes me a moment to process this. To convince myself that everything is good.

My own heart is beating out of control.

A few feet away, her nightgown is still on fire. It is in my line of sight, and I see that the white dress is charred and black. I clutch her closer, thankful that I got it off in time. I know that she will have sustained burns on her legs, but with any luck, they won't be so bad. She's alive. That's all that matters.

I notice then that the flames from the burning log have caused the carpet to catch on fire, along with the wooden floorboards beneath it. The house is going to burn down, unless I put out those flames. But I'm somehow in no hurry to move.

I continue to lie against Scarlett's body, panting for air and bleeding all over her. I realize that I am gripping her body so tightly that my fingers are digging into her abdomen. I remember the cigarette burns that Mr. Brown used to put into her stomach. Is it possible that she somehow trained herself not to feel the pain from the cigarettes? Is that why the fire didn't bother her? Does her mind not process the pain from heat and burns?

She places one of her hands against the gash on my arm to try and stop the bleeding, and uses the other to embrace me.

"Thanks for helping," she says softly. "I'm sorry that you got hurt."

I lift my head off her chest so that I can look into her face, and determine if she's lucid. "Scar—"

"I'm not Scar," she interrupts angrily. "I'm not Serena. I'm the strong one. I'm the one who killed the baby. Benjamin's baby."

My heart twists and constricts. "The baby?"

"She couldn't face it. She couldn't deal with it. That's why she needed me. She was only twelve, and I was so much more. I'm her mother, and I'm her father. I'm her sister, and I'm her brother. I take care of her. So we don't need you, Cole."

Using both hands, she puts pressure over the deep wound on my chest. "You don't have to bleed for me. Remember that. You never have to bleed for me, because I am so very good at bleeding. I can bleed, and bleed, and bleed, like a river in Egypt. I bled out that baby for her, in a tiny airplane bathroom. I flushed it down the toilet, dead."

"Oh my god, Scar," I whisper softly.

"I am not her!" she says again. "I'm the one who does what needs to be done. I'm not afraid, Cole. I'm the girl he wanted me to be. I'm everything. Look at me." She tilts her chin up and gazes at me in a frenzied way, with her eyes darting back and forth between mine. "I'm the girl you're waiting for her to be. You think she needs to grow up, and heal. She doesn't. Because I'm already here, and I'm grown up, and I'm healed. I can't be injured, and I can't be scarred. I'm pure white snow. I'm ready for anything. Everything."

I am growing lightheaded, and I should probably call an ambulance. But I somehow feel like I need to know *her* more than I need a blood transfusion and stitches. "Who are you?" I ask her hoarsely.

"I'm a killer, Cole. I'm the crack running through her mind. I'll show up every time she needs me; every time she's pushed so hard that she breaks." She lifts one of her hands to my cheek, and places her bloody fingers against my temple. Her fingers lightly brush against my hair as she stares deep into my soul, absorbing the data from every secret corner

"So if you ever want me," she whispers. "Just break me. And I'm yours."

Her hand slides into my hair as her lips crash against mine in a salty kiss of ash and smoke. The kiss drowns out my whole world, until I feel like reality is but a dream. I no longer exist. I am drowning in her, even while the fire continues to burn and cackle near us. We need to get out of here. I am bleeding, and the house is burning, but there is simply nothing more important than her lips.

She is crazy. By her own admission, she is cracked, and she is completely insane.

And somehow, this is the moment when I become certain that I am completely in love with her. I have sensed this before, this person lingering beneath the surface. I never knew she existed, but I felt her. I thought I saw a shadow of her, inside Scarlett's blue eyes. They were so clear, and so cloudy at the same time. There had to be more than she was revealing.

And now I see.

She's a murderer. She saved my life. She is strong. She is soft. So soft that she needed to break herself in half to save her softness from ruin. I wish I could have protected her from everything that life has thrown at her, but it seems she's found a way to protect herself. And that means I really will never lose her.

She isn't fragile glass; she is fire-forged steel.

I kiss her back, zealously. If I am about to bleed to death, I want to spend my last few minutes in her arms. I hold her body close, ignoring all my pain and injuries to pull her against me. I cling to her desperately, ignoring the fire that is closing in on us. I don't even care if we both burn to death here, tonight. It would all be worth it for this kiss.

Knowing this side of her doesn't scare me. It only enchants me deeper. I loved her because of this, before I even knew of this—because it's something that exists inside me, too. In some of those nightmares that won't let me sleep? This is the person I become in those nightmares. I become desperate and capable of anything. I become unafraid. I feel like she is the missing part of me—the part I have always needed to become whole.

I can feel it in her kiss. I suppose she kissed me once before, when I got her the laptop. Or maybe twice before, if you count that brush of our lips under the bleachers. But she was hesitant, tentative, cautious. She was sweet, childlike, innocent. She was afraid.

Now, she's an entirely different person. I've never been kissed like this before. By a girl who has absolutely no fear of anything. No fear of death, of fire, of pain. She is unreal.

She's all woman and power. She is larger than life, and I know that I will never let her go.

Tonight, she killed for me. I'll always be willing to do the same for her.

A noise from the side distracts me, and I realize that my thoughts may have been a little premature. Professor Brown has risen to his feet, and he looks monstrous; his clothes are aflame, and his face is smashed in beyond recognition, and he lets out a roar that is inhuman. There are flames behind him, from where the log fell, and they are making him look like he has a blazing aura of power, and he is about to destroy us both. My first instinct is to cover Scarlet's body with my own, protectively.

But that won't get us anywhere. At this point, it's kill or be killed.

Rising to my feet shakily, I run over to the fireplace and grab one of the iron pokers. But when I turn around, my heart leaps into my throat. I see that the professor has gone after Scarlett instead of me. She rises to her feet, standing only in her underwear, but she looks so ready for his attack that she might as well be wearing battle armor. Her naked skin is covered in my blood, which is dripping down her stomach and resembling war paint. Mr. Brown has almost reached her when I lift my iron poker and rush toward them, but before I can land a blow, Scarlett lunges forward.

Her hand darts out violently and I hear him scream.

It takes me a moment to realize that she has shoved her index finger into his eyeball. She used his own momentum to impale his skull on her hand. The horror of this is not lost on me, and I recoil slightly from the sight. However, I am more focused on her safety, and actually making sure this man is dead. So I raise the iron poker and reach out to smash him over the head.

He is moving, so I miss and get him in the shoulder. The man bellows in rage, but he ignores this as he strikes out at Scarlett again. His fist gets her in the side of the face, and she stumbles backward. He pursues her, but she twists her body around and leaps on him, grabbing his head and sinking her teeth into his neck. She rips out a chunk of his flesh like a wild animal, while the man throws back his head and screams, trying to push her off.

My mouth goes very dry at the sight of a man's neck between Scarlett's teeth, but I focus on the situation—Mr. Brown's clothes are still on fire, and she has none. I smash the iron poker into his back before reaching out to shove myself between him and Scarlett. When I am sure that she is away from him, I turn around and swing the iron poker down into his head, like a sword. He finally falls, crumpling into a heap on the floor. But I am not taking any chances. I lift the poker and use my entire body weight to bring it down forcefully again.

And then again.

And then again.

The feeling of his skull caving in is satisfying. The man's whole body quakes and quivers, like an insect dying. I swing again, and again. I don't intend to stop until I see brain matter spilling out.

"Cole!" Scarlett shouts at me, grabbing my arm. "You're injured. That's enough! We need to get out of here."

I see her quickly rubbing something on herself, and I look at her in confusion.

"We can say that he sexually abused me," she explains, showing me the piece of flesh from Mr. Brown's neck that she has been rubbing on her underwear. "I have enough... damage, in that area, from Benjamin. They should believe me."

"Blame his death entirely on me," I say firmly, grabbing her hand. "I'm going to take the fall for this. We'll say it was self-defense. He *did* stab me."

"More evidence never hurts," she says with narrowed eyes. "Believe me."

"Come on," I tell her, coughing as the fire closes in around us. "We have to leave. Now!"

"Wait!" she says, looking toward the library sofa in panic. "My laptop! I have to get my laptop."

"No! The fire is spreading too fast."

"I need it, Cole. You got it for me."

When she begins moving into the flames, I find myself reaching out to grab her. I wrap my arms around her midsection tightly, beneath her naked breasts.

"Let go!" she says, struggling against me. "I need that computer! *Cole!*"

"I'll get you another," I promise. "Come on. I'm bleeding a lot, and if you keep struggling like this, I'm going to pass out, and you're going to have to drag me out of here."

She abruptly stops fighting, but as soon as I let go of her, she lunges forward, heading into the flames. I anticipated this, since she doesn't feel fear or care about getting burned, and I grab her arm just in time, slamming my other hand into the back of her head and knocking her unconscious.

I reach out to catch her as her body slumps. Lifting her limp body into my arms, I grunt in pain as I walk out of the library. I hear the sound of sirens in the distance, and this is comforting. Maybe I will survive this after all. Scarlett stirs slightly after a few steps, so I must not have hit her as hard as I thought.

"Cole?" she mumbles, clearly dizzy from the blow. "Oh god, it hurts." She moans and grasps a handful of my shirt, and is startled to find it soaked with blood. "Cole! What's happening?"

"You feel the pain?" I ask her softly. Her voice has returned to normal.

"My legs," she says with a gasp. "Cole, you're bleeding!"

"I'll be fine," I assure her, although I am assured of no such thing.

"And why am I naked?" she asks feebly, putting a hand over her breasts. "Oh my god, my head hurts."

"Just get some rest," I tell her, leaning down to

place a kiss against her forehead. "The danger is over now. Mr. Brown is dead."

"What?" she gasps. "How?"

"I killed him."

She lifts her fingers to touch my chin, but her hand falls limply to her side. "Cole," she says as tears gather in her eyes. "What's going to happen now?"

"I don't know."

"Please," she says softly, before letting her head roll against my chest. "Cole…"

"Hmm?"

"Don't ever leave me."

"I won't. Promise."

She falls asleep in my arms as I walk, and I see Mrs. Brown standing in the darkened kitchen and staring at us.

"You killed my husband?" she asks in a dark voice. "You killed Jeremiah."

"Yeah," I say as I walk past her, holding Scarlett close protectively. "You're welcome."

My knees begin to buckle under me as I walk, and I know I haven't got much left in me. But I manage to get Scarlett outside of the house, and I see the paramedics running toward us before I let myself completely collapse to my knees.

"Help her!" I tell the paramedic who is rushing to my side with a stretcher and gently taking Scarlett out of my arms. "She's badly burned." The moment her warmth leaves my chest, I find my upper body crashing roughly to the gravel driveway.

The world spins around me. Somehow, I know that I have survived once again.

Chapter Thirteen

sophie shields, 2016

Holding a lighter in my hand, I use my thumb to roughly spin the wheel and jab the button so that the fluid inside catches fire. A little flame ignites at the opening with a *poof* sound, and I watch it wavering for several seconds before I release the button and let it die.

I perform this motion again, and again, staring at the little flame.

Fire never really bothered me, but I still remember the look in Cole's eyes whenever he caught sight of the tiniest spark. If he walked into the room even now, and saw this lighter in my hand, he would pause for a moment and grow serious and contemplative. Cole wasn't afraid of much in this world, but the sight of fire always made him hesitate.

Playing with the lighter is just a distraction.

Zack's computer is sitting in my bag just a few feet away, calling to me. I have the strong urge to turn it on and dig up more information about Cole—especially that hospital footage. But I know that if I get started, I'll be up all night, and I might be too tired to attend the funeral. I already have dark circles under my eyes and trouble keeping them open.

So I flick the lighter closed. And open.

I often think back to the night that our last foster home burned down. I don't remember everything that happened, other than Professor Brown choking me and Cole trying to make him stop. I don't know exactly how the fire started, other than what Cole told me later. I must have blacked out, because I only remember waking up in his arms, burned and confused. I remember those few days we spent in the hospital, and how badly Cole was injured. They had to give him so much blood.

It was all my fault, wasn't it?

Cole had already been through enough, but because of me, he had to suffer even more. He had to kill the professor to protect me, and go to prison for it. The fire that took his parents had already been giving him nightmares for years—but being stabbed and needing to bludgeon a man to death? That sort of thing will wreak havoc on a young boy's mind. It's a wonder he didn't need more therapy.

The look on Mrs. Brown's face at the trial still haunts me. She hated us so much.

Tossing the lighter aside, I fall back onto the bed. I have already brushed my teeth and peeled off my jeans, and I just want to crash. I am tired as hell after the flight and emotionally jetlagged from this crazy day. My body is here, in this time zone where Cole no longer exists, but my mind is trapped in several years ago, when we were inseparable. All my muscles are limp with exhaustion, but my thoughts are racing with a jumble of memories and questions.

When I really try to think of all the people who would want to hurt my brother, it's a little staggering. Cole didn't really go through life causing or seeking trouble, so I have no idea how he made so many enemies. To be fair, I suppose, many of his enemies were originally mine.

My eyes are closing when the phone beside my bed rings, causing me to sit up abruptly. I reach to the side and answer it, trying to think of who would be calling.

"Hello?" I say, fighting back a yawn.

A familiar woman's voice filters through the receiver. "Agent Shields."

"Shit," I curse, leaping off the bed and blinking the sleep out of my eyes. "How did you find me?" The question is stupid. I am upset at myself before the words have even finished leaving my mouth, but I am too tired to form any other sentences.

The woman laughs, a musical sound. "Well, isn't it obvious? We had someone who actually came in to work today do it. Your colleagues were very excited for the opportunity to pry into your personal life."

Looking around sheepishly, I place a hand in my hair. I try to remember my recent credit card transactions and whether there was anything embarrassing on there that they could gossip about in the office. No, I didn't use my credit card to check into the hotel. They must have traced Zack's phone and financials. I bet he just made a purchase downstairs at the gift shop—a midnight snack, most likely.

"Sophie, I want you to know that we're all a little concerned. There was some airport security footage of you using a computer in a very public location. You know that your contract prohibits…"

"I don't care, Luciana. You can fire me if you want."

"Yes, well, maybe it's about time we revised your contract. You're not a little girl anymore, and you're not going around and stealing sports cars and drawing attention to yourself."

"I never stole a sports car. There is no conclusive evidence that I ever stole a sports car."

My boss sighs. "Sophie, we know about your brother, and it's totally understandable that you need some time off. We all know how close you were."

"It's not a big deal," I say stubbornly. "Did you ever think that maybe I just came to Cali for the sun?"

"Will you just stop? We have your personnel files, Sophie. We know that your foster brother went to prison protecting you from abuse when he was fifteen years old. We know that you hacked into that prison to get him out so he could study architecture at MIT."

"I never hacked into a prison," I tell my boss. "I don't know where you're getting all this, but…"

"Shut the fuck up, Sophie. I hired you *because*

of all that crazy shit you did, and how loyal you are. You may not talk about your past or private life, but we all care about you, okay? I care about you. So just take all the time you need, and be careful out there. Give me a phone call if you need any help. You have friends here at the agency."

Her kindness makes me pause. "You're not firing me, Lopez?"

"No! Why would I fire you? So that you can go and work for the FBI or Homeland Security? I know they have been trying to recruit you for years. You're the best we've got, Shields. I'm... sorry if I'm hard on you, sometimes."

A sad smile settles on my face. "Thank you. That means a lot."

"Just don't kill anyone? Okay? When you find out who is responsible..."

"I'll try my best," I say softly as an image of Benjamin comes to my mind.

"You're not a field agent, Shields. You don't have all the required training..." Luciana sighs. "Look, just access Zack's cell phone, okay? I will send you the coordinates of someone who can hook you up with a gun, and some other equipment you might need for your personal protection."

I am surprised. "Are you allowed to do that?"

"Protect my agents? I'm supposed to do that."

"Thank you, Lucy." I pause, shaking my head. "You're... awesome."

"You have no idea how awesome! Hey—I know you're upset at Zack. Don't ask how I know. But keep him around until this blows over, okay? You shouldn't be alone right now. I'll hook him up with a gun, too, since he has advanced weapons training."

"That sounds good. Hey, Lopez? When I get back, your morning mocha lattes are on me, for like, a year." As soon as the words leave my mouth, I remember that Cole has handed me the reins of his company. How much work will I need to do here? Am I even going to be able to return to my old job?

"How about my evening chardonnay?" Luciana suggests. "It would be nice to actually hang out with you after work sometime, *and talk.* Especially after a hard day. There aren't many other women in our department, and it would be nice to vent about all the shit I have to deal with."

"Okay," I tell her softly, hoping that it's true. I feel like I have been uprooted from my life. Do I owe it to Cole to stay and continue his affairs? I can't deal with thinking about this now. "In the future, I will be less of an antisocial asshole and buy my boss drinks after work."

"Good. Take care of yourself, Agent Shields."

"You too, Lopez."

When I place the hotel phone back down into its receiver, I look at the curtains thoughtfully. Maybe I have had friends all along, and just never really noticed. I never imagined that anyone would have my back or be there for me in a disaster like this. But I never imagined a disaster like this, either.

Lying back on the hotel bed, I wrap my hands around my middle. Warm and fuzzy feelings swirl around in my stomach, and I think this must be gratitude. Being away from Cole made me really closed off to the world, but losing him again, in such a final and terrible way, is somehow opening me up to people again. It's easy to get through each day alone, putting up walls around myself, but when something like this happens… the walls come down. The truth comes out.

It's times like these when you realize that you need people—and that certain people have been there all along. You just needed to stop shutting doors in their faces.

Speaking of doors, there is a knock at mine— but it is not the front door of my hotel room. It's the adjoining room that Zack is staying in. I hesitate for a moment, unwilling to coax my muscles to move and leave the comfort of this bed. Why am I so tired? But he knocks again, and I groan as I push myself up to my feet and sluggishly move along the wall. I am only wearing an oversized t-shirt, but Zack has seen me in worse, and I don't really care. Grasping the doorknob, I slide the latch aside and unlock the door to pull it open.

Zack moves into my hotel room, and he is holding a tray of fast food. It is warm, and fresh, and it smells delicious. I look up at him questioningly.

"You haven't eaten since yesterday," he explains. "You've been running on coffee and booze."

Is Zack one of those people I've been shutting out? Is he really a great guy, but I just haven't been able to appreciate it in my self-obsessed blindness? After all, he is here. He came all this way to look out for me and to take care of me. I realize that he has taken care of me a lot lately, and I haven't been paying much attention. Maybe it's even… a little understandable that he acted so crazy and hid my letters. I might have done the same thing if someone I cared about deeply was lying to me.

Okay, maybe I wouldn't have done that—but I can understand his anxiety. He gave me so much energy and attention, and I barely gave him the time of day. *I used him, didn't I?*

"Sophieee," he says in a singsong voice, reaching for a French fry. He holds it out to my lips with a smile, as if I am a child. "You've gotta eat something."

I stare at the fry, which is a classic crispy golden brown. What is it about French fries that is so irresistible and alluring? But I've already brushed my teeth, and I don't think I have the energy to do it again.

"I'm really tired," I tell him.

"Yes, because you haven't eaten."

Moving over to the bed, I lower myself back down onto the mattress with a sigh. "Thanks, Zack, but maybe I'll just wait until the morning."

Zack frowns. "No, you really need to…" He is interrupted by a loud buzzing sound, and he puts the tray down and pops the French fry into his mouth before reaching into his pocket to check his phone. "Hey, Soph? What does this mean?" He holds the screen out for me to see.

When I read the text message, I laugh softly.

Shields,

You will not find any guns in the trunk of the car that you didn't steal.

-L

"That's just my boss messing with me," I explain to Zack. "She decided not to fire me after all, and she's hooking me up with some gear to help out. She's even throwing in a gun for you."

"A gun?" Zack repeats, his eyes growing wide, like a puppy staring at a treat. "What kind? For me? When do I get it?"

"It's probably there waiting now. Or at least, she's sent it there, and she figures that by the time we can get there, it will have been delivered."

"When can we go?" Zack asks. "Can we go now? Sophie, I haven't held a gun in… months. It's the only thing I'm good at. And I'm really, *really* good at it."

My face softens, imagining what it must be like for Zack to be injured and out of work for so long. Having received an honorable discharge, he would be eligible to receive disability benefits from the VA if he applied, but he has been determined to find meaningful work and contribute to society. He doesn't know that since we were set up on a blind date—by his old boss and Luciana—I kind of have been his job. They both thought it would be good for us. Zack wouldn't leave the house at all after losing his leg, not even for physical therapy. Lucy didn't think it was safe for me to live alone, considering my job and my history.

Maybe now that he knows, I can try to hook him up with a real job that gives him some satisfaction. Feeling a little guilty, I nod. "We'll go first thing in the morning. I need to take a little nap."

"Isn't it better to move fast?" he asks. "I just wouldn't be too happy if those guns got into the wrong hands."

"Maybe," I say, glancing at the French fries. A few hundred calories in the tank could keep me going for another few hours.

"Hey," Zack says suddenly. "I got distracted by the guns, but I wanted to tell you something. I'm not upset about the marriage thing. I understand that you probably had your reasons for never telling me that you were married."

Turning away from him, I look toward the wall. "The funeral is tomorrow, Zack. I should probably get some rest."

"I know. I know how important Cole was to you, and… I'm so sorry I kept those letters, Sophie. I didn't know what I was doing, and if I could go back in time…"

"That means a lot, Zack."

"But it still hurts. I can't help it. I just proposed to you this morning, and to learn that you've been married this whole time…"

"We—we got married for financial and legal reasons. It wasn't like that. I was fifteen."

"So, you never slept with him?" Zack asks.

I don't respond. The silence is heavy in the room.

"Sorry, that's none of my business," Zack says. "But—why didn't you ever get divorced?"

This question is even worse. I shrug. "What does it matter now? He's dead."

"It matters to me," Zack says. "Because I still love you, Sophie. I just want to know you."

"You wanna know me?" I ask as a slow smile spreads across my face. Turning over and sitting up, I reach for the French fries and shove a handful in my mouth. They are so salty that I can feel them burning the insides of my cheeks and gums, but they are also sinfully delicious.

"Silly, Zack. If you really want to know a woman, you've got to meet her family. And if she doesn't have a family… well, then you've got to meet her car."

"The stolen car?" he asks me suspiciously.

"I did not steal a car," I tell him, but I think that the smug look on my face might say otherwise. "Come on. Call me an Uber."

"You look crazy right now," he tells me with a headshake as he follows my command.

"I feel crazy right now," I tell him as I pull myself off the bed and grab my purse. I am too tired to pull on my jeans, so I march to the door in my oversized t-shirt. *Whatever.* It's California, and no one wears real clothes. I'll just call this beach attire if anyone asks. I even go a step further and slide my feet into flip-flops.

Flip-flops.

Do you have any idea how that feels? I usually have my feet packed tightly into high heels all day or suffocating in sweaty running shoes at the gym. But out here, on the west coast—you can get away with wearing flip-flops and it's not weird. I wiggle my toes, amazed at their freedom.

"Okay," Zack says with a worried smile, looking up from his phone. "It's on the way."

"Great," I tell him, leaving the room. "Are you coming?"

Chapter Fourtneen

sophie shields, 2016

Zack lets out a low whistle as the garage door lifts.

I had to bite my lip as I punched in the code to enter Cole's house and discovered that it's still my birthday. I did all this while trying very hard not to look at the actual house. I can't bear it right now. I'm just here for the car and the guns.

"Sophie, what is this thing?" Zack asks as he ducks to step into the garage.

"It's a Bugatti Veyron," I explain to him proudly.

"Holy shit. I was expecting a Volkswagen Beetle or a Mini Cooper." He steps forward cautiously, inspecting the vehicle. "I didn't know you were such a car enthusiast!"

"I'm not," I tell him as I lower the garage door

to lock us inside, for some privacy.

"How can anyone own a car like this and not be a car person?" Zack asks.

Smiling, I pull the car keys out of my purse and press the button to open the car. I then move to run my hand over the sleek hood of the vehicle. The paint is still as shiny as the day I first got it, and there isn't a speck of dust anywhere to be seen. Cole kept it in good shape for me. "It was a gift," I explain to Zack.

"From your brother?" he asks, a little jealous.

"No way. Cole couldn't afford this back then."

"Then who?" He is now at the back of the vehicle, fiddling with the rear of the car. "And how do I open the trunk on this thing?"

My lips quirk upward at his innocence. "The trunk is at the front of the car," I explain to him as I pop it open. When I do, my own eyebrows lift. It's a small trunk, but Luciana managed to pack it with goodies for me. It's divided down the middle into two sections, like his and hers weapons closets, complete with concealed carry permits. My side contains state-of-the-art electronics, while Zack's side contains firearms. I can't help feeling a little emotional at this sight; she really does care.

Zack limps over to my side and nearly trips when he sees one of the containers. He rips it out of the car and opens it up, pulling out a rifle and nearly shouting in joy.

"Are you kidding me?" Zack says as he strokes the rifle lovingly. "Are you fucking kidding me? The Mk 12 SPR! This is my baby. One of the most versatile guns I've ever used, that has saved my life on more than one occasion. I don't know who you work for, Sophie, but she's a goddess."

"I agree… but it does seem like overkill. Does she really think we'll need any of this?" I muse out loud.

"Who cares?" Zack asks. "Free toys! It's like Christmas."

It's uplifting to see him so excited, and I am happy we made the trip tonight. I am still tired as hell, and I may have briefly napped on the way over here, but it's worth it for this. I notice there are at least two smaller pistols, and I pull one out to check it out.

I am a little puzzled by how many items Luciana included. I almost wonder if she knows something about Cole's death that I don't. Are we actually in serious trouble? If so, being at Cole's house is a rather safe place, structurally, although it is also a very likely place for any assailants to look…

"We should probably carry these ones around," I tell Zack, handing him a small Beretta. "I don't think you'll have any use for the rifle, but she probably just put it in here to make you happy."

"If only I'd had one of these babies with me when I lost my leg, instead of the heavy piece of crap I was using…" Zack quickly assembles the rifle, adding the scope and the suppressor. "God, look at this thing. Isn't it beautiful? Do we have to give it back? I don't care, I'm never giving it back."

I laugh lightly at this as I give in to my own temptation to check out the sleek silver laptop that Agent Lopez left for me. I bring it close to my face and stare at the little machine while I feel the weight carefully. Computers sure have changed since I was young, but I already know that we are going to have some fun together. Zack's laptop is old and sluggish, unable to keep up with the demands of my fingers. This powerhouse will do a lot better.

"Did you just smell that computer?" Zack asks me.

"Maybe," I say softly. "There's something special about fresh metal."

I replace the computer and skim the other items in the trunk, retrieving a cell phone. Luciana knows that I haven't owned one for years. It's funny how I thought I was walking out on my job and surely going to get fired, and instead, I've ended up with renewed ties to my work, and even with them helping *me* out in a personal matter.

But is it my job, or just Luciana? It doesn't matter. I am grateful.

Checking the Beretta's magazine for bullets, I place it in my purse, along with the cell phone. A huge yawn overtakes me, along with a wave of tiredness. Moving around the car to sit in the driver's seat, I lean back, enjoying the feeling of being in a familiar environment. I can even recognize the smell of the car when I breathe in deeply. I run my hands over the leather, remembering the way it felt to drive this beast.

Zack enters the passenger side of the car and takes a seat, hugging his rifle to his chest. The car is pretty small, and he is a big guy, so there isn't a lot of room for the gun, but it's kind of adorable. "Do you want to take it for a spin?" he asks.

"Oh, no way. It's not insured. It costs a fortune to insure this thing." I gesture at a beat-up older car sitting further back in the garage. "That's my car for actually driving around. The Hyundai Elantra. I'm not insane."

"So you *did* steal this?" Zack asks.

"No. But it is… a trophy." Reclining in the comfortable seat, I gaze at the stylish dashboard fondly. "There was this big shot real estate developer who was trying to screw Cole over when we were younger. It was one of his first massive projects, and the guy was going to use his designs for an entire subdivision while paying him peanuts. The jerk was established, and had lawyers who would crush Cole if he tried to complain. So I negotiated a better deal."

"Oh, man," Zack says, wincing. "What did you do?"

"Nothing too ridiculous. I just seduced the developer, and set some cameras up to take photos of us in compromising positions. I threatened to show the photos to his wife if he didn't make good on his agreements with Cole, and of course, he stood to lose a lot more money in the divorce. I was feeling kind of vindictive, so I told him to throw in the car, just to add insult to injury. He signed it over to me, and I knew that we would be okay from that point on. I could sell the car if we were ever in real trouble. But we never were again. It was just one success after another, after that, so I just kept the car as a memento."

"I see. So you got it from blackmail."

"Negotiation," I correct.

Zack shakes his head. "I can't believe I've been

living with you for so long, and I didn't know the first thing about you. Geez. If I had known… I probably would have proposed a *lot* sooner."

"Why?" I ask teasingly, running my hands over the steering wheel. "Because of my sexy Bugatti?"

"Because of your sexy brain."

His response makes me pause. Cole used to say things like that to me. "Sometimes, I drive it anyway," I tell him softly as I tighten my grip on the steering wheel. "When I'm feeling really depressed or insecure, and I need a little ego boost. Insurance or not, I would take it out onto the highway, just to get that feeling. Of being free, and powerful. Of breaking the rules. It reminds me that I'm not useless."

"Useless?" Zack asks. "Why would you think that?"

I shrug. "Cole did so much for me. He sacrificed and he suffered for me. No one ever cared like that before. I needed to know that I was an asset to him, and that I could protect him, too. This car is a symbol of that. That I was maybe worthy of him. Worthy of everything that he gave to me, because I could give back a little something, too."

"I can't imagine you ever feeling unworthy, Sophie."

"It's an abandonment thing. My parents didn't consider me worthy enough to keep. How could anyone else? And… Cole wasn't just anyone. He was special. He was so amazing at everything he did. Achievements came so easily to him, while I was too afraid to even make goals in the first place."

Turning to the side, I look out of the car's

windshield at the nonexistent scenery. A halfhearted smile touches my lips.

"Zack… I really loved him."

"I know. I can tell."

"Wish you could've met him," I say as I lean back against the car seat and pull my knees up onto the cushion, "under other circumstances than him being lowered into the ground."

"Me too," he says. "He must have been pretty cool if he's this important to you. Hey, Soph, you look tired as hell. Do you want to go into Cole's house and get some rest?"

"No!" I say a little harshly, as though stricken. I shake my head and close my eyes. "I can't. Not ready to go in there."

"Did you live here for a while?" Zack asks.

I nod in response.

"Well, do you want to go back to the hotel and get some sleep?" he asks, but my chin is already falling to rest against my shoulder.

Zack leans forward and places a kiss against my hair before squeezing one of my hands. "I don't mind sleeping in a million-dollar car with you. As long as I've got a pistol and an Mk 12 with me, I can sleep just about anywhere."

"One point four million," I mumble sleepily.

"Hmph," Zack grunts. "This car is more expensive than most of the houses I've slept in. It would be nice if it came with a bathroom and a kitchen, maybe a backyard with a hot tub, trampoline for the kids, and a barn for the horses. Not that we have kids or horses, but if we had a trampoline and a barn, we'd have to get some kids and horses, wouldn't we?"

"Yeah," I mumble, not entirely sure what he's saying. *Something about a trampoline?* I like trampolines. I just have to wear a sports bra.

"For what it's worth," Zack says softly, "I wish that Cole was still here, Soph. I wish you could walk into that house right now and see him reading the newspaper or watching television, or whatever it is that Cole normally does. I hate to see you this sad."

I fall asleep with an image in my mind of Cole reading the newspaper. Except he didn't read the newspaper. He was on the newspaper. And the newspaper said he was gone.

The newspaper in my mind goes up in flames. So does the trampoline.

Chapter Fifteen

sophie shields, 2016

Waking up in cramped quarters, I feel like my whole body is stiff and aching. I reach up to rub my neck before wiping a bit of dried drool off the side of my face. Feeling a hand squeeze my shoulder, I groan and bat it away.

"Five more minutes, Zack."

There is a low, masculine laugh. "I'm not Zack."

My eyelids shoot open. The voice hits me like a lightning bolt to the heart, and I turn around so violently that my arm slams into the side of the steering wheel. "Cole?" I whisper.

There is a boyish grin on his face. "Thought I told you, Scar. I'm indestructible."

"But..." In my shock, I move closer, and my elbow hits the car horn, causing a loud blaring noise to make me jump.

And then I really wake up. I am hyperventilating as I turn to the side and see Zack lying there, hugging a machine gun like a teddy bear. His eyes are wide open in surprise at the sound.

It was just a dream. I curse and hit the steering wheel.

"Hey, shh," Zack says, reaching out to rub my back. "You okay?"

"No," I say angrily, pressing my forehead against the wheel. "No, I'm not."

Today is my brother's funeral. It's a terrible day to wake up. Most bad days consist of not wanting to get out of bed, but this day is so bad that I don't want to get out of the car—and I want to kick Zack out, and put this car on the bottom of the ocean. Then I want to go back to sleep.

It is also the funeral of my best friend. Someone I abandoned and neglected for years. I've always heard people say that death will make you regret the time you've wasted, holding grudges, not appreciating your loved ones—not spending enough time with them. I regret everything. I regret it so much that it's burning a hole through my insides. Cole's time here was so short, and I had the power to make him far happier than he was. If I had been just a little stronger… we could have been happy.

Today is the funeral of my husband.

Sudden images come to mind of the old Indian practice of sati. Hindu and Sikh women would throw themselves on the burning funeral pyre of their dead husbands in a gesture of undying loyalty and love. I always considered it barbaric, but then again, it's easy to consider such things barbaric before you actually have a dead husband. Today, it feels like the most natural thing in the world. Maybe if I had been a better wife, a present wife, or a goddamned wife at all, Cole would still be here.

Don't I deserve to die for that?

Thoughts and feelings from my youth come rushing back to me. Thoughts I banished years ago, at his request. I promised Cole I would stop considering suicide—but haven't I been emotionally dead for years? Letting my hand dangle off the car seat to where my purse sits on the floor, my fingertips brush the cool metal of the gun. Cole died to gunshots.

Wouldn't it be poetic and fitting if I chose the same fate?

I believe Miranda would get everything that Cole left to me. That's good. She has children. I could ask Mr. Bishop to draw up some documents quickly, and leave this car to Zack, along with all of Sophie's belongings. I suppose I'll need multiple wills for multiple identities…

"Sophie," Zack says, running his hand over my hair soothingly. "What are you thinking?"

I hesitate before responding. "Do you know what sati is?"

He shakes his head. "What's that?"

"Nothing. Never mind."

Raising an eyebrow, Zack reaches for his phone and searches for the word. He misspells it, but is able to find the definition anyway. After skimming the definition, he looks up at me with wide eyes. "What the hell?"

"Just… a thought."

Zack stares at me for a long moment, his face growing creased with tension. "Do you really hate me that much? Am I really such a pathetic second prize that you would do that to me?"

Turning to gaze at him, tears prick my eyes. I never really considered his feelings in all this. How much has Zack suffered due to my inability to trust others or open my heart? Am I currently doing to him what I previously did to Cole? What kind of monster would I be to leave him now? But wouldn't he be better off without me?

"Listen, Soph," Zack says, clearing his throat. "It's almost morning. You need to get some coffee and breakfast in you. You're running on empty and your emotions are running high; of course you're going to think about crazy shit. Let's put the brakes on that until we're fed?"

"Sure," I mumble.

"Are there any breakfast places within walking distance? Actually, it might not be safe to walk. We could always take your Hyundai."

I glance over at my beloved old car. It was the first vehicle I ever purchased, and I have real memories of driving it and spending endless hours behind the wheel. Often with Cole beside me. Unlike this ridiculous flashy sports car, I have an actual emotional attachment to that little beater.

"Also, weird question, Soph. Do you have any idea what you're going to wear to the funeral? I didn't bring anything black."

"Oh, shit," I murmur, rubbing my eyes with one hand. There is a very classy black dress in my walk-in closet in Cole's house. Every time I needed to be taken seriously in a professional situation, that was my go-to outfit. I can even picture exactly where it is in the closet, because Cole let me design those closets myself. I frown, glancing at Zack. Cole has some black suits that might fit Zack, but I'm not sure how I feel about raiding his wardrobe.

I think that would make this day even worse, if that is possible. Walking into Cole's closet and being surrounded by all his clothes and all the memories of times he wore them. Remembering what each garment meant to him? The bold ties he wore on days when he felt nervous before a big presentation. The casual sweats he wore around the house, for eating white cheddar popcorn and watching martial arts movies. The ridiculous costumes he wore for cosplaying his favorite anime characters. The warm pair of pajamas he would wear for when we drove up to his cabin in the mountains. I'm not strong enough to handle all that right now. It would break me.

"We can go shopping after breakfast," I tell Zack quietly, grateful that he reminded me. After all, Annabelle's going to be at the funeral, and it's probably best if she doesn't see me looking like I'm homeless again. I also need to talk to the detective, so wearing normal grieving wife attire could help expedite that. Clothes are so important for facing the world.

I guess I would like to have a new dress—especially if it ends up being the last dress I ever wear. I'll need some shoes, too. I find myself imagining the particular outfit I should wear before shooting myself in the head. Should it even be my head? I think, if I'm wearing the right dress, it won't matter where I shoot myself. It will still be stylish. What would make a really great fashion statement? The perfect death dress is hard to find, and should be shopped for months in advance and pre-ordered, like wedding dresses.

Where do I go to shop for something like that? I'll have to look it up online.

My fingers are caressing the gun in my purse, but I suddenly pause. Lucy would be so upset if I used her gifts for self-destruction instead of self-protection. What is wrong with me? Why am I thinking like this? I promised Cole I would never think like this.

"Soph?" Zack says, putting down his rifle so that he can reach out and grasp both of my hands. "Will you look at me for a sec?"

I turn to the right, looking at him, but not really seeing him.

"The lawyer mentioned something about a semen sample. Cole had his sperm frozen?"

No. Not this. Shutting my eyes tightly, I hold my breath for several seconds before responding. "He wanted kids," I say finally, choking out the words. "He wanted them so much. He had no family remaining. Neither of us did."

"Sophie, if you wanted…"

"No, no, no," I say quickly, interrupting and squeezing his hands aggressively to try and stop him.

"If you wanted to use his sample…"

"Zack, please!" I beg, my voice breaking. "Please don't."

"I would understand. I would understand if you wanted to keep him alive like that."

I burst out crying. My breathing is short and shallow as a violent sob shakes my shoulders. I clench Zack's hands so tightly that my nails dig into his skin, almost drawing blood.

"I would be here for you," Zack says. "Always. I just want you to think of good things, okay? I want you to think about life, not death."

Tears are sliding down my cheeks. I fight it. I fight it so hard, but it conquers me. All the emotion that I've been holding back comes out in a flood, and I don't know if I can ever stop this onslaught. Turning back to the center of the car, I rip my hands away from Zack and slam my fist into the center of the steering wheel, causing the horn to blare again.

The loud sound causes my body to tense up, and my tears slow down. I punch the horn again until my tears abruptly stop. I breathe, trying to regain composure.

"Sophie," Zack says, reaching for me again, but I push his hands away.

"Just shut the hell up!" I hiss, turning the key in the ignition. Why not drive this car? It is a car. It's also a special occasion. They say you only get married once, but that's not always true. What is true, is that Cole's not going to have any more funerals. Might as well drive there in style.

"Fuck this," I say, slamming my hand up to hit the garage opener on the sun visor of the Bugatti.

"Wait!" Zack exclaims as I push the shifter into gear. "Everyone's going to be looking at this car, so you should probably let me put the rifle back in the trunk…"

But the car is already rumbling to life under us, and I am already peeling backwards out of the garage. Cole is dead. So is Scarlett Hunter, and Serena Powell. What the hell does it matter what Sophie Shields drives? She'll probably be dead soon, too.

Chapter Sixteen

sophie shields, 2016

As I park my car and stare at the gravestones, I swallow.

I dreaded coming here so much that I delayed and delayed, and now the funeral service is almost over. But I am in no hurry to see my brother's body being lowered into the earth. I am sure that Miranda picked out a very elegant box to put him in, and invited all the right people—thank god she was there to take care of those arrangements.

It feels a little unreal to think that this is the last time I will get to see him. Or be near him. Sitting in the car, in my new black dress and shoes, I feel my stomach turn with fear and nausea.

I can still remember the first time I saw him.

My thoughts drift back to that day, when my social worker introduced me to my new foster family.

I was prepared for the worst and trying to keep my expectations low, but the social worker was very hopeful. She spoke highly of a man she referred to as "the professor" and said that she'd recently had some success in placing another intelligent teenager in that home.

She showed me a photograph, and they looked like a sweet old couple. A regular Martha and Jonathan Kent, or Marilla and Matthew Cuthbert—the kind of seemingly loving family that every orphan dreams about, until they actually get one. The social worker said there were lots of books in the house, and that was the only thing that made me feel like the situation could be worthwhile.

When she described Cole, I was annoyed. She made him out to be some kind of golden boy, and I thought I would hate him on sight. I thought he would be superior, privileged, and entitled, and that I wouldn't speak more than three words to him for the remainder of our lives in that home. But then I saw him. He looked like he was carrying the weight of the world on his shoulders, and his bones were cracking, but he didn't mind. He could handle it. He could handle anything.

And then he shook my hand.

Everything changed for me in that moment, although I didn't know it at the time. Maybe I should have known, from the way that nature shuddered beneath me. For when the earth moved that day, so did my soul. It was like I'd always been made up of pieces; large, disjointed sections of a human mind, moving together, or apart—and I could suddenly feel the rift between them all. I looked into Cole's eyes, and I suddenly knew a little more about what I was. My whole world was shaken up, along with my innermost essence, and I was never quite the same.

I wish I had known; but we never really know when we are meeting the people who will shape what we become, until long after we have been shaped by them.

At the time, I thought that what I saw in him was anger. I understood anger. His eyes were dark, with a deep, brutal, unbridled kind of rage. But it wasn't anger at all, and it wasn't unbridled. More than anyone I have ever met, Cole had complete rein over his emotions. He was calm. Utterly unaffected and calm.

I was intimidated by the power of what I saw inside him. It was a new experience for me. He was not physically intimidating back then: he was barely taller than I was. He was very lean and slender at age fourteen, and he didn't develop any real bulk until years later. But when he touched me, and the earth quivered, I swear that there was also a tiny jolt of electricity between us, carrying unspoken words.

I think it was love. I think that's what I saw in his eyes.

A capacity for love far surpassing anyone I had ever met. Love, loyalty, and a devotion that would last until the very day he died. I know that he never stopped loving me. He never stopped writing letters, even if I didn't receive them. I never should have allowed myself to believe that he stopped writing letters. I know him. Deep down, somehow, I have always known him.

Later on, I remember looking up the earthquake online to make sure that it had really happened, and I wasn't just imagining it all. It had. The quake had registered as a 5.2 on the Richter scale. I suppose it's a very human tendency to assign meaning to arbitrary events, but I was absolutely convinced that the planet was somehow communicating with me. The earth was trying to tell me something about Cole, and I didn't understand it at the time.

Is it too late? Is it really too late for me to demonstrate that I return all of his devotion?

I reach for my new black purse, which I had to buy to match my shoes and dress. It contains only a few items, among which are my red Scarlett wallet, and the gun and cell phone that Agent Lopez gave me. I hold the purse with both hands as I watch all the other cars that are lined up around the perimeter. I see that the people gathered around one particular gravesite have begun to leave.

My grip on my purse tightens. I am glad they are leaving. I don't want to have to interact with any of the visitors who are just here out of obligation or a sense of propriety. I only want to see the people who really cared about Cole. The people who are going to stay until the very end, until the very last clump of dirt is placed over his coffin.

"Sophie," Zack says from beside me, and I realize that he has placed his hand over mine. "You're not still thinking about that crazy shit you said earlier, right?"

I shrug in response, biting my lip.

"Don't let yourself go down that rabbit hole. I know how you feel, Soph. Since I lost my leg, the thought has crossed my mind. More than once. But you're the reason that I hang on, and hope for things to get better. I can't be this fucking useless forever. And now, today… on the first day that I haven't felt useless in months, holding a gun in my hand again, being of some service? You're thinking this way? Please, don't."

"Zack, I had a really rough childhood. I never thought that I'd get this far, go to school, get a good job working for the CIA, have a boyfriend…" I shake my head in frustration. "But I'm still really messed up on the inside. I'm just this stupid, lost little orphan with no real purpose. I have no idea what I'm doing or where I'm going. And I'm not… okay. This—" I gesture out at the funeral service I'm missing, "this is just a reminder of how much I've screwed up everything."

"Guilt will make you do crazy things," Zack tells me. "Trust me, I know. But don't make rash and permanent decisions out of guilt. You didn't let your brother down, Sophie. I'm the one who kept his letters from you. You should blame me."

"I screwed up long before that. It was my fault that letters were the only way we could communicate. I pushed him away. I put a whole continent between us."

"You can't focus on that now. He knew that you cared. You need to concentrate on finding out who shot him. If you give up now, then you'll let the bad guys win."

"They killed him. They already won." Turning off the car, I sigh and toss the keys into my new purse before slinging it over my shoulder. "Whatever. I have a date with a tombstone."

Stepping out of my car and into the sunlight, I enjoy the fierce feeling of my new black heels hitting the asphalt. I used Scarlett's credit cards for the first time in years, and I wasn't sure if they would work, but they did. The black dress is elegant and simple, with a boat neck and lace sleeves.

Overall, my outfit was designed to match the gun in my purse.

Zack moves to my side and offers me his arm, and I shake my head to decline. I think it's very important that I do this on my own. Walking briskly toward the gravesite, slightly ahead of Zack, I pass many older men and women who are leaving the service.

Only Miranda, Mr. Bishop, and Annabelle are still standing near Cole's grave as the casket is lowered into the grave. I see that Annabelle is covering her face with her hand as she cries softly. When I approach, Mr. Bishop moves forward and touches my arm.

"We waited for you to throw the first handful of dirt onto the coffin," he tells me quietly.

I want to refuse. My first instinct is to refuse.

But I have great respect for Mr. Bishop, who was always good to me. The muscles in my forehead are clenched so tightly that it's giving me a killer headache. I can't even look down at the grave without my head throbbing madly.

We'll all be returning to the dirt someday. I'm in no rush to put myself in an early grave.

Cole's words echo in my mind, from some distant, ancient conversation.

I'm going to fight, and struggle, and treasure every moment of life I've got.

Standing here, at his grave, is causing our whole lives to flash before my eyes. I can see and hear everything so clearly, as if it's happening again right before me. It's like a movie.

Life is going to be great. Why not? We can do anything.

His grave is just a television screen, playing reruns of our greatest moments.

It hurts. Deep in my chest, where I keep everything locked away, it hurts like hell. I can feel his voice, pulling, tugging at my heartstrings, forcing me to feel all these unbearable emotions.

It's driving me insane.

From a few feet to the right, I hear an annoying sobbing sound. How can Annabelle be crying so hard when she barely got to know him? They didn't spend almost a decade together. He never got stabbed, burned, and incarcerated protecting her. He never prostituted himself to afford her basic needs. She never broke him out of prison. She never stole a million-dollar car just to impress him.

But perhaps that's why she has all the more reason to cry. She never got to know him as well as she could have, and all their potential years together have been stolen. The potential of a thing is often more beautiful than the actual thing itself. But not in this case. The years spent with Cole would have been more magical and filled with love, laughter, and excitement than she can even imagine.

She should cry. And so should I.

"Mrs. Hunter," says a voice from behind me. "Do you have a minute to discuss your husband?"

I glance over my shoulder to see the detective standing beside Zack. I turn back to the grave without responding. Moving closer and stepping around the casket, I study the letters carved into the tombstone.

Cole Hunter

1987–2016

Extraordinary architect, husband, friend

No. No. *No!* This can't be right. Why would anyone do this? It doesn't make sense. I shouldn't be standing here right now and looking at this offensive piece of rock. It's a lie. It's blasphemy. Who dared to carve such revolting words into stone? There must be some mistake. I reach out, tracing the letters of his name, searching for an error. C-O-L-E. The letters are etched so clearly, so carefully, and the edges are sharp under my fingertips. If there's an error in spelling, doesn't it mean that this is all a mistake? Doesn't it mean that Cole isn't really here, in this casket? H-U-N...

I stop then, and let my hand fall to my side. I

turn to let my eyes dart madly between the other people standing around the grave, making fleeting eye contact with each of them. I'm searching; searching for something, and I'm not sure what. My lips are parted slightly, questioningly.

"Mrs. Hunter," the detective says again. "It would be very helpful to the investigation, if you have any time to spare…"

"She doesn't care," Annabelle says bitterly. "Look at her. She doesn't care at all!"

I turn back to look at this woman who is accusing me of something so vicious. For a moment, rage floods my chest and causes my ears to burn. I imagine putting my hands around her neck and choking the life out of her. How dare she say such a thing? If only she knew how much I care.

Miranda gently pulls her back from the grave and steps in front of her. I am not sure if she is protecting Annabelle from my harsh glare, or protecting me from her harsh words.

"Scarlett, honey," says Mr. Bishop. "Will you throw the dirt onto Cole's coffin?"

I look down at the dirt, and back up at the Jewish man. The tradition must be important to him. He has known Cole even longer than I have, since he was a small boy. I suddenly realize that I must look emotionless and terrible to all of these people. I *am* terrible. I don't deserve to be here. I don't deserve to live. And why would I want to? Without him? I have barely been living at all. I have been just going through the motions. I have been doing all the things I think I should do, and none of the things I actually want.

Placing my hand on my purse, I think of the gun inside. I close my eyes briefly, imagining it. Death has always been so seductive and peaceful. No more pain, no more noise. And Cole is already there, ahead of me, as usual. He wanted me to come home and live with him again. But failing that, and since it's too late… could I be buried here with him?

Glancing at Mr. Bishop, I realize that I never made that will.

Thinking about suicide as an adult is very different from thinking of it as a child. Mainly because of stuff. You have all these belongings that need to be properly distributed, and it feels like it's wrong to die without doing the paperwork first. Then that paperwork becomes one more chore that never gets completed, and by the time you have a chance to get around to it—the moment is gone, and you no longer want to die.

But one of the major benefits of suicide is that you no longer need to do paperwork once dead. So putting off death until the paperwork is done kind of defeats the whole purpose of dying. I feel fairly confident in Mr. Bishop. He'll take care of things for me. The whole point of dying is to be free and untethered. And to show everyone, including Cole, that I care. I care so much about him that I don't care about anything else at all.

I slide my hand into my purse, reaching for the gun.

Zack immediately moves to my side and touches my wrist. "So—" he begins, but catches himself. "Mrs. Hunter. Weren't you saying that you were free to meet with the detective around noon?"

I was saying something like that. But that was before. Zack's voice is easy to ignore.

My fingers close around the gun, and I am comforted by the cool metal grip.

As I look down at the casket, I imagine Cole's body lying inside. I try to picture the gunshot wounds. "Miranda?" I ask softly. "Where was he shot?"

She pauses before responding. "In the head, dear."

"How many times?"

"Twice."

I think it would be poetic if I shot myself in the head, to mirror Cole's injuries. But I don't think I can manage to do it twice. Once will have to be enough. I am sure that it would make a good headline. My only concern is that Zack is standing rather close to me, and his hand is touching my wrist. His body looks poised to grab me if I try anything. I knew I shouldn't have shared my intentions with him. Releasing the gun, I pull out a napkin instead, and hand it to Zack.

"Please give this to Miss Nelson," I instruct him.

He seems wary and hesitant to move away, but he knows that handing the napkin to the crying woman would be the polite thing to do.

"Throw the dirt," Zack orders me softly, "on his grave. They're all waiting for you."

I know he is trying to distract me, but I do feel like it's the appropriate thing to do. For Mr. Bishop, at least. I lower myself to the ground, as gracefully as I can in my black dress, until I am kneeling beside the grave. I reach for the dirt and gather up a very large handful. A few small trails of sandy material slide out of my fingers, and I stare at them thoughtfully.

No. I'm not going to throw the dirt.

That would be saying goodbye. I refuse to say goodbye.

I let the sand fall back into the pile, and I push my dirty hand into my purse. I can already feel the bullet entering my brain. Where should I aim it from? Under my chin? Into my eye? Inside my mouth? My temple? Yes, the temple is the classiest choice. I see Zack moving toward me, so I know that I need to be fast. My hand is shaking, but I need to do this. I inhale sharply.

I don't care anymore.

Pulling the gun from my purse, I slam the cold metal nozzle into the side of my head. I shut my eyes and begin to press down on the trigger when the oddest thing happens. Amongst Miranda screaming, and Mr. Bishop yelling, there is something else. Another sound. Another… sensation. I am a whisper away from freedom when curiosity hijacks my finger; just for a millisecond. It is the most difficult thing in the world to do, once I have begun, but I pause.

I pause just to make sure that I'm not imagining things. Just to make sure that I haven't really gone insane. In that pause, I realize that my chest is heaving with frightened breaths, and there are tears sliding down my cheeks.

And the earth is shaking.

I open my eyes, just in time to see Zack knock

my hand away from my skull, and wrestle the gun out of my hand. But it doesn't take much wrestling, because my hand has grown limp. I am staring at the freshly dug dirt around the gravesite. It is trembling. The tiny rocks are moving—dancing. Shivers of amazement and understanding run through my spine. I watch Miranda grab Mr. Bishop's arm for support, and Annabelle stumble backwards in her heels and fall flat on her ass.

Is this real? *Yes.* The earth is shaking.

Tingles spread from within my chest to my fingers and toes. My whole body hums to life with electricity and… hope. Tilting my chin upward, my eyes move to gaze at the sky as tears begin streaming from them endlessly. I fear I must look like a cartoon character in one of Cole's anime shows. But also, a smile touches my lips. I remember what Cole said to me in my dream earlier today.

"Thought I told you, Scar. I'm indestructible."

I begin to laugh softly as I watch and feel the earth shudder. I place both of my palms flat on the ground, as though I am soaking up the power of the earthquake. It's a sign. It has to be. I laugh. I laugh loudly. I laugh hysterically.

"He's not dead," I declare to everyone in the vicinity as the earthquake dissipates. "He's not dead!"

"Scarlett," Miranda says softly, as she covers her face with both hands. "Oh, honey."

"You crazy bitch!" Annabelle shouts. "Who brings a gun to a funeral?"

Crawling forward, toward the grave, I reach for the casket, which has not yet been fully lowered into the ground. I try to pry it open with my bare hands. "He's not in here!" I say with utter conviction. "He can't be. He's not dead. He's not."

I feel myself being pulled away from the casket and restrained by two large men. I struggle, but a pair of handcuffs are being roughly locked onto me. "Stop!" I shout, wrestling against them. "Open the casket! I need to see what's inside. *Miranda!* Open the casket!" When she stares at me with wide eyes of disbelief, I begin screaming. "Cole isn't in there! You don't know him. None of you know him! He's too strong. He's too strong to be killed by a fucking bullet!"

"Mrs. Hunter," says Detective Rodriguez calmly. "I think it's a good time to bring you into the station now. We need to ask you some questions, and give you a chance to calm down."

"I'll come with her," Zack says at once, tightening his grip on my left arm. "I'm sorry about this, Detective. She hasn't been dealing with this whole situation very well."

The detective grunts as he begins dragging me back to his police car. "We will need to keep her in custody for a while. Then we'll have her committed to a psychiatric facility."

"Understandable," Zack responds softly.

"I'm not crazy!" I shout at him, kicking his prosthetic leg with my new high heel and causing him to stumble. "Cole's alive. You better believe it, Zachary."

"No, Scarlett. You need help."

Chapter Seventeen

cole hunter, 2003

I am walking cautiously through a darkened hallway. There are doors on either side, and I am holding a metal pole containing an IV bag that is attached to my arm.

"Cole," says a female voice, echoing in the distance. "Can you hear me?"

"Yes," I say in response as I head toward the sound. "Where are you?"

"Please come and find me. Hurry."

I start moving faster, because it sounds like there is panic in her voice. But as soon as I round a corner, a gust of heat hits me in the face. I raise my arms to protect my eyes and stumble backwards, nearly tripping over my own feet and the metal pole. I grab the wall to steady myself, but the wood is hot to the touch. "Hello?" I call out, confused and afraid. I try to take another step, but smoke enters my lungs and I begin to cough violently.

The building is burning, and it's spreading fast. Smoke is seeping into the hallway from under all the doors, and I can feel the heat on my bare feet that indicates the floor below is already ablaze. The tiles beneath me are weakening and growing warped, and I am suddenly paralyzed and rooted to the spot. The structure is collapsing beneath me and falling apart beneath my feet.

"Cole," says the woman hoarsely. I can tell she is in real physical pain. "Please! *Cole!*"

I overcome my terror and race toward the sound of her voice. "Where are you?" I call out.

"Over here! Cole, please!"

Entering one of the doorways, flames immediately surround my entire body. All I can see is fire. I squint and keep moving forward, until her outline becomes clear. The woman is standing in the fire, and she's reaching out to me. "Cole," she says, with both hands extended. "Cole, please..."

She is wearing a white dress. Her hair is dark, and the tendrils at the bottom are all ablaze, with flames traveling up to her ears. Her hair is burning. Her dress is burning. She is going to be consumed. Is it Scarlett? I peer closer.

"Baby, please help me!"

It's my mother.

My heart sinks. I try to take a step forward, into the toxic thickness of the smoke, but it feels like I am swimming through lava. My mother keeps screaming for me. She keeps screaming as she is burned alive, and there is absolutely nothing I can do. The flames twist and crackle into an inferno that causes the house to disintegrate under me, and I begin falling into blackness. I reach out to grab on to something, trying desperately to move forward so I can help her.

It seems like all hope is lost, but then I grasp her hand. "Mom!" I call out, gripping her hand tightly with both of mine. I'll never let go. I'll save her, somehow. But I squeeze so tightly that her hand turns into ash. *"No!"* I scream as the cloud of ash filters through my fingers, falling all around me like snow. I breathe her in, tasting the cinders and soot. "No! Come back..."

The ash falls, and so do I. My arms flail frantically, reaching for something, anything. But I just keep falling. Falling into blackness.

Falling into oblivion.

Until I wake up.

Sitting up abruptly and gasping for breath, I find myself in blinding pain. I am in a white room, with white sheets covering me. A hospital. I clutch my chest with both hands, and let out a murderous scream at the pain in my chest.

"He needs to be sedated! Quickly."

I see a woman in powder blue scrubs moving to my side and grasping a transparent tube, with a syringe in her hand. "Calm down, Cole," she says in a gentle voice. "You're safe now. You're in the intensive care unit, and you're going to be fine."

The sedatives begin to work quickly, and I fall back against the pillow. "Where's Scarlett? Where's my sister? She was badly burned..."

"She's healing well. You're the one who got stabbed. Now, we're going to need you to rest, okay? When you're feeling better, the police will need to speak to you, along with the fire department."

The fire department. I've spoken to the fire department once before. The images from my dream come rushing back to me, and I remember. My mother died. My father died. I failed them. Everyone was dead. I can't fail another person. Never.

I can feel myself slipping under, and I grasp for the nurse's wrist. "Scarlett," I demand. "I want to see Scarlett. I need to see that she's safe."

"I'll let her know," the nurse says softly, touching my forehead. "Just hang in there, kid."

Chapter Eighteen

cole hunter, 2003

"Cole," says a soft voice.

I feel a flood of pain throughout my body, and I groan in response.

"Are you… awake?" she asks me.

When I pry my eyes open, I see that Scarlett is lying in the hospital bed beside me, with her arms wrapped around my body. There are tears sliding down her cheeks. "I never meant for you to get hurt. I'm so sorry."

"Shh," I tell her, putting my hand in her hair and ruffling it fondly. I grunt at the effort it takes to move my arm. "It's nothing at all. It's just a scratch."

"Just a scratch? You nearly died."

"No way!" I say with a laugh, and my laughter hurts so much that I begin coughing violently. "Didn't

I ever tell you? I'm indestructible! Ouch! Ah, ow, ow, ow, ow."

"Somehow, I'm not totally convinced," Scarlett says, touching my bandages with concern.

I grip one of my stab wounds, and suck in air sharply through my teeth at the throbbing pain. "Dammit, that hurts. But yeah, I'm totally indestructible. For real."

"If you say so," she says in a skeptical tone, hugging me tightly and burying her face in my shoulder. "I came to your room to visit you dozens of times over the last few days, and you were never awake. You were just... dreaming."

"They kept me sedated," I explain with a groan. "But that's okay. Dreams are really important to the healing process."

"Cole... you were screaming in your sleep."

"Oh. Well," I say thoughtfully. "When you're seriously injured, emotionally or physically, you need the most potent and crazy sort of dreams to heal your wounds."

"Did I... do something? Did I hurt you?" she asks me haltingly.

"No. Why would you ask that?"

"Because I don't remember very much. Sometimes I have these moments where I get so angry—and then I just black out. I don't really remember what happens in those moments, but usually, someone gets hurt."

"You didn't hurt me," I assure her. "Did you talk to the police yet?"

"Yes. I'm scared, Cole. They've been

investigating the fire. They said that it's suspicious that your family died in a fire, and now so did Professor Brown."

I sigh, and immediately grimace at the pain from sighing. It seems like I can't breathe too deeply yet. I wrap my arm around Scarlett and hold her tightly against my side, thankful that she isn't on the side with the stab wounds. Leaning over, I place a kiss on her forehead, although I groan at the effort it takes to move.

"Don't worry about the legal bullshit, Scar. Things will be fine. We will be fine. It was all in self-defense. We have enough evidence of that."

"But what if we get in trouble? What if we get separated, Cole? We'll have to run away. I can help you find a new identity. I've done it before. We can plan our escape, as soon as you feel better."

"No," I tell her through gritted teeth. "We'll never be able to support ourselves without turning to more crime, and then we'll really get in trouble. We'll get lost in the system, going straight from foster care to prison. The system is fucked up, and it's designed to make us fail—but I'm not going to let that happen. I have an inheritance, Scarlett. I have an inheritance that I can access soon. We'll be okay."

"I don't want to deal with the police and investigations and all this bullshit. Run away with me, Cole. We can live on our own, and I can make it work. Trust me, I can do things…"

"I know what you can do. But we did nothing wrong, Scar. We're not going to get in trouble. Trust me. We're going to be fine." Another wave of pain hits my chest and I let out a guttural groan while grasping the bandaged areas. "Shit, shit, shit."

"Are you okay?" she asks, her eyes darting down to my wounds with concern. The machine tracking my heart rate starts beeping rapidly, and Scarlett jumps off the bed. Only then do I see that she is also wearing a hospital gown, and there are bandages on her head, neck, and legs. "I'm going to get the nurse," she whispers, before running from the room.

"Scar," I croak out in a miserable rasp. "Scar!"

But she is already gone. I allow myself to cry out in pain and writhe in the bed, letting out a low, pathetic whimper. "Scar..." I murmur softly, missing the warmth of her body beside me. One of my hands grasps the sheet where she was just lying, and I twist the fabric up in my hand. I realize that there is a metal railing on the other side of my bed, and I clench it tightly with my fist, until my knuckles turn white. I see a kaleidoscope of colors all over the ceiling.

"Scar..."

Chapter Nineteen

cole hunter, 2003

"Good evening, Cole Hunter."

I am drugged and dizzy, and it takes me a minute to realize that someone is speaking to me. It is a man's voice. I open my eyes and try to move my head, but I am way too groggy after surgery.

"Do you know who I am?" the man asks.

Blinking slowly, I try to focus my vision and lift my head to see him. He is a tall, slender blonde man with a bit of grey at his temples. I feel like I have seen him before… somewhere. Is he a teacher at our school? A social worker? Oh, man, I really don't want to deal with a social worker right now.

"Can we talk another time?" I ask, my speech slow and slurred. "I'm in pain."

"No. I like right now," he says, moving closer with the hint of a smile. "I've come a very long way to meet the boy who burns down houses."

"I don't... I didn't..." Groaning, I turn away from the man and shut my eyes. I just want to sleep. Is he from the press? I really don't want to deal with a reporter right now—especially one intent on making me out to be a boy arsonist.

"You see, my name came up in the investigation. Quite a lot, actually," the man tells me. There is a slight clicking sound on the floor as he moves closer, and I realize that he walks with a cane. "Can you tell me why my name came up so much?"

Turning to look at him with frustration, I try to grab the railing of the bed to sit up, but I feel so weak. I feel like I am still missing most of the blood in my body. I sigh, and it still hurts way too much to exhale, even jacked up on a ton of morphine. "I don't know," I tell him weakly. "Why? What do you want?"

"I want to know if you've heard of me," the man says, leaning over my bed. "You certainly seem curious enough about my activities."

"Look, mister. I am not curious, and I don't give a flying—"

"But you do. A little bird told me that you're simply fascinated with me."

I pause. *Does he mean to say...*

"Benjamin Powell. That's my name."

My eyes grow wide. I am too drugged to keep it cool and avoid displaying shock and horror.

"I see. You do know who I am." The man reaches out to touch my shoulder, and I flinch. "Do you happen to know anything about a young lady named Serena? She's my daughter, you see, and I can't seem to find her."

Clamping my lips shut tightly, I glare at the man. "Who said—I was curious about you?"

"There was a laptop computer at the scene of the fire, and while it was damaged, they were able to retrieve some information. It turns out that my name was one of the most frequent searches made on that laptop. Can you tell me why that might be?"

Oh, shit. I really fucked up this time.

Scarlett was running back through the fire to collect that laptop, and I stopped her. She knew that there was evidence of her identity on there. And it's evidence that *I* put there from frequently digging into her past and digging up information on this monster. Now he's here, standing before me, and I wish I'd run back through the fire for the damned computer.

But how did he know about that? The investigation wouldn't have been released to the public, would it? No, but a hacker could easily access that information. This man has money and influence, and he could easily get someone to search police databases for information that might lead to finding Scarlett.

Did I just blow her cover? I'm an idiot. I need to try and fix it.

It might not work, but I'm desperate. I have to say something.

I cough weakly. "There is a girl I know named Serena. She has light brown hair, almost blonde? She's very smart?"

"Yes. That would be her," says the mayor.

"Okay, yeah. She told me about you, and how

she ran away. So I looked you up. I promised her that I wouldn't tell…"

"Where is she?" Benjamin asks, leaning forward. "Where does she live?"

The wheels are turning in my brain, but not as fast as they normally do. He really doesn't know yet? He hasn't figured it out? I guess Scarlett Smith was an actual person, and when Serena assumed her identity, she was very thorough. If he hasn't seen her yet, there's still a chance…

"She goes to a Catholic school downtown. Our Lady of… something. I took her out on a few dates. What's this about?"

"You took her out on *dates?*" he nearly roars, and his eyebrows lift hideously. "Where did you take her?"

"I—I took her to the movies. For ice cream. Why? Is Serena in trouble?"

He sneers at me, and reaches down to grab my arm that's been recently stabbed. "You fucking pervert! Stay away from my daughter. Do you hear me?"

I wince at his grip. "Yes, sir."

"Where does she live?" he asks me. "Where did you pick her up?"

Taking quick, shallow breaths, I clench my teeth together. What kind of a grown man gets upset about a thirteen-year-old girl going out for ice cream? Oh, yeah. Rapists. Rapists do that. "We just met at the mall," I gasp out, trying to sound like a dumb teenager. "But I think she said that she lives near her school? Our Lady of… whatever."

"Good," he says, turning away and walking to the door. But he pauses, and turns back. He looks at me thoughtfully before stepping close again. "I don't want you ever going near my daughter again. She's a good girl, and she doesn't need any teenage dirtbags putting their hands all over her."

"I didn't do anything like that."

"Mm-hmm," he mumbles, reaching out and touching the bandage on my chest. "Let me tell you something, boy. I have friends everywhere. Friends on the police force, friends who are judges, friends who are doctors. Don't be surprised if you find yourself sent to prison and locked away for a very long time. So you better never speak to my daughter again, you hear me? Leave her the fuck alone, or else."

"What if…" I mutter angrily. "What if I'm not scared of you?"

"Then you'd better think about that pretty little sister of yours," he says, ripping the bandage off my wound. "I saw in the news that you were injured protecting her? Well. Let me assure you. If you piss me off, I will have her killed, and there will be nothing left to protect."

With that, he slams his fist down into the stab wound that I just had surgery to repair.

I scream loudly at the pain as blood starts trickling out between my stitches.

Benjamin smiles at this before turning to walk away. "Have a good evening, Cole Hunter."

I press the bandage back over the wound and grasp the railing of the bed to help me sit up. Wincing, I rip the IV out of my arm. Some blood squirts out in the wake of the needle, but I ignore it as I watch Benjamin leave the room.

Staring hatefully at his back, I know that I'll have to do something about him someday. But that day is not today. I am too wrecked by Mr. Brown and the fire. And I need to think of Scarlett. I push myself off the bed and walk through the halls of the hospital, heading in the direction of her room. As I press on my chest wound, a trickle of blood is seeping between my fingers and leaving a path of droplets behind me, like breadcrumbs.

My steps are unsteady, and often the blood hits my feet, or I step on the trail of blood. I am still dizzy, but I need to find her. Glancing behind me, I try to make sure that Benjamin isn't following me. I find that I have to pause and lean against the wall, for I am out of breath. It is difficult to breathe.

When I do this, I hear a crashing sound coming from somewhere nearby. There aren't many people walking around the hospital at this hour, so the sound startles me. I look around until I see a supply closet. Glancing around the hospital to make sure no one is nearby, I take a step toward the closet, then I pause. I quickly walk down the hall a bit further, and turn a corner, so that the trail of blood leads somewhere else.

Then I wipe my feet off on my ankles before returning to the supply closet, trying not to drip any blood on my way there.

"Scar?" I say softly, outside the door, before turning the knob. When I open the door, I see that she is huddled in a corner, holding a broken broom handle out as a weapon.

"I saw him," she says, as tears well up in her eyes. "I saw him and I panicked. How did he find me?"

"He hasn't found you yet," I tell her, moving forward to wrap my arms around her. "I tried to mislead him… but you can't let him see you."

She returns the hug fiercely. "I switched my chart with the girl in the bed beside me who had a burst appendix. I told her to cover for me and say her name was Scarlett if anyone asked. Oh, Cole. You're bleeding!"

"No, I'm fine," I tell her, as I try to think of what I can possibly do to fix this situation. I feel responsible. After everything she did to escape…

Looking around the closet, I notice some stationery. Pens and notepads, probably used by the nurses. Releasing Scarlett, I move over to them and grab one of each, trying to avoid getting blood on the paper as I begin furiously writing.

"What?" she says. "Cole? What are you doing?"

"You need to get out of here," I tell her, rubbing my eyes. "Look, things have changed. I said something stupid, and he threatened me. So… you need to run."

"Run? Where will I run to? Cole, I can't leave you now. You're injured."

"I'm writing an address, and a note for someone I trust," I tell her. "He's my father's old lawyer, and he's a really good man. Ezra Bishop."

"What makes you think he'll help me?"

"He's the person in charge of managing my inheritance. On this note, I'm promising him some money and a vacation property in exchange for taking care of you. I'll sign it over to him as soon as I receive the funds."

"Cole, you can't do that. Those things are all you have."

"And it's my choice to do this, Scar." Finishing up the note with my signature, I hand it to her. "Fold this and keep it safe," I tell her, then I hesitate. "Wait. One more thing."

Reaching for another sheet of paper, I don't care too much if I get blood on this one. I scribble the note quickly, to my friend Levi, Mr. Bishop's son. I ask him for a favor, remind him that he owes me, and add a quick threat to the end. After I write my signature, I press a bloody fingerprint into this one, enjoying the aesthetic. I think it makes it look more serious.

Turning around with the letter, a wave of dizziness hits me and I stumble back into a row of cabinets. "Ugh," I say, groaning as Scarlett helps me to stand.

"Cole, you're not okay," she tells me with concern.

"I will be." Folding the letter into a small square, I hand it to her. "Here, take this. You'll want to give it to Levi, Mr. Bishop's son."

"What's this for?" she asks me.

"He's an expert at Krav Maga. He's going to teach you while I get better. Okay?"

"Cole, I don't want to leave you…"

"You need to. You need… you need a new identity, Scar."

"But I can't go through that again. I've been

doing so well in school."

"Me too. Look, Mr. Bishop is the only person on the planet my father trusted, so I know that I can trust him. This is the only safe place I know." After saying these words, I pause. "I hope he'll agree to take care of you. He should. He was bugging my parents to sell him that vacation home for years! I wish you could have seen it, Scar. It's a huge hunk of land my family owned in the mountains. It's so secluded—like an hour's drive in any direction, from any kind of civilization. It's total paradise."

"Cole, if you're about to inherit paradise, you can't sign that away for me."

"Naw. I still have the memories. It just would have been nice to go there someday. There are hot springs, and even a little geyser. When I was little, I thought it was the best place on the planet. I asked my mother why the earth was boiling, and she told me that giants were making soup."

"That's adorable," she tells me.

"Yeah," I say, giving her a crooked smile. "The hot springs were cooking pots that belonged to giants who used to live there. And when the giants left the mountains, they forgot to turn off their stovetops—the volcanoes."

"Your mother sounds so lovely," she says with a forlorn expression.

"She was. I still dream about her all the time."

"Cole, I don't know if I can do this. I can't leave you, injured, in the hospital…"

"There are no other options. You have to go. I'll write you a letter," I tell her. "Let's promise that whenever we get separated, we'll write each other letters?" When she nods, I do too. "Good. I'm going to send the letter to Mr. Bishop's house. Trust me, you'll be safe there. Just—be careful of Levi. He's a good kid, but he goes crazy over pretty girls."

"Okay," she tells me softly. She moves closer and puts her arms around my neck, hugging me tightly. "Thanks for taking care of me."

I return her hug fiercely. "Just be careful. Please."

"Am I really going to learn to fight?" she asks me softly. "I don't know if I'll be any good at it."

"You will be. I know you will. Now go, get out of here."

Her face looks heartbroken as she steps away from me. "Cole, you better take care of yourself. If anything happens to you, I don't know what I'll do."

"You'll keep on fighting," I tell her. "I know you will. Somewhere inside you, there's a fighter, and she's capable of anything. You don't have any clue how strong you really are. You'll be okay, Scar. No matter what. With or without me."

"No," she says defiantly. "You're wrong. Without you, I'll just give up. So do whatever you have to do, Cole Hunter. But in the end, once the danger passes, you better come back to me."

"I will," I promise her. "Always."

Chapter Twenty

sophie shields, 2016

Considering that I'm handcuffed in the back of a police car, I feel surprisingly optimistic.

The sun is shining. I'm wearing a gorgeous black dress and heels, and I feel like an aristocratic lady being chauffeured around by her driver. The backseat is rather comfortable, surely made that way by dozens or hundreds of detained criminals squirming around to soften the cushions for me. I can't help smiling.

I don't really care if I end up in a psych ward.

I feel like someone just turned on all the lights, and the world is good again. I feel like I have just been given a second chance at life. I am not analyzing it at all, but just leaning back and enjoying the afterglow of my humbling experience. I can't remember the last time I had such hope and certainty that things were going to be okay.

When the detective pulls up to the police station, he parks on the side of the street a few buildings away. I am curious about why he has done this. Does he want to grab a donut first? I look around, searching for a shop that sells donuts and coffee. Coffee would be nice. Somehow, for the first time in months, I don't feel totally desperate for the caffeine. But a donut would also be nice. With sprinkles.

The detective clears his throat.

I look at the rearview mirror questioningly, and I see that he is glancing back to make eye contact with me.

"Mrs. Hunter," he says in a hard voice. "I would like to ask you a few questions before taking you in."

"Sure."

"What led you to conclude that your husband was alive?"

I look at him with puzzlement. "What led you to conclude that he was dead?"

He glances away briefly before looking back at me. "You were about to kill yourself, and then you stopped. You just seemed to... know something. But how did you form this opinion? Your decision—what evidence was it based on, exactly?"

"Detective Rodriguez, I didn't even see a body."

"I can show you the crime scene photos."

The smile returns to my lips. "Have you ever read *Romeo and Juliet*? It seems to me that people have been faking their deaths for hundreds of years. And that's *with* bodies. They didn't even have

Photoshop back then. What makes you think that photographs would convince me?"

"You seemed to believe that Cole was dead up until a few minutes ago."

I shrug. "Can you blame me? I wasn't thinking clearly. When I saw the newspapers, I reacted emotionally instead of logically. Then when I got to the morgue... I trusted Miranda's verification of the body."

"And now you don't?"

"No. I think she's wrong. I think that you're all wrong."

"Why?" he asks me.

Looking away from the detective, I shake my head. He has no idea of half the things that Cole and I have been through, and it wouldn't be wise to tell him that I've changed my identity several times. "Why not?" I say simply. "If you can prove to me that he's dead, definitively, then I will gladly admit I was wrong and go back to trying to kill myself."

"You just... you seem to have changed your mind very rapidly, based on very little information. I just want to know if you're emotionally stable, Mrs. Hunter. I could understand if you have some kind of a hunch..."

"A hunch?" I repeat with a scoff. "Please don't call it that. I simply know." Gesturing behind us, I give him a disapproving look. "You can't belittle what happened back there. It was *a lot* of information. It was thousands of terabytes of information, concentrated to a point, hitting me all at once. *I know*."

His eyes in the rearview mirror look sad, but interested. "I want to be able to understand. Can you please explain exactly what happened at the gravesite?"

"I don't need to explain it."

"Look, Mrs. Hunter. I am a superstitious man. I shouldn't be, as a detective. I should be more practical and fact-oriented than that. But I've seen things, you know? A lot of death, a lot of murder. I've seen the kind of things that would make even the toughest atheist burn incense and sacrifice a goat to survive the night. I've seen situations so bad that all you can do is pray that you'll get out alive, so you might as well pray, and pray hard. I've even seen some of those prayers get answered." He pauses. "But what I haven't seen is a woman put a gun to her head, and get stopped by an earthquake."

There is something very vulnerable about his eyes as he speaks, so honestly and openly. I feel slightly compelled to give him an actual answer, instead of just avoiding the question flippantly. I grow serious as I gaze at his reflection in the rearview mirror. "The earth... it just spoke to me. It happened once before, but I didn't listen. This time, I will."

He stares at me for a long moment before responding. "What did it say?"

I look away. "It's hard to describe, exactly. It was a feeling. A feeling that I should live, and that I was wrong."

"You ever think that maybe you just *wanted* to feel these things, and attributed them to a random event?"

"Of course. I mean, I thought that the first time it happened, but now, it's happened again. Both times, it had to do with Cole. How could this possibly be random?" I shake my head, leaning back in the seat and glancing out at the blue sky. "Detective, I believe that all of nature speaks to us. It's up to each individual to listen closely and interpret these signs. Most of us are too busy, distracted, caffeinated, and consumed by the minutiae of our lives to pay attention. I just got lucky that this message was so loud and clear that even I couldn't miss it."

The detective continues to stare at me in the mirror for a long moment. Then he places his hand on the headrest of the passenger side chair, and turns back to look at me face-to-face. "Okay," he says, quietly. "I just needed to talk to you a little, so I could be assured that you are clearheaded and rational. I was a little worried that you might be crazy."

Lifting my wrists so that he can see my handcuffs, I give him a sarcastic smile. "I'm pretty sure you do think I'm crazy, Detective. I know I caused a bit of a scene back there, but I just wanted to see the body. Seeking evidence is important, you know."

"I'm aware of that, Agent Shields. I just needed to check if you were mentally stable, or if your judgment was compromised."

My eyebrows lift upward. "Wait, what? What did you just call me?"

He smiles. "Oh, did I forget to mention that? Your boss called and asked me to put my whole department at your disposal. I was a little skeptical at first, but Agent Lopez assured me that you have great instincts, and when there's a computer in front of you, you can do the work of ten men in one tenth of the time. Sounds like a sweet deal. Let's see if you live up to the hype, Shields."

"I don't understand. I'm a hacker, not a detective."

"Your boss thinks you're more than qualified, and she wants you to get some field experience. You're now the lead consultant on this case— unofficially, due to the conflict of interest. I look forward to collaborating with you on this investigation."

"Why would she be interested in this case?" I ask him.

"It's a high profile case, Shields. You know this more than anyone. The victim was the personal architect of many important foreign dignitaries. He designed secure bunkers for heads of state, and impenetrable military compounds. There are a lot of people who could want him dead."

"Or captured," I murmur under my breath.

"I'll set you up with an office," the detective says, "and I'll return your purse, your cell phone, and your gun."

"My gun? You're giving me back my gun?"

"Sure."

"Dude. I just tried to kill myself in front of you."

"Well, suicide isn't illegal in the United States," he says with a shrug. "Besides, you changed your mind, and you seem like you're thinking sensibly. You might be extremely emotional and clinging to the existence of the supernatural, but I can understand that, considering the circumstances. Most people who just lost a loved one are eager to talk about life after death, and heaven or hell, for comfort. How is this any different? Some detectives even consult with psychics and mediums when they're really stumped on a case, and they swear it helps. Who am I to judge?"

"So what you're saying is that you think I'm crazy, but you find crazy people interesting."

"Pretty much."

Sighing, I lift my handcuffed wrists behind my head and rest on them comfortably. "So I'm kind of your boss now? I knew there was a reason I felt so relaxed back here, like I was being chauffeured around by a personal driver."

"Don't push it, Shields."

"Well, Rodriguez, let's get started. Is there any chance at all that Cole was kidnapped? Was there a body? Did it go missing?"

The detective hesitates. "I just want to make one thing clear. We can't turn this into a manhunt. You're able to use all of our resources to find the killer, but you can't have a personal agenda to prove that someone who was murdered is alive. I'm not going to be able to explain that to my captain. Okay?"

I frown at him. "Fine."

"It's now your job to find out who killed your husband," Rodriguez says.

"Oh, he's not really my husband," I explain to

him. "It was a fake marriage. Cole is actually just my foster brother."

The detective grins. "Are you sure about that, Agent? I don't know many sisters who are so eager to off themselves for their brothers. I think you need to reevaluate your fake marriage."

A small smile cracks the corner of my lips. "Well, if he's alive, maybe I will." Shoving my wrists forward, I tilt my head to the side expectantly. "Now remove these cuffs, Detective. And get me a donut. With sprinkles."

"What? I'm not your errand boy. I'll take off the cuffs, and you can get your own donut."

"I nearly just *died,* Rodriguez. Maybe that wouldn't have happened if you weren't concealing information from me, or delaying information— testing me, or whatever. And for the record, I'm still really, *really* sad. So if you know what's good for you, you will do as I say." With a sweet smile and a soft whisper, I speak the words again, slowly. "Get. Me. A. Donut."

His tanned face scowls at me as he opens the door of his police car. "What the hell have I gotten myself into?" he grumbles. "I can tell it's going to be a pleasure working with you, Shields. I hope you're *half* as smart as they all say you are."

When he steps out and slams the car door, I wait for a feeling of pleasure at this little victory. But I feel nothing. I find myself staring out the window blankly. "I am smart," I mutter to myself. "Or... I used to be." I frown and look down at my metal-encircled wrists. "I will be, once I've eaten my damned donut."

Chapter Twenty-One

sophie shields, 2016

I sink my teeth into the vanilla glaze with strawberry sprinkles and make a face. It is overly sweet, and does not taste anything like what my body really craves: caffeine. Why did I get this again? I don't even like donuts. It must have been partly to exert power over the detective, and partly for a modicum of comfort in this whole ordeal. Power has always been of greater comfort to me than sugar.

The detective was thoughtful enough to get a box of twelve, and I am determined to stuff them all into my face for absolutely no reason while I stare at this computer screen in this small room. Rodriguez has given me access to everything he's gotten so far in the investigation, and it isn't much. As I am sitting here in my black funeral dress with mascara staining my cheeks, I can't help wondering if I am too close to this case to work on it. Every bit of information I access makes me feel a pang of emotion. Nostalgia, guilt, jealousy, regret, fear, nausea. Is my reasoning compromised?

Usually when I'm sitting in front of a computer, all those feelings disappear and I can simply focus on my work. Today is different. My mind is scattered and my thoughts are racing. I ebb from hopeful to devastated within seconds as I read the eyewitness reports of Cole's murder. The nurses describing all the blood and commotion, and how there was nothing they could do to save him.

Please. Please. Let him be alive, somehow. Let this all be some huge, ridiculous conspiracy. He saw a murder or a drug deal, and he's in witness protection. The coroner made a mistake, somehow. I need a coffee. No.

I will stop drinking coffee if he can only be alive. I will try to be more honest with everyone in my life. I will face everything that scares me, and be a better person.

Oh god. That's bargaining. One of the five stages of grief.

Am I grieving?

No. No, I can't be grieving. Because that would mean he's dead, and he's not dead. I have absolutely no reason to grieve.

Shit. That's denial.

But why shouldn't I be in denial? I wonder this

as I try to access the hospital security footage again, from around the time he was murdered. There are only empty halls. No masked shooter, no screaming nurses. Did someone overwrite the footage with a loop? Did someone prevent it from recording at all? Or did it not really even happen? I frown as I try a few different methods of retrieving a deleted feed. This should be a lot easier than it is. Did the police already mess with it and screw it up? I will need to discuss it with the detective.

When the door opens, I am surprised to find Miranda entering the room, along with Zack and Mr. Bishop.

"Oh, sweetie," Miranda says as she rushes over to my side and hugs me tightly against her chest. "I'm so sorry. Why would you even think of hurting yourself? Please don't ever do anything like that again. You'll break my heart."

"I won't," I say, squeezing her arm. "Everything is going to be okay."

Zack storms over to my side and rips my purse away. "I drove your Bugatti here," he says angrily. "The detective told me that he returned your gun. What the fuck?"

"It's okay. Rodriguez knows who I am," I inform Zack.

"That shouldn't matter. You are not okay, and you shouldn't be working on anything right now. You need help."

"You're right. I do. In fact, I texted my boss about the situation, and she'd like to offer you an official job. If you stay with me and help out as my bodyguard and assistant, you'll get a paycheck from my employer, and they may consider hiring you for future freelance opportunities."

Zack clamps his lips together firmly. "A job would be great, but that's not what I'm talking about. What you did back there…"

"Forget it," I tell him. "Sit down."

"I will not sit. You just tried to—"

"Zack, you need to improve your résumé. Do you want to be able to put working for the Central Intelligence Agency on there? Good, now sit down and help me out."

He glares at me. "I'll sit, but we're going to talk about this later," he says in a hushed voice.

The detective enters behind them all, shutting the door and clearing his throat. "Agent Shields, you have good friends. Mrs. Walters and Mr. Bishop came to the station demanding your release, but I informed them of the situation. Your bodyguard is also very devoted. I thought that we should all meet and discuss the investigation. Many of you have valuable information and insight to share with Agent Shields, and get us started moving in the right direction."

"Why isn't Annabelle here?" I ask them, not that I really want to see her. "Didn't she want to help out?"

"Sweetie, we came because we were worried about *you*," Miranda says brokenly. "Annabelle is just upset about the whole situation."

"I see."

"Scarlett," says Mr. Bishop nervously as he places some folders down at the desk. He removes his wire-framed glasses and cleans them neurotically. "I—I don't know how I feel about discussing this all now. Do you need some time?"

"I'm fine, Mr. Bishop. Please tell me anything that might be important."

"Well, I have Cole's will with me. Near the end, he had a very bad feeling about things. He was very worried. He left you this letter—are you sure you're ready to see this now?"

"Yes." Reaching up, I run a hand through my hair. "I'm so sick of Cole's stupid letters."

"Well, this is more of a note. He considered it of utmost importance that I get this to you."

I shrug and nod. "Sure. I'll check it out."

"Wonderful. Let me just see here, if I can find it in these files." He replaces his wire-framed glasses and begins to hunt for the paper. Mr. Bishop is a small and meek man, but he has surprising strength through the worst of situations. The year he took care of me, when I was younger, was one of the first good years of my life. He was kind and gentle, but a strict father who was very involved with his children's lives. It was almost painful to be part of such a loving family, after so many bad experiences. My mind drifts back to his son, Cole's boyhood friend. I can still see his eyes grinning at me under his motorcycle helmet, and feel his leather jacket under my hands as we tore up the highway.

"How is Levi doing?" I ask Mr. Bishop.

"Oh," says the older man, looking up in surprise. "He's doing very well, Scarlett. You know how he is. Won't settle down. A real playboy, breaking hearts everywhere he goes."

"That sounds like Levi," I respond fondly.

"He wanted to make it here for the funeral, but he is all tied up with work in Karachi."

"Karachi?" I say, remembering Cole's emails. "There's a building project there with angry investors—"

"Yes. The megacity housing complex. Levi was there to keep things in line for Cole, and try to prevent a lawsuit. Or to deal with the lawsuit, if it happened."

Nodding, I turn to make eye contact with the detective. "Look through flights and communications with Pakistan in the last few days. See if you can find anyone suspicious. That could be a good place to start." I know that Cole had great confidence in Levi and sent him to deal with difficult projects that were getting out of hand. Levi always had a thick skin and the ability to diffuse the most heated conflict. Or to win, if it came to blows. Cole trusted him implicitly— except when it came to women.

The detective scribbles a few words down. "Sure."

I reach for my purse to make some personal notes on my phone, but Zack holds onto it tightly.

"Stop," he demands. "If I'm getting paid to be your bodyguard, that means protecting you from yourself."

"I'm fine, Zack. I only did that earlier because I thought that Cole was dead."

"He *is* dead."

"Did you look inside the coffin?"

"No, but Sophie... I can call you that, right?

Everyone knows?" When I nod, he leans closer. "You're acting crazy. Your behavior is so… volatile. You need to take a step back from this and relax."

Ignoring Zack, I turn to Mr. Bishop. "Did you find Cole's note?"

"No. I think it's here—no—ah! All right, here it is, my dear." He hands me the little piece of paper, and I am immediately puzzled.

"Mr. Bishop, this isn't Cole's handwriting."

"He was very ill, my dear. He could not see to write properly, and he dictated it for me."

My eyebrows draw closer together. It is difficult to imagine Cole being so ill. The note itself makes me frown even deeper.

Dear Serena,

If I'm gone and buried, please take the pin out. We always promised we would.

Unconditionally,
Cole

That's all? That's all he had to say in his final sentences to me? My eyes burn.

"This doesn't make sense," I say finally.

"He was feverish and ranting. He was barely coherent, but he begged me to write that for you," Mr. Bishop says.

"Exactly like this?" I ask. "You're not missing anything?"

"Well—no. I don't think so."

"Who's Serena?" Zack asks as he scoots closer to peek at the note.

I am frustrated that he is prying into something so personal. "It's my name."

"Jesus. Another one?"

"It was my first name, Zack. A shortened form of the name on my birth certificate."

"Actually, that reminds me," Miranda says, and she looks around at all of us hesitantly. "Cole had a very big argument with one of our major clients a few days before his death. Before his illness got worse. They were fighting about that name."

"Which client?" the detective asks. "You didn't mention this before, Mrs. Walters."

"I did, Detective. Just not the particular details. The argument concerns Scarlett," Miranda says softly. "It's about the senator. Do you mind if I speak about him, sweetie?"

I recoil slightly. "I don't think he's involved in this, but go ahead." Placing the note down on the table, I try to mentally prepare myself for anything that she might say.

"Cole refused to accept Benjamin Powell's proposal for the name of the development project. At the ribbon cutting ceremony, they had it out when the senator found out that Cole had gone against his wishes and renamed the building."

"What was the name?" the detective asks, his pen poised.

"Serenity Towers," Miranda says softly. "That's what Benjamin wanted to name the project, from the very start."

Anger floods my bloodstream and makes my vision red for a moment. I swallow down a bit of bile. "Why? Why would he—why would Cole agree to design a building for that man? Why would he betray me like that, Miranda?"

"Oh, sweetie. Cole never betrayed you. He was trying to take Benjamin down. But… obviously, he failed. And I think Benjamin might have found him out, and done something about it."

My chest is heaving with rage. Serenity Towers. Seriously? That sicko. How *dare* he?

"I don't understand," the detective says as he takes a seat at the table. "Agent Shields? What is the deal with this senator? You two have history?"

I pause before speaking, because it is difficult to find the words. "It's not important, Detective."

"It sounds important to me. Please do share."

Dammit. Exhaling, I remind myself that I am in a room filled with many people who already know, or almost know. Many of these people, I trust. Miranda and Ezra Bishop are like family. When Benjamin nearly found me thirteen years ago, Mr. Bishop was the one who gave me shelter. Zack—well, he cares about me, and I have lied to him. He has been there for me through all this, and he deserves to know.

Only the detective is really a stranger. As I stare at him, I remember the brief conversation we had earlier when I was locked up in the back of his police car. He's a good man. He's cautious. I glance down at the donuts. He's also kind. Is it possible that he could genuinely want to help? I've spoken to detectives before, when I was young, and it left a bad taste in my mouth. But if I don't tell him, Miranda will have to, and it's probably better directly from me. I suppose even Miranda and Mr. Bishop don't know all the details.

"Okay," I say quietly, bracing myself by physically grasping the edges of the table. "Benjamin Powell was my father, for a time. He adopted me when I was nine years old. I lived with him for three years, during which he repeatedly molested me. Almost every day. His wife knew, and she did nothing." I glare into the detective's eyes, as if to deliver the story directly into his brain, like little daggers of data. "I spoke to law enforcement many times, but he had too much clout for them to take me seriously. He was powerful. I ran away when I was twelve, and lived on the streets, until I could take on the identity of Scarlett Smith. I met Cole shortly after that, in a foster home. Unfortunately, Benjamin found us—well, he found Cole after we were involved with a fire. Cole was trying to protect me, and he told a lie about how he had dated someone named Serena, so that Benjamin wouldn't discover that it was actually me, in the hospital, just a few rooms away, with my hair dyed black…" I take a deep breath. "To make a long story short, Benjamin used his connections to get a judge to put Cole in prison for arson. He's always been trying to ruin Cole's life, and trying to find me. He nearly has, a few times."

There is a little silence in the room after I finish speaking.

"Why didn't you tell me all this sooner,

Miranda?" the detective asks. "This helps a lot. Now we have our prime suspect."

"I told you from the start that I believed it was the senator," Miranda says in a shaky voice. "The rest of it wasn't my story to tell. Cole was hell-bent on getting revenge for what Scarlett went through all those years ago. He only agreed to work with Benjamin because he thought it would allow him to get close enough to finally get the evidence to take him down, and put him behind bars for life."

I grab a donut and take a very large bite, chewing viciously for comfort. The sugar on my tongue does nothing to soothe my inner turmoil. "I think I need a… smoke," I mutter, remembering my bargain not to drink any coffee.

"You don't smoke," Zack tells me.

"Maybe I should start," I say quietly.

"Why don't you take a break, Agent Shields," Detective Rodriguez suggests. "I didn't realize how complicated this case would be for you. Maybe you should get some rest, and I'll look into Benjamin Powell."

"I already did," I tell him. "I couldn't find anything. If Benjamin did this… he's going to get away with it. The way he gets away with everything. He's smart."

"Not this time," Detective Rodriguez says. "I promise, Shields. I'll send my whole department after him, and we'll find something to nail him."

"Good luck," I say with a sick smile, and a sicker feeling in my stomach. "I've only tried for almost two decades." Grabbing Cole's note, I crumple it up in my hand before taking my purse from Zack and stuffing the note inside. "If you'll all excuse me, I'm going to go get a smoke. Or a drink. Some fresh air. A brisk jog. I just need, like, five minutes. Please."

"Sure thing, honey," Miranda says gently, taking my hand and squeezing it. "Take your time."

"I'm coming with you," Zack tells me.

I'm about to protest, but I am too drained. "Sure."

Chapter Twenty- Two

sophie shields, 2016

Standing outside the police station, I suck in several quick, shallow breaths of fresh air. Looking around, I search desperately for something, anything to take my mind off all this. I see a row of shops, all of them selling various things that I could put in my body to alter my state of mind. Coffee, booze, cigarettes, fast food. I am hyperventilating. Placing a hand on my chest, I stumble forward awkwardly, switching directions in midstep. I need something to help me. A shot of tequila, 5-hour ENERGY, or a Big Mac. My eyes dart around the urban landscape erratically, until I see a man walking along the street without a shirt.

For a moment, I am startled by the sight of so much skin. Then I remember that I'm in California. He is walking away now, so I continue to stare. There are intricate tattoos covering his muscled back—a pair of angel wings, rippling with his every step. The detective's words pop into my brain.

Most people who just lost a loved one are eager to talk about heaven and hell for comfort.

Is Cole with the angels now? Is he somewhere else? That thought does not bring me any comfort. Not in the slightest. But somehow, staring at the man's tattooed body has a strangely hypnotic effect on my mind, and stirs some kind of sensation in my stomach.

When I feel a hand on my back, and I turn to see the concern in Zack's eyes, I barely hear the words he's speaking.

"Sophie? Hey. Are you doing okay?"

Reaching up to grab his face, I pull him down until his lips crash against mine. Stepping closer, I allow my body to press against his until I can feel the hardness of his muscled chest and abdomen against me. I kiss him hungrily, tasting and probing like an addict. It all swirls around in my brain. I can see it all, playing like a movie on fast forward. I can feel it all.

The textures, the sounds, the tastes. They hit me. Hard.

Benjamin's expensive cologne. Smothering. Levi's leather jacket. Freedom, danger, weightlessness. Cole's soft lips, his impossible tenderness.

His rage.

Zack's hands tighten around my waist, partially in surprise, partially for balance, and mostly in desire. I can feel the heat of his manhood pressing against my navel through the expensive but thin fabrics of our funeral clothes. I can smell his arousal, and feel a little perspiration beginning around his neck, beneath my fingertips. I am swept away in the sensations until finally, my fear and anxiety disappear, and I feel nothing. I feel calm.

My mind is clear. My mind is blank.

When I pull away, I can taste the heaviness on his breath and see the need in his half-lidded eyes. I feel better. I feel refreshed.

"What was that for?" he says in a husky voice, adjusting his pants and looking around to see if anyone was paying attention.

"Oxytocin."

"Excuse me?"

"I didn't think eating any more donuts would help."

"So you decided to eat my face?"

"Basically." I pause. "And also, I'm sorry for kicking your leg earlier, when you were trying to restrain me. I didn't mean to hurt you."

"Soph," he says quietly, tightening his grip on my hips. He slides his hands over my back and looks at me unhappily. "You only really hurt me by putting a gun to your head."

"I know. Look, I'm really messed up. This is bringing a lot of bad stuff up for me. Just bear with me while I get through this, okay?"

"And then we'll go back to our life in DC? Together?"

"Maybe." I breathe out heavily. "Maybe." Stepping away from Zack, I cross my arms and turn to look at the police station. "Okay. So I've been thinking that you were right. I should have read those letters. They could really help in all of this."

"Do it as soon as we get back to the hotel," Zack suggests.

"I will. Also, I'm going to have to talk to Annabelle. I'll ask the detective to set up a meeting with her. They should already be following up on this Pakistan lead—but maybe I can privately talk to Levi and see if there's anything that he can tell me. He should be open with me. We have history."

"What kind of history?" Zack asks.

I turn to him with a smile. "He rode motorcycles."

"Damn. That kind of history."

"Yeah. Anyway, I think that as long as we stay—"

I am interrupted by the sound of a clearing throat. Turning to my left, I am surprised to see Detective Rodriguez standing near me. How did he get here so fast?

"Sorry to interrupt," he says to us, "but you two should probably go."

"Go?" I ask in confusion, a little worried that I might be off the case. "Why?"

The detective moves closer to Zack and speaks in a low whisper. "You need to take her back to the hotel."

"What the hell! What's going on, Rodriguez?" I ask in annoyance.

Turning back to me, he looks down uncomfortably. "Senator Benjamin Powell is on his way here for questioning. Right now."

All the blood drains from my face.

I open my mouth and try to speak, but the words won't leave my throat.

Zack nods briskly, taking my arm. "Okay. We're going to get out of here."

"No," I manage to choke out. My whole body feels limp, and I am unable to fight against Zack. I try to force out more words. "Let me stay."

"What? That's not safe," Zack says.

I clench my teeth as I turn to the detective. "Why," I say haltingly, fighting down a bit of bile. "I told you I don't think it's him. Why did you...?"

"He argued with Cole shortly before the homicide. We need to talk to him. You don't need to be here."

"Detective. Can I try—try to help?"

Rodriguez hesitates. "I'll put him in an interrogation room and you can watch from behind the glass. He won't know that you're there. Do you think you can handle that?"

"Yes," I say in a robotic voice.

"Thank you. It could really make a difference. You know him, and you'll be able to interpret his facial expressions and tell us if you think he's lying." The detective pauses. "Are you with me, Shields?"

"Yes."

"Good."

When he begins moving to the station, I try to follow, but my feet feel like they are made of lead. My legs refuse to move, and an odd coldness is spreading through my body. I feel like I have been turned to stone and fused into the concrete

No. Shit, shit, shit. No.

Chapter Twenty-Three

sophie shields, 2016

"He will be here any minute now," Zack says.

I carefully study the empty chair in the interrogation room. "There must be others."

"Sorry?"

"Other girls. Other children. It's been so many years—I can't be the only one."

"No," Zack responds. "It's unlikely. For people like him, harming others is a habit. It's a wonder that he hasn't been caught already."

"He has too many friends in high places. He has enough money to make people keep quiet."

"Why didn't you go after him harder, Sophie? With your skills, I'm sure you could have taken him down."

A little shudder touches my shoulders. "I just wanted to run, Zack. I never wanted to see him again, or be near him. I couldn't deal with it. The idea of spending time with him in a courtroom…"

"Do you know how many despicable people are walking around for that reason?" Zack asks me. "These guys get away with everything because their victims can't deal with the emotional strength it takes for a confrontation."

"I don't mind confrontation. But I didn't want to look at his hideous face."

"And you're ready to look at him now?"

Inhaling deeply, I shrug. "I need to be. For Cole. Besides, he can't see me, so that makes it slightly less sickening. I can be detached."

"I'm right here, Soph. We're in a police station, and everyone is armed. You're totally safe."

"No. I am not, nor have I ever been safe. The moment I forget that, and let myself relax…" I trail off, because the door to the interrogation room is opening.

A slender cane is the first thing to enter the room, its rubber tipped bottom colliding with the tiled floor. It makes no sound at all, but I flinch anyway, ever so slightly. Next, I see the tips of stylish leather shoes stepping into the room, along with sharp knees under a pair of grey slacks. My mind is registering every detail so carefully that it feels like the scene before me is happening in slow motion, although I logically know that everything is moving at a normal speed.

When I see the man's hand gripping the top of the cane, I have to fight the urge to take a step back. So much time has passed. He was already so old before. I was expecting to see someone looking wizened and weak, but I can tell from the way he grips the cane that there is life and energy in his body.

Benjamin has always reminded me of a skeleton. He is very thin and gaunt, but this is part of the deception. He comes across as kind and meek, but he is actually very strong and muscled beneath his baggy clothing. I can tell that he has been staying active and taking care of himself, even though he is presenting the image of being tired and acting his age. No. Benjamin is still strong. It requires a lot of strength to restrain another human being, and I have no doubt that he is still capable of this.

When he steps fully into the room, I notice the unevenness of his gait. Back when I knew him, he never walked with a limp. It was only when I caught a brief glimpse of him a few years later that I noticed he was using a cane. My eyebrows draw together and grow tense. I feel like I should know how he got injured, but my memory is fuzzy. I know that on the last day I lived with him, his leg was in a cast. There is an entire three-day period where my memories are incomplete.

I remember using makeup to cover the bruises on my neck and wrists.

I remember sitting on the floor of a tiny, filthy gas station restroom as I read the instructions for a pregnancy test.

I remember stealing Benjamin's credit card to

buy myself an airline ticket to get away.

I remember Benjamin finding me. I remember him screaming at me. I remember a hotel.

I remember a balcony. I remember climbing up onto the railing, and feeling the wind in my hair.

I remember a flash of Benjamin's white bone sticking out of his pant leg.

I remember walking away. Running away.

"Sophie," Zack says, and my head snaps toward the sound of his voice. "They're starting."

Blinking in confusion, I realize that I've been completely zoned out. I also realize that Zack's missing leg is on the same side of his body as the leg that Benjamin injured. I stare at Zack's leg thoughtfully, wondering if that had something to do with why I was first attracted to him. Why I got close to him.

Guilt.

"Thanks for taking the time to come in for questioning, Senator," says the detective.

I turn back to the room, and see that Detective Rodriguez is seated across from Benjamin Powell. I realize that I have been holding my breath, and I force myself to exhale so that I can refresh my oxygen supply. *Concentrate, Sophie. You are not that weak little girl you used to be.*

"It's no problem at all, Detective," Benjamin says in his deep, somehow harmonious voice. Every syllable is filled with warmth, and there is a mild, peaceful look in his eyes that makes you want to trust him. He has an honest presence about him, like your favorite uncle or teacher who regularly offers solid and life-changing advice. It is no wonder that people hang on his every word. "Cole was an incredible architect, and an amazing young man. I will be happy to do anything I can to help." His thin lips pull together tightly in something akin to a smile. A carefully rehearsed, sympathetic smile. "In fact, I've already asked my people to set up a scholarship fund in his name for the best and brightest young people who are interested in architecture."

"Bastard," I whisper under my breath.

"That's very generous of you, Senator. You seem like a very charitable man. I believe I read about another scholarship program that you started?"

Benjamin hesitates. "Yes. In honor of my daughter, Serena."

I feel my face twitch at the sound of my name on his thin, ghostlike lips.

"Oh! I didn't know you had a daughter."

"I adopted her when she was a young girl. My wife was not capable of having children, you see. Serena was particularly gifted in the computer sciences, and I know that she would have had a bright future if her life hadn't ended prematurely."

"I see. How did she die, Senator?"

Benjamin leans in closer, as though it is difficult to speak about this. "She took her own life, Detective. I am afraid to say that my Serena was a very disturbed girl. I tried my best to make her happy, and to provide her with all the luxuries that a little princess deserves. But in the end, there was something dark and damaged in her soul that I simply couldn't heal." The senator touches his temple and combs away a few wisps of white hair shakily. "I loved her, though. God, I loved that sweet little girl."

I lift both of my hands to my face, pressing them firmly against my eyes and cheeks. I force my face into my hands so hard that I am sure there will be a permanent imprint of them on my face forever. I suck in deep breaths, trying to fight against the urge to scream.

The scream has been sitting inside my chest for years. It's a loud, shrill, piercing sound that I feel inside my chest, reverberating in my ribcage, begging to be released. I am sure that if I screamed at the top of my lungs, as loud and long as I want to scream, Benjamin would hear me through the soundproof booth. All of Los Angeles would hear me.

Zack places his hand on my shoulder, but I grab his wrist and twist it. "Don't touch me," I whisper, but I immediately release him when I realize it is only Zack. "Sorry."

He looks disturbed and upset. "I'm... I'm here for you, no matter what."

I frown. "Hey. How did the detective know about the scholarship fund in my name? I never mentioned it."

"He must have done some quick research online?" Zack suggests.

"That sounds so awful, Senator," the detective is saying. "I can't imagine what it feels like to lose a child."

"I was never same after my little girl died, Detective." Benjamin sighs and reaches up to loosen his tie. "Do you mind if I stretch my legs?"

"Go ahead," Rodriguez says with a hand gesture.

When Benjamin gets up, I watch his movements carefully. Every muscle in my body grows tense, even though there is a glass between us. My fists clench into little balls. The senator moves back and forth in the room idly before heading precisely in my direction. A small, almost imperceptible gasp escapes my throat as Benjamin stares at me through the glass.

I know that he cannot see me, but it almost feels like he can. Are they absolutely, one hundred percent certain that this two-way mirror cannot be seen through? By anyone? If he looks closely enough...

"Sorry for getting distracted in my line of questioning, Senator. This is about Cole, after all. How did you meet him?"

Benjamin's thin lips curl upward in what can only be described as an evil smile. It sends a shiver through my body. "It's funny you should mention that, Detective. After my little girl died, I went crazy. I found myself searching the whole country for her, refusing to believe that she was actually dead. That was how I met Cole Hunter. It turns out that he had been dating a young girl matching my daughter's description in a suburb outside of Los Angeles. It was a false lead of course, and the little girl attending Catholic school was not my Serena. My heart was crushed."

Benjamin reaches into his pocket and pulls out a sleek leather wallet that matches his shoes. He clutches it tightly in the palm of his hand. "I never gave up hope, though, Detective. I still have the suicide note that my sweet Serena wrote to me. I read it every now and then, and tell myself that there is no way. There is no way that a girl so smart, so beautiful, so full of love and life, could kill herself. Maybe, even if she really intended to die, she somehow survived her own attempt. What do you think, Detective? Have you ever seen someone change their mind or fail at suicide?"

Rodriguez clears his throat. "Well…"

"Oh my god," I whisper in horror, afraid that he can hear me. "Zack—"

"I know."

Benjamin keeps talking, and he keeps looking directly into the mirror. Directly at me. "Most of us get deeply depressed, don't we, Detective? But the will to live is almost always stronger than the desire to give up. People don't give up so easily, do they? People keep trying. It's in our nature. People keep living, no matter how hard it gets. We almost can't help it. Don't you think so, Detective?"

I study Benjamin's facial expressions carefully, moving closer to the glass. There are a few new lines around his eyes, but the same sharp, calculating irises buried inside a sheath of aging skin. His eyebrows are lowered in concentration as his lips curl ever-so-slightly at the corners.

"Do you see this?" I ask Zack. "He's interrogating the detective. He's watching his facial expressions through the mirror."

"Yeah," Zack says quietly.

Rodriguez stutters. "Well, Senator. I suppose I hadn't thought about that very much. Are you asking these questions in relation to Cole? I know you worked with him recently. Did he seem depressed to you?"

"He did seem… off. I kept in touch with him over the years, since I met him when he was a boy. He seemed a lot healthier and more energetic in the past. That's why we fought, Detective. It was our first opportunity to work together, and Cole didn't seem to be putting his heart and soul into the project. I erected Serenity Towers as a monument to my little girl, and my love for her. Cole knew that, but he didn't share my vision. He even refused to name the building as I wished. I spoke to Cole in detail about what I wanted, and I really thought that he was just the man to give me my building. I thought that he could understand my feelings. He had recently suffered the loss of someone he cared about deeply, as well, you see."

"Oh?" the detective asks. "Who might that be?"

"His wife," the senator says softly. "I know that Cole loved his wife deeply, and was broken up by her leaving him. That's why I thought he could understand how much this building meant to me. I may not have been the greatest father on the planet. I may have made mistakes, but what father doesn't? If there was a chance that my little girl was out there, somewhere in the world, I wanted this building to be a message to her. I wanted it to be an apology."

"That's—that's a beautiful sentiment," the detective says softly. "I'm sorry that Cole didn't design the building strictly to your specifications."

"He did the best that he could," Benjamin says, turning to glance at Rodriguez, "considering that he was a man with a broken heart. He wasn't healthy, Detective. He was only half the man he used to be, when he was younger. Do you know what a broken heart will do to a person? Being abandoned by someone you love. Do you have any idea what that's like?"

"I have some idea," Rodriguez responds.

Benjamin turns back to look at me, and places his palm flat against the glass as he speaks. "That's how I felt when I lost my little girl. It's funny how a child can come into your life, and change everything. Having a daughter—it makes you a better man. Because there's nothing you wouldn't do to protect her. To find her."

My eyes dart over his face, scanning frantically for information. I find him to be hard and stoic, as though he is playing poker. The only hint of emotion is the thin sheen of unshed tears in his eyes. Somehow, even that seems intentional. His attention to detail is remarkable. His hand on the glass— familiar, with a scar running across his palm, in a gesture of peace. I gulp down a lump of fear in the back of my throat, admitting to myself that these words—they are for me.

He is speaking to me.

"I thought that if I could build something beautiful enough, in her honor, that my Serenity would forgive me," Benjamin whispers. "That's all I've ever wanted; her forgiveness. And even if she isn't here, on this planet anymore, maybe those buildings might be tall enough to stretch to heaven and send my love to my little angel." He removes his palm from the glass, and begins to trace a heart on the two-way mirror.

It looks like he is pointing directly at me, and it makes my stomach churn with nausea. I take a step backward, warily.

"But I know she isn't gone. Somehow, I know that I would feel it if she were gone. We have a sixth sense like that, about the ones we love, don't you think, Detective?"

Rodriguez clears his throat, and looks in my general direction. There is a tiny twitch of concern in his eyebrows. "Perhaps."

Benjamin smiles. He saw it. He saw that tiny twitch of concern in the Detective's face. He's won.

"Sometimes, I just know that I'm going to see my daughter again," the senator says, stepping closer to the glass.

I take another step backward.

"I just feel her presence, you know?" Benjamin says with a soft voice and knowing smile. "I feel her close to me. Sometimes, I think she's so close that I could almost reach out and touch her."

That's it. I'm gone. Stumbling backwards, I crash into a table and curse before darting for the door and running out of the room. One of my ankles twist slightly in my black heel, and I reach down to rip my shoes off in two quick, fluid motions before continuing my flight.

I can almost hear Benjamin laughing behind me. Is he laughing, or am I imagining it?

I am going insane. I can hear his laughter inside my skull.

It reaches every corner of my brain, and I want to scream.

All I can do is run. I run, and run, and run. I run until I can't breathe.

I feel like I am nine years old again, helpless and alone.

I keep running, even when I can no longer breathe.

I keep running, even when I can no longer stand.

All I know is how to run.

Chapter Twenty-Four

sophie shields, 2016

My body won't stop shivering.

Sitting naked in the cold, empty bathtub, I hug my knees against my chest as my mind jumps and cartwheels between flashes of the distant past, the present, and the future. My hair is hanging limply and sodden around my face like a haphazard curtain. I am staring blankly through the wet and stringy tendrils, at the patterns on the bathroom wall. The tiles are a creamy-beige color, with a pearly finish, but I can still see the walls of a filthy gas station bathroom from my childhood.

After wandering around for hours, running and walking down busy streets, through parks filled with palm trees, and along the water, I found myself heading back to the hotel. I didn't know where else to go. My feet were growing sore and raw, and I only had my heels with me. I considered returning to Cole's house and firing up all its emergency security measures, but I didn't want to risk being seen by anyone who might be watching the house.

On my way back to the hotel, it began to rain a little, soaking my hair and my new black dress. I had to put my heels back on because the bottoms of my feet were getting tender. However, walking in high heels requires a lot of strength and balance, and after wandering around for hours, I was far from being able to walk at my usual brisk, confident pace. I had to wobble forward miserably, one step at a time, with each step being excruciating.

When the door to the bathroom opens, I jump a little.

"Sorry to startle you. I knocked, but there was no response," Zack says with concern. He looks over me, as if to make sure that I haven't slit my wrists or tried to hurt myself, before moving to my side and crouching beside the tub. "You're shaking, Soph. Didn't you want to take a shower?"

I don't respond right away.

When I finally part my lips to speak, they feel cracked and dry, and I can't find any words to push between them.

Zack reaches out to touch my shoulders and brush my hair away from my face. "God, you're freezing. Let me turn on the water."

He turns on the tap and tests the temperature

with his hand as the water begins to fill the tub. At first, I feel the sharpness of cold water against my toes, but then, slowly, the warmth begins to build as the water pools around my feet. Zack reaches for a clean towel and allows it to get soaked with warm water before gently using it to clean and warm my face and neck. He wraps the towel around my shoulders before reaching for the hotel soap and beginning to slather my feet. He carefully washes away the debris I had accumulated from walking around barefoot, before turning off the water and letting the dirty water drain out of the tub. I immediately miss the warmth from the half an inch of water that I had been sitting in.

Why had I been sitting in an empty tub, anyway? I stare at the faucet and taps in confusion, wondering why I hadn't turned them on. Am I really that absentminded?

When Zack begins to refill the tub with warm water and gently splashes some over my arms and knees, I begin to remember who I currently am, and where I am, in this moment. He brushes his hand over my temple, combing his fingers through my tangled hair. Slowly, my body and mind begin to thaw as the warm water surrounds my hips and thighs.

I hadn't even realized that I was frozen.

Turning my head to look at him, I try to actually focus on the man sitting before me, and not all the ghosts of men inside my head. I see the deep concern on Zack's face as he tries to take care of me. Reaching out, I grab Zack's hand and squeeze it in thanks.

"You still have those guns Lucy gave us, right?"

I ask him hoarsely.

"Yeah," he responds, gesturing to his belt. "Don't worry."

Nodding slowly, I look around the bathroom, trying to gather my bearings and formulate a plan. "Okay," I say softly, deciding that I've had enough of being weak and pathetic.

I reach into my mind and flip the switch. I feel better now.

I stand up, ignoring that I am naked, and grab another towel, drying myself off before wrapping it around my body. "Did I receive any phone calls?" I ask Zack, aware that I left my wallet and phone with him when I ran out of the police station.

"Yes. Levi called from Karachi at the request of his father, and said he has some information for you. He says you can call him back anytime, but it's not urgent, because he has everything under control."

"Of course, he does. Anything else?" I walk into the bedroom, using the towel around my shoulders to dry off my hair.

"Uh, yeah," Zack says, following behind me. "Mr. Bishop sent you some more details about Cole's will, and Miranda called reminding you that you're in charge of the company now, and that she could really use some help if you could come into the office tomorrow morning, or whenever you're feeling better. Or if you have a break in the investigation."

I nod, tilting my head forward to wrap the towel around my scalp and roll up my hair before slinging it back to hang behind me. I grab the handle of my backpack and toss it onto the bed before arranging some pillows for back support. Finally, I climb up onto the bed and dry off my hands and arms on the towel I'm wearing before reaching inside the backpack for the stack of Cole's letters.

"You're going to read those?" Zack asks.

"Yes. I could use some privacy."

"I don't think it's wise for me to leave you alone with the way the senator..."

I look up at him. "Make yourself useful and get me a coff—er, chocolate milk."

"Chocolate milk?" he asks in surprise.

"Yes. I'm cutting back on caffeine."

"Since when?"

"Zack, just get me something to drink. A bottle of water would be fine. I'm going to work on this, okay?"

"Sure," he says finally.

I wait for him to leave the room before reaching for a letter. My hands don't shake or hesitate as I reach for the flap and open the thin sheath to retrieve its contents. I unfold the letter calmly and allow my eyes to soak up Cole's familiar handwriting.

This isn't the way it's supposed to be. It always used to feel like Christmas morning to receive a letter from Cole. As long as I remind myself that he is still alive, these words do not have the power to upset me. Anything that's broken can be fixed, as long as he is alive.

Benjamin's words come hurtling back to me.

Somehow, I know that I would feel it if she were gone. We have a sixth sense like that, about the ones we love, don't you think?

It felt like he was directly mocking me. But there is another possibility. Maybe that's just the way he is, and after three years of living with him, I have picked up some of his thinking. Am I like him? I don't care. Am I *right?* Is there a chance that Cole is alive, or do I just think so because I faked my own death? If he is gone, what's the point of anything?

I push this doubt from my mind and focus on the words before me.

Dear Scar,

I got it. I actually freaking got it. Can you believe this?

They selected my designs for a megaproject in the new DHA city outside of Karachi. It's going to be one of the biggest projects I've ever worked on. Bigger than Tokyo. Bigger than Germany. Dozens of apartment buildings and condominiums, on virgin landscape. I really feel like I am making a contribution to the world—helping to build a whole new city. A master-planned, self-sufficient city, better than any ever built.

As I write this, I am staring at an unopened bottle of champagne—your favorite kind. I know I should celebrate my success, but without you here to share this bottle, I don't feel like it's right to open it up. I wish you were here. Victory doesn't feel the same without you. It feels like... it isn't victorious enough.

Could we meet up? Just for a day or two. I can fly over there for a weekend and we can grab some food and talk. I would love to discuss this project with you, but more importantly... I just need to see you. It's been too long, and I don't know how much more I can take. Letter writing is all good, but I would give anything just to sit close to you and look into your eyes. We don't even have to talk.

Sitting with you in silence is one of my favorite things to do.

I miss that brain of yours. Miranda has some cool ideas for this project, but most of them aren't going to be in the budget. I'm going to try to convince the developer that spending money up front will alleviate maintenance costs in the future, but you know how these guys are.

I keep trying to imagine what you would say if you were involved in this. Would you give me crazy ideas to make everything more complicated and frustrate the hell out of me? Tell me how each unit needs to be wired with cameras because women can't be trusted to be honest about domestic abuse. Tell me how we should have wireless monitors hooked up to the collars of family pets, triggering emergency lockdown measures based on their elevated heart rates. Tell me anything.

I miss the way you always made things complicated.

I allow myself to get lost in carefully reading the words, and even reading between the lines. Sometimes the most important words are the ones that go unspoken, and I know Cole well enough that I can see the hidden meaning behind each sentence, and feel everything he felt while writing.

Taking a deep breath, I dismiss this letter as unimportant and skim the rest of it before placing it in the beginning of a "read" pile. Someday, when all of this is over, I will go back and carefully read each letter for personal reasons. But I need to be professional now. I pick up another letter randomly, but this time, from closer to the middle of the pile. I don't think reading them chronologically will help.

Dear Scar,

Karachi is killing me.

I'm getting too old for these deadlines. I'm cracking under pressure. What is wrong with me? You know the way I used to be—I used to thrive under intense working conditions. I used to rise to the occasion, no matter how many sleepless nights it took to get to the finish line. I used to become superhuman whenever I needed.

Now, I'm just a mess. Do you think you could call me? Sneak away to a payphone somewhere and call me. No one will ever know. I just need to talk to you. There's no one who knows me better than you do. There's no one who knows exactly what to say to give me clarity and pull me out of this funk.

More and more, I've found myself turning to Annabelle for help. Lately, I have been telling her a lot about you. I hope you don't mind, but it feels good to open up. I promise that I am not telling her anything that would compromise your safety; I learned my lesson about that.

She's been a great help, and a great listener. Annabelle thinks that I should reach out to you, and that it would be healthy if we talked or met up. She thinks I need some sort of closure...

My eyebrows pull together in confusion. He spoke to Annabelle about me? Why did she seem so surprised when she met me? He must have referred to me as his foster sister, and left out the part about the marriage. I select more letters and read them quickly, allowing a clearer picture to develop in my mind of the last few months of Cole's life.

One thing is clear: he was in a very vulnerable state. I can't fathom what type of despicable person would want to hurt him when he was already at his lowest.

I carefully sort the read letters into different piles, indicating which ones might have information that could be of use to the investigation, and which ones are mostly personal. I am so focused on my reading that I jump when my cell phone rings. I am not used to having a phone anymore.

Reaching out to grasp the device, I see that it is the detective and I accept the call.

"Rodriguez."

"Hey, Shields." He sighs. "Rough day today. How are you doing?"

"Fine," I say harshly. "But I can't work with you. I don't trust you."

"Why not?"

"You betrayed me," I accuse. "You told Benjamin that I was there, behind the glass."

"I did no such thing, Shields! It's insulting that you would even suggest that."

I know it's not his fault. I could see the honesty and shock on his face in the interrogation room, but I need to be angry at someone. It's part of my method; anger will keep me sane. It will help me cope and keep me focused.

"Agent Shields, I don't know if he really knew you were there, or if he was just bluffing. He's a twisted fuck, and he could have just been playing games to mess with us…"

"He knew," I tell the detective. "There's no mistaking it. We both know that *he knew.*"

"It doesn't make sense for him to know, Shields. No one at the station would have divulged that information."

"It was more than that," I tell him in a snappish voice. "Benjamin seemed to know things. He seemed to know about what happened at the cemetery. How I almost…"

Shit.

It clicks in my mind at the same time that I'm sure the detective is realizing it. Reaching for a bunch of Cole's letters in one particular pile, I drop the phone onto the bed and put it on speaker as I rummage through the letters, scanning them.

"Annabelle," I say softly, with wonder. "She could have communicated with Benjamin."

The detective is quiet for a moment. "Do you

think so?"

"Something doesn't add up about her. Cole spoke about her in some of the letters he sent to me, but she seems… different."

"How so?"

"Cole said she's involved with holistic therapy. Some clinic with an artsy name—*The Mind Mechanic*. I glanced at their website, and it seems like they are aimed at overworked businessmen. Workshops and private coaching meant to unburden and cleanse to enhance the creative process and remove stress barriers." When I first read about this, my first thought was that it's the sort of thing I would tease Cole about. Then, I realized that he must have been really miserable, lonely, and desperate if he even tried new age therapy.

He was probably having trouble sleeping again. I glance down at the letters, and idly touch the pile that mentions Annabelle. "She just sounds so wise and supportive from the way he described her. Was she pretending to be nice to him when he was alive for some reason? For his money? Is she a charlatan, or did she just take off her mask and reveal her inner bitch when he died?"

"You're sounding a little jealous, Shields."

"I realize that, but I'm serious. How else would Benjamin be able to reference what happened at the cemetery?"

"If this is true, it means you blew your own cover, Shields. If you hadn't put the gun to your head, he never would have made the connection between Scarlett Hunter and the twelve-year-old girl who left him a suicide note and disappeared."

I can't respond to this ironclad logic.

"Luckily, there's still a way out for you. He doesn't know about Sophie Shields. I can scrub your name from the investigation, and you can lay low for a little while, before returning to your cushy job in DC. How does that sound?"

I press my lips together, thinking about this. When Zack reenters the room, holding a bottle of water, I hold up my finger to indicate that I am on a call.

"No," I tell the detective finally. "Not yet. I want to know what happened to my brother."

"Your husband."

"Whatever!"

Zack makes a face, tossing me the bottle of water. I catch it and roll my eyes before untwisting the cap and drinking. I am surprised at how thirsty I am.

"So, Shields, are we still working together?" the detective asks. "Do you trust me?"

"Of course. I was just blowing off steam."

"Aren't you delightful?" Rodriguez mutters. "How the hell did Cole ever put up with you? I'll never understand."

But somehow, the way he says it makes me think he likes me.

"I'm going to look into this Annabelle chick," he says. "For now we'll assume that she could be working for or with Benjamin. Can I call you back in a few minutes?"

"Sure."

Hanging up, I look at Zack curiously. "You

were gone a long time considering that you only brought back a bottle of water."

Zack smiles. "Did you get a lot of reading done?"

"Yes."

"Good. I got you a surprise."

He steps away to the door, and I am surprised when a bellboy enters pushing a cart containing trays of hotel room service dinners. There is even a bottle of white wine in an ice bucket.

"Dinner is served," Zack says, reaching over to lift one of the metal lids to reveal a plate of cooked lobster in a creamy sauce, topped with a sprinkle of parmesan cheese. There is a bit of pasta on the side. "Lobster Thermidor," Zack explains.

My first experience with Lobster Thermidor was while playing Sims. My character was a chef, and Lobster Thermidor was one of the best dishes she could cook. I am both surprised and impressed, and slightly embarrassed that the bell boy is witnessing me sitting here in just a towel. Zack gives him a tip, and he leaves, while I inhale the delicious food.

"This looks amazing," I tell Zack. "Much better than just a bottle of water."

"You've had a rough couple days, and I thought that you needed some proper nourishment."

"Nourishment doesn't have to be lobster, Zack. This seems a little extravagant."

"Hey, I am employed now, so I have a little extra spending money, don't I?" He grins at me. "I wanted you to relax and get pampered a little. I want to remind you that life is good."

Oh. So that's what this is about.

Zack unscrews the bottle of wine and pours a bit into a glass before offering it to me. When he sits on the side of the bed and begins massaging my sore feet, I am momentarily startled, but then grateful. I sigh at the sensation, allowing the tiredness and pain to be kneaded out of my muscles. I take a small sip of the wine, which happens to be a chardonnay. A good pairing for lobster.

"I was thinking about the way you kissed me earlier," Zack says softly. "I don't think you've ever kissed me like that. I'd really like to do that again."

Ripping my feet away, I place the wine glass down on the night table a bit abruptly. "Zack, I still have so many letters to read and so much work to do. The wine is a nice gesture, but I can't afford to relax too much."

Zack sighs. "I know. I'm sorry. Did you find anything good in the letters?"

"Not too much. I'm a little suspicious of Annabelle—I think you heard some of that conversation. The detective is looking into that for me."

"Something about her did seem off," Zack says with a nod. Then he frowns. "Hey, can I ask you a question?"

"Sure."

"What did he mean by 'take the pin out'?"

This question catches me off guard, and I stare forward vacantly, remembering the past. I shake my head, unable to speak about it. I do not realize that Zack is moving toward my bag and retrieving the crumpled note.

He reads it out loud, clearly and questioningly. "Dear Serena. If I'm gone and buried, please take the pin out. We always promised we would. Unconditionally, Cole." He pauses and looks at me. "What does that mean? Is it some inside joke?"

Hearing the words read aloud like that causes my face to scrunch up in thought. The phrasing is strange, and it doesn't sound like Cole. *If I'm gone. And buried.*

"Is it like a pin number for a bank account you guys shared? A safe or a safety deposit box?" Zack asks.

I stare at him in confusion. "No."

"It seems like an odd note for someone's final words. I suppose he didn't know they were his final words, but he must have had some idea if he wrote you a note at all. He didn't even say that he loved you." Zack shrugs. "I guess I was just expecting something a little more epic. A little more dramatic. It was his last chance to reach you. I just thought... he wouldn't hold back."

I look at Zack with puzzlement. "What did you say?"

"Hold back?"

Then it hits me. The pin. Buried. "Zack! You're brilliant."

"I am? Why?"

"It's... a code. For a code breaker." I smile.

"Are you sure, Soph?"

"It's a game. Cole's playing a game with me." I throw my legs off the side of the bed and move to gather my clothes. "I need to get out of here."

Before I can start getting dressed, Zack grabs my wrist. "Sophie, please. Stay and eat with me first. Then we'll go anywhere."

"I can't. Cole could be alive. He could be out there somewhere, waiting for me to find him. What if he needs help?"

Zack looks at me sadly. "Your husband is dead. Your brother is dead. You can't waste your life pining for a dead man. I'm right here, and so is our lovely dinner. Let's just sit and eat for a minute, and try to relax and enjoy ourselves, okay?"

"No. I've got an idea and I need to check it out. If I'm right…"

"Whatever it is can wait. You need to take care of yourself better, and let me take care of you. You've been running all over this city in the rain. You just had to watch the interrogation of the monster who ruined your childhood. You need to take it easy for five minutes, Sophie. Just sit and eat with me. It won't hurt anything. You don't need to be in such a crazy rush."

I look into his sincere face and hesitate.

"You're always running off to do something. Well, there's no use in running off to chase down a ghost. I'm right here." He steps forward and places my palm on his chest. "I'm flesh and blood, and breathing. I'm a warm-bodied human man. That's got to be better than a ghost—the ghost of a man you haven't seen in years. He was already gone, while I've been right here beside you, all along. A ghost won't keep you warm at night."

My lips part slightly to respond, but I'm not sure what to say. Am I chasing ghosts? The idea chills me to the bone. Am I insane? When my phone rings, I hastily rush to pick it up.

"Detective?"

"Hey, Shields. I'm having some trouble getting in touch with Annabelle, so I'm driving to her house to see if I can talk to her. Do you want me to text you the address?"

"I actually have something else I need to check out, based on the note Cole left for me."

"Oh, really? Do you think it meant something?" he asks.

"Yes. Can you handle looking into Annabelle while I follow this lead?"

"Of course. I wouldn't be much of a detective if I couldn't handle one entitled blonde."

A small smile touches my lips. "You think she seems entitled?"

"She's a plastic princess. For the life of me, I don't know what Cole saw in her."

For the second time, I hear alarms going off in my brain at the Detective's words. The way he just spoke about Cole almost makes me wonder... were they friends? Is this personal for him? Is that why he's being so nice to me?

"Do you know what he saw in me?" I ask the detective, before I realize how suggestive that sounds.

"Sure. You're batshit crazy. Just his type."

My smile blossoms into a full-fledged grin. "You knew him well, then?"

"I... well, we met a few times. He always

seemed like a smart guy, but I suppose even the smartest men can be dumb when it comes to women."

"Do you mean me, or Annabelle?"

"Both," the detective says with a chuckle. "I'll keep you posted, Shields. Text me if you find anything."

"I will."

When I hang up, I see that Zack is standing a few feet away and looking at me sternly, with his arms crossed over his chest. "You're not going anywhere until you eat, young lady. I have been worried sick about you all day, and I am not letting you leave this room unless you're well fed."

Glancing at the room service, I feel guilty for rushing out without at least trying the lobster. Zack has been so thoughtful and sweet, and I have to accept his kindness.

Still, it feels like there's a fire lit beneath me, and I need to move.

"Two bites," I say, negotiating.

He nods. "If you can stop after two bites, then you're welcome to leave. It looks *really* good."

Chapter Twenty-Five

sophie shields, 2016

It is a bit disconcerting to pull into the parking lot of my old high school driving a Bugatti. I can still remember what it felt like to be a teenager in this place, and how miserable I was back then. I didn't really imagine that I'd ever be successful, or own a car at all; I was never completely certain I could survive the week. As the car pulls to a halt in a teacher's reserved parking spot, I place a hand on my side, over the scars that were burned into me by Mr. Brown's cigarettes.

Covering the damage with tattoos did help put that part of my past behind me, but being in this schoolyard brings it all back. I remember the pain. Fire burns slowly, especially such a weak fire. Just barely touching the cigarette for a moment wouldn't have done too much harm. But I remember the way he held it there, purposefully, and pressed it in deep. I remember the gleeful look in his eyes as he gained pleasure from tormenting me. It was like he was trying to burn holes right into my bones, to match the holes in his soul.

For the life of me, I will never understand how people can get off on harming a child.

In some ways, Mr. Brown was more frightening than Benjamin. At least Benjamin pretended it was done out of love, and it was almost possible to believe that he just couldn't control himself. Sometimes, I wanted to believe that. At least he made a sick attempt to soothe the wounds afterwards with gifts and attention. The professor just had a demon inside, unleashed by booze; he never even remembered what he'd done in the morning, so he could never acknowledge it or apologize.

I suppose I am lucky that neither man was my real father. There's a sort of freedom to having no father at all, and being able to imagine that you could have come from anywhere or anyone. Being born to a truly bad man must be a terrible burden to bear. I don't think I ever would have gotten over it if Mr. Brown was my flesh and blood—these scars I wear would have been a lot heavier.

Stepping out of the car, I walk to the front to pop open the trunk and retrieve an item. My hand clenches around the wooden handle of a slender implement. I had to stop by a hardware store on the way over here to purchase it. If my hunch is right, this could give me some much-needed answers.

Shutting the trunk, I walk briskly out into the football field.

It's nighttime, and the stars are peeking out from gaps in the clouds. I remember all those beautiful things Cole said to me in this field, all those years ago, and how much those words meant. I remember all the promises we made. I sometimes tried to tell myself that they were the silly promises of children, but maybe I was wrong. *No.* If he really meant to send me back here from his deathbed, then it must have meant just as much to him.

Enough thinking.

When I reach the goal post in the far south side of the football field, I search for letters carved into the paint. It seems like they have repainted it sometime in the past thirteen years, so I am unable to find the carving. This disappoints me, until I reach out and run my hand over the pole.

My fingertips graze over the bumps and scrapes of time, and I wonder if I'm crazy.

Did Cole ever write on this pole at all? Was I just imagining it all?

Feeling an odd impression beneath the paint, I pull out my cell phone to use the flashlight. I use my fingernail to scrape away some paint, and peer closer, until sure enough, I see it.

2003

CS

PIN

I get a little shiver of victory. My thumb moves over the word *PIN* hopefully, praying that this is what Cole was talking about—and somehow knowing that it is. I look down at the earth below the goal post with interest, wondering what, if anything, lies beneath. This feels more real than it did at his tombstone. Somehow, I know that these letters are the real marker of a grave—of our grave. Maybe we both left part of ourselves dead and buried in this field, all those years ago.

There is no freshly dug dirt to guide me, so I just look directly beneath the letters. Grasping the handle of my shovel firmly, I plant it into the grassy earth and drive it in with the sole of my running shoes. I dig my first few shovelfuls of earth out aggressively before I begin to wonder if I'm crazy again. Is there really something physically buried here, or was it just symbolic?

I plant the shovel in again, and press down with my sneakers.

Removing several considerable scoops, I begin to wonder how deep I will dig before giving up. What do I even expect to find? A map to buried treasure? If the map itself is already buried, isn't that kind of redundant?

No. I want to find a map to Cole. It's possible that he managed to come back here and hide something in recent months—a contingency plan of some sort. With Zachary stealing his letters, he needed to make sure that I would be the only one capable of finding his instructions. Whatever it is must be highly classified: copies of evidence he managed to gather on Benjamin, just in case? Something to do with his stressful project just outside of Karachi? I know there's really big money involved with that.

Whatever it is, I wonder how he decided to bury it? A USB key sealed in a Ziploc bag would be good enough for me.

I just need some sort of direction. I need to know where to go next. What to do.

When several minutes pass and I am still digging, I begin to grow frustrated. He didn't bury it six feet deep, did he? That seems unnecessary. And what if it was a few inches to the right or the left, and I missed it? I want to scream and pull my hair out in frustration.

"Damn you, Cole!" I shout into the empty field. "Why do you always have to be so dramatic? Why couldn't you just send me to a wall safe concealed behind a painting or something? That's a classic! But no, your death note has to lead me to the middle of a football field. And yes, I do know that *Death Note* is one of your favorite anime shows. Stop changing the subject!"

At first, my rambling is kind of fun and relieves some of my stress, but then I am stricken by the idea that I might actually be talking to a ghost or spirit. I shudder and keep digging. That's not it at all. I just know Cole so well that I can imagine exactly how he'd respond.

What if there are bones buried here? I don't know why this thought crosses my mind. It's a stupid thought, because if Cole killed someone, I am sure he'd find a better place to bury a body than in our old high school football field. I keep digging, getting more annoyed with every scoop.

It's not Cole's fault. Maybe I just misinterpreted his note.

My emotions are wavering between hopeful and disappointed every time I dig a bit of dirt out. I clench my teeth together and dig faster, trying to make something appear with sheer will. When my shovel clinks against something, I pause, almost in disbelief.

I toss the shovel aside and kneel down beside the hole I've dug, leaning forward and clawing dirt off with my hands. As I uncover a shiny item, I gently brush dirt away with my fingers, feeling a bit like an archeologist discovering evidence of ancient civilizations that lived beneath my high school. There should be a posh voice in my head doing a BBC voiceover for this dig.

As Sophie carefully uncovers the urn, it looks to be made of a glass material that was popular for alcoholic beverages in the twenty-first century. This particular transparent cylinder is branded with the mark of its manufacturer, and logos celebrating libations, much like the designs seen on ancient Grecian jugs depicting Bacchus or Dionysus. Upon careful inspection, as she removes the bottle, it seems to contain a small item that Sophie estimates to be a digital key holding important data that could be used to incriminate...

Oh, hell no.

Sitting back abruptly in the dirt, I stare at the item in my hands. The first crushing realization is that it is not something Cole planted here recently. It's an old vodka bottle belonging to Professor Brown. Cole must have left this here for me back when we were still in high school—before he was sent to prison.

This shatters my hopes a little.

There is no USB key. No flash drive. No SD card. Just a few pieces of paper rolled up. A message in a vodka bottle. If it was written in 2003, around the time that Cole carved our initials into the goal post, it probably won't have any useful information. It won't lead me directly to Cole, or to the person who made an attempt on his life, or to any of the reasons behind any of this.

It's going to be useless.

And Cole might actually be dead.

Chapter Twenty-Six

sophie shields, 2016

I sit on the ground for a minute, with the vodka bottle lying in the grass before me. I almost wish that it still contained some vodka. It takes several deep breaths before I can gather the courage to reach forward and unscrew the rusted cap. The paper inside is yellowed with age. I think I know what this is.

Someday, when we're both ready, let's promise that we'll come back here. Then, if we're both confident that we are strong enough, we'll take the pin out of the grenade.

Whatever is contained in this letter is so overwhelming that Cole had to keep it locked up for over a decade. We were supposed to be dealing with all of this together, but now I'm here—alone. At least he remembered.

I bet you're going to forget all about this in a few days.

Although we have been through so much together, we never really went back to that moment and reconsidered our decision. Sliding my fingers into the vodka bottle, I carefully retrieve the tender old paper and remove it from the bottle. I unroll it so that I can read the words, and use my camera flash to help me in the darkness of the field.

Holding my breath, I try to prepare myself for this. But you can never be prepared for unleashing emotional grenades; especially when your emotions are already in turmoil.

Dear Scarlett,

Do you want to know a secret? Everything I've ever done in my life, from the moment we first met, has been for you.

I don't know how many years it will be until you open up this bottle, but I do know one thing. Everything I do from this moment, to the day I finally inform you of this letter's existence—it will all be for you. And everything I do after you read this letter—it will still be for you.

The question is this:

Is it enough?

I have to pause and look away, because all my airways feel suddenly very constricted. I try, but I am unable to breathe. Is it enough? Is he serious? He was always way more than enough. Even if he did the bare minimum he was capable of doing, it was more than most men giving every ounce of their effort.

And when he really tried?

He could build entire cities.

Who does something like this? Something so impossibly romantic. Who buries a love letter in a time capsule for the girl he likes in high school? Who still loves that same girl, thirteen years later, and still writes her letters once a week?

This is hard. I would love nothing more than to just put this letter in my pocket and walk away. Maybe I could look at it later when I am drunk and emotionally numb. It's not important. These words are purely the sentimental ramblings of a fifteen-year-old boy, and can offer nothing to the investigation. But if Cole sent me all this way, I owe it to him to read it. I clench my teeth together as I allow the pin to slide out of the grenade.

You are the love of my life, Scarlett. I knew that you were going to be from the first time I saw you. I know that it was destiny for us to meet, at precisely the moment we did. I know that you knew it, too.

Do you know how broken I was? I was lost, and floundering, and pretending to function. I couldn't sleep. But the day you walked into my world, I was instantly a better person. Just being close to you made me stronger. Your love gave me purpose, and I am always motivated and excited when I'm close to you.

I will always remember how the earth moved when you touched my hand.

That was all you, Scar. The earth shakes just for you.

A chill runs through my spine at his mention of the event. Especially in light of what happened today, I feel like it is fate that I should find this bottle now. Will this help me to understand what the earthquakes mean? Is there a key or a legend enclosed? Did I interpret the signs correctly? I am curious, and I want to know more. Cole always had all the answers.

The words of this letter are shockingly relevant—pun intended—and I feel myself needing to pause every few sentences to process them and breathe.

Maybe the first earthquake was our theme song, and the one today was just a reprise.

This idea makes me smile.

Most couples have a song, don't they? We have a natural disaster.

Please don't hate me for waiting. Don't hate me for not telling you all this today, or yesterday. I wanted to. I wanted to so badly. But the truth is that I don't know what the future holds in store for us and I need to know that before I make any more promises.

If I can't be the person I need to be, then I will never tell you about this letter. But if you're reading this, I hope you know that you're in a lot of trouble.

When I wrote these words and sealed them away in this bottle, I also vowed to lock away some of my deeper feelings for you. Because frankly, I'm scared shitless about how much I feel for you, and I don't know what the hell to do about it.

Young love? Does that ever work out? You just turned fourteen yesterday, Scar. We're both pretty smart, at least academically. But emotionally, I think that we know nothing at all.

I just want us to last. I just want it to be us, at the end of our lives, together. If we started now, how high are the chances that we would fuck it up? Pretty high, I think. Neither of us has any experience with being in a relationship.

I don't want to be your guinea pig. I don't want to be your crash test dummy. I want you to go out into the world and love others, and get your heart broken, and fail. I want to be there to pick up the pieces, every time. I want you to see what other men are like, so you never wonder if the grass is greener with someone else.

We need to learn how to love, before we can love each other.

If you've opened this letter, it means that I'm going to make you mine, Scarlett. I'm going to stop holding back and hit you with all of my passion and devotion.

I'm going to make love to you tonight, and every single night from now on.

It's already killing me not to touch you, sometimes. I feel like once I started, I would never be able to stop. Do you feel the same, Scar? If you don't, I'll find a way to make you fall in love with me. I'll dedicate my whole life to it, every waking minute.

There's no going back now. I'm never letting go of you, and never letting anything come between us. I would do anything to protect you, and protect our love. I would kill for us to be together. I would die.

I would conquer the world for you.

"You stupid, fucking bastard!" I curse as tears flood my eyes. I look around for something to take out my frustrations on. Dropping my phone, I grab Mr. Brown's old vodka bottle and slam it into the goal post. The glass makes a satisfying sound as it smashes into smithereens. "I hate you, Cole!" I scream into the empty football field. "You stupid asshole. Why did you do this to us? You wasted all the time we could have had. I was ready. I was always ready! I didn't want you to conquer the fucking world for me. I just wanted you. Totally and completely, one hundred percent all-in."

At the same time, I know it's true. He's right. Cole was wise beyond his years, and if we had tried to begin, back then… there's a good chance that everything would have been ruined. Cole might never have been able to accomplish as much as he did, and build so many great monuments in dozens of countries. I might not have an amazing job for the CIA.

I know he did it to protect me. To protect us both.

This letter is like an insurance policy for our hearts. By sending me here, Cole is cashing in his insurance policy. What does that mean? Who is going to reimburse me for all the love that has been lost over the years? All the love that was promised and never realized?

Cole had better be alive. When I see him again, I'm going to punch him right in his stupid face.

Against my better judgment, my eyes are drawn back to the letter. My hand shakes as I retrieve my phone flashlight.

I keep on reading.

There are going to be dark times ahead. But if you're reading this, it means that I am absolutely certain that we can get through anything. I never enter an arrangement unless I feel that success is guaranteed, because I cannot abide failure.

I don't know if I've already said these things out loud, because you were just so beautiful and brilliant that I couldn't resist. But here they are anyway, in writing.

Are we older now, Scar? Are we strong, and rich, and stable? Are we still best friends?

Okay. At the time of writing this, maybe we're not best friends yet, but we will be soon. Like, maybe tomorrow. I'm going to be the best friend you ever had, for the rest of your life.

There's no getting rid of me, my love.

I hope to god that something critical didn't change, that could get in the way of my plans for us. But it doesn't matter. I am ready, and it is time to give us a try. To really give it a try. You let many buried truths out of the bottle when you opened it. You've released them, and they are spoken, and they are real.

And they cannot be denied.

I will wait for you. I may only be two years older than you, but I feel like I have lived a lot more in some respects, and I know what I want. What I want is you. Even if it takes you a decade to find this bottle under the football field, I will wait for you. One decade, or two, or three—but please don't make me wait that long. I will lose my mind.

Because from now on, you're my end game. You're the girl of my dreams, my partner in crime, and my muse.

Someday, Scarlett Smith, I'm going to marry you. I hope you don't mind. I'm going to be the father of your children. I hope that sounds cool. We are going to be a family. A real family, like the one I once had. Like the one you should have had. Who, other than us, deserves this more? Who, other than us, can value this more?

We will have the greatest love you've ever known. The greatest love you've ever seen. It will be just like those books you're always reading, except better— because it's truth. I can feel it already, right here, between us, brimming, teeming, bursting at the seams. Can you feel it, Scar?

And if somehow, life is cruel enough to separate us... rest assured that there is nothing to worry about. Nothing can keep us apart for too long. Not hell or high water, meteor showers, the rapture, or the goddamned apocalypse.

You can look for me at the end of the earth, if it ever comes to that.

I'll always be there, waiting for you.

Unconditionally yours,

Cole Hunter

He signed it with a bloody thumbprint. He always had such a flair for the dramatic. I bring the letter to my lips, and hold it there for a moment, like a fourteen-year-old girl.

I did not realize how tightly I was clenching the paper and my cell phone until I read the final words, and the muscle tension in my hands disappeared. Exhaling, I allow my whole body to sag and collapse backward onto the grass. I look up at the stars and I feel a laugh rumble in my throat. The laughter grows until I am laughing loudly, hysterically, with my arms stretched out.

"Fine!" I say with a smile up at the sky. "I'll look for you at the end of the earth. But you better be alive, buddy. You better be. You can't just give a girl a letter like this and die."

Alone in the middle of the football field, I hug the yellowed paper against my chest. I forgot the way that everything Cole says and writes sounds like wedding vows. Maybe that's the reason I barely noticed that Zachary was trying to suggest spending our lives together. When I've already had one man in my life who made such honest and devoted vows of loyalty—vows that he never broke—how could I even notice the efforts of anyone else?

I inhale deeply, and somehow, the air tastes fresher than it has ever been.

No one can see, so I can just be honest with myself in this moment. As the clouds drift across the sky, a bit of the moon peeks out and illuminates the sky, highlighting the outlines of the clouds.

Staring up at the moon makes me feel so peaceful and complete. I don't get much time to look up at the night sky anymore, at home in DC. But now, precious childhood memories come rushing back to me. I used to go for walks by myself and talk to the moon when I had no home, no friends, and no family. The sense of companionship this gave me was incredibly comforting. The moon always made me feel important and connected. She made me feel loved.

How could I ever feel lonely? The moon is the best friend a girl can ask for. How could I ever feel abandoned, or care about the fact that I have no human family? The moon is the best sister a girl could want. She always listens, and she always seems to care deeply. Sometimes, I swear she even tries to help out. As I got older, and busier, I forgot the wisdom of my youth.

"Please let him be okay," I ask the moon softly. "Wherever he is, please watch over him for me." Reorganizing the pages of the letter and folding it up carefully, my finger grazes against something cold. I am surprised to feel a metallic item that I hadn't noticed before, taped to the back of one of the pages. I guess I had been too focused on the words themselves. Getting out my phone camera, I shine a light on the paper to reveal a delicate gold chain with a crescent shaped pendant. There looks to be a diamond in the center of the crescent moon.

It is a familiar symbol, for Cole bears a similar design tattooed on his body. Touching the pendant reminds me of touching his skin, and I get a little shiver of amazement. How does Cole know exactly what would mean the most to me in every moment? Being psychic or telepathic is one thing, but adding time travel to that is way too overpowered. I had just been speaking to the moon an instant before finding this! My fingers caress the pendant lovingly. This is more than déjà vu. This is more than magic. This is more than coincidence, fate, or divine intervention. This is more than anything imaginable, other than the most elusive and precious power known to man:

Love.

A great love. Just like he said.

Gently removing the necklace from the paper, I

fumble with the clasp in the dark to fasten it around my neck. Then I look back up at the sky.

"I'm going to find him," I declare, before placing my hand over the necklace. "Dead or alive. And I could really use some Moon Crystal Power right about now."

Chapter Twenty-Seven

sophie shields, 2016

I sip my coffee as my Bugatti barrels down the desert highway at twice the posted limit. I had to give in to my cravings at the last gas station, to help me stay awake. After leaving my high school, I found myself unable to drive back to the hotel. Instead, my car was being pulled in the other direction: north-east. The moon was hanging high in the sky, beckoning me, guiding me.

Long ago, I remember driving up north with Cole. Whenever he was most stressed out and overwhelmed, that's what he would do, to clear his head. Just drive. Drive out across the mountains and deserts. Drive through small towns that are barely on the map. Drive through surreal landscapes that would inspire the soul and take your breath away.

He would drive to the middle of nowhere. He would drive to the end of the earth.

So, where exactly is that? The end of the earth?

I've been mulling it over in my brain.

I even used the Google Maps app on my phone to search for the "end of the earth" but the only result I got was a church in New Jersey. That's way too far to drive, and I highly doubt Cole would be there. But it does have a good review on Yelp. Apparently, that church is an excellent place to pray for your sins in order to avoid burning in hell—if you trust the Yelp reviews.

My natural inclination is to head in the general direction of Death Valley. It seems appropriate, considering the circumstances. Besides, I know that Cole always loved the topography. He spent so much time in cities, creating concrete landscapes and being immersed in a geography of flawed structures built by other humans. He always found it refreshing to look upon natural, virgin terrain. Perfection.

"Scar," he would say in wonder. *"If there is a god, he's a fucking amazing architect. And if not, and this is all just random natural forces and tectonic plates, millions of years of erosion, and glaciers— that's pretty fucking amazing, too."*

Thinking about how passionately Cole loved the world makes me smile. But when my brain starts to dig up everything he's ever said about natural landscapes, I remember him gushing about his favorite place. His parents' old property in Nevada.

Would he have gone there? He used to say that it was nothing short of paradise.

I squint with effort as I try to remember the address. Red something. Red Canyon, Red Mountain, Red Rock… Red Earth? Could it have been Red Earth Lane?

And the vacation cottage would have been at the end of the road. The end of *Earth* road.

"Yes!" I say, slapping my palm against my steering wheel victoriously. I think I might actually be driving in the right direction. That's partly luck, and partly because it was just Cole's favorite direction to drive. If we'd ever had more time, maybe we would have driven all the way up to the mountain hideaway he gave to Mr. Bishop in exchange for my safety.

I am grabbing my phone to GPS the address when the cell phone vibrates against my palm with an incoming call. Glancing out at the empty road ahead before looking down at the phone, I feel worried to see that it is the detective calling. It is well after midnight, so I am not expecting good news. *I hope Zack is okay…*

"Hey, Rodriguez."

"Shields…" He sounds tired as his voice trails off. "You were right. Something was off about Annabelle."

"Yeah? What did you find?"

"Her body."

"What?"

"Annabelle is dead."

I slam on the brakes and pull over to the side of the road. "What are you talking about, Rodriguez?"

"There's more." The detective exhales slowly. "Sophie, she was murdered days ago."

"Days? But we saw her earlier today at the funeral—oh. Oh, shit."

"That wasn't Annabelle."

"Who was she?"

"I am not sure yet, but I have my people looking into it. When I got to Annabelle's house, no one answered the door, but I heard a whimpering sound inside. It turns out that her dog has been starving for a week, shitting on the floor and tearing apart the kitchen for scraps. I called it in, and not too long after that, Dr. Annabelle Nelson was found dead in her office at a health clinic in Anaheim. Someone has been calling all her clients and cancelling their appointments, so no one noticed she was missing work."

"She didn't have friends who were worried?"

"No. She seems like a lonely workaholic."

"That's definitely more Cole's type of woman than the girl who was at the funeral." I pause. "So, who was she? She must have been fairly close to him if she knew to impersonate Annabelle. I guess Miranda and Mr. Bishop had never actually *met* Annabelle. Why would she be interested in Cole? Who's been cancelling the appointments? Did the doctor have an assistant, or a secretary…"

"Yes. Let me see here…" The detective pauses. "A Miss Brown. Brittany Brown."

"Brown!" I nearly shout at the detective. "Are you kidding me?"

"What?

"Detective! Brittany Brown, as in the daughter of the man that Cole went to prison for killing?"

"Shit."

"He was protecting me," I explain to the detective. "We also burned down her childhood home."

"I'm sorry, Shields. I may not have needed to bring Benjamin in after all. He might not be involved in this at all, other than the building named after you."

"I don't know," I say quietly, glancing in my rearview mirror. "I never know what to expect from him."

"Do you want to come to the crime scene?" the detective asks. "I know you didn't get a chance to see Cole's crime scene, because you got here a little late and we had to work fast to give the hospital back their ICU room. But I would love to have your input on this one. I can text you the address."

Hesitating, I look out at the open road, and up at the desert moon for advice. "I don't know…"

"This location is called *The Mind Spa*—it's the female-targeted version of Annabelle's other holistic clinic, *The Mind Mechanic*. They are beautiful offices—it looks like Cole designed the buildings for her, and that's how they met. She seems… like she was a really good doctor. Really cared about reducing the stress levels of her patients to improve their overall health."

"She sounded really wonderful in Cole's letters," I say softly. "I was jealous. Why did Brittany leave the body there, for us to find so easily?"

"Well, my guess is that she's trying to draw you

out. She probably sees you as responsible for her father's death, just as much as Cole."

"I am." Biting my lip, I look around at the darkened desert with indecision. "Detective, I'm actually not in L.A. anymore. I found some information that led me to think that I should check out one of Cole's houses upstate."

"Upstate? Like San Fran?"

"Around there," I say, lying. I don't want the Detective to know about Nevada. I trust him, mostly, but at the same time, I can't be too careful. If Cole's hiding, and going to such great lengths to conceal his whereabouts from everyone, including me—it wouldn't make sense for me to announce it to every stranger who asks.

"That's a long drive, Shields. You could have flown."

"I'm in a Bugatti, Rodriguez."

"Fair point. Still, I could have hooked you up with a faster trip. Why didn't you let me know?"

"It was kind of spontaneous. Besides, you were finding dead bodies." I sigh. "Do you really want me to come back to check out the crime scene?"

"No," the detective says. "It's not important. You should chase your lead. Besides, she was murdered pretty brutally, and it's not a pretty picture."

"Are you sure?" I ask him.

"Absolutely. I was told to trust your instincts, and if you think there's something special up in San Fran, then by all means. You should go there. Just keep me posted, and keep Zack close in case of any trouble."

"Suuure," I say, looking at the empty seat beside me. "I will."

"He's not there, is he? Shields!"

"I'll be fine. I'm a big girl from Washington D.C., where the bad guys have suitcases instead of surfboards. You worry about your crime scene."

"Will do."

"And Detective? I'm sorry about Annabelle."

"All part of the job, Shields."

When we hang up, I sit on the roadside for a minute, feeling awful. Another dead body. *Another?* No. The whole point of me driving out here is that I didn't think there was a dead body to begin with. But now, as more deaths start to pile up, and we have a suspect with serious motive, it starts to seem less likely that Cole is still alive.

I just don't understand, why now? Why would Annabelle—er, Brittany, do this now? Maybe her life just took a terrible turn for the worse, and she decided to lay blame on Cole and me. Maybe she has nothing left to lose, and her anger has been building to a breaking point all these years.

Glancing at the moon again, I sigh and consider calling Zack to tell him about Nevada. But I can't bear to hear anything negative right now, especially about how I'm chasing a dead man.

But am I? Why would he give me that note, and lead me to that letter...

I might just be seeing things that aren't there. Fabricating meaning from the mundane. I need to remember that Cole was fifteen when he wrote that last letter to me. As he lay on his deathbed, he might not have even remembered the contents of the letter, other than pouring his heart out to me. He didn't know that any of this was going to happen, and he might not have meant to use it as a secret code.

Mentioning the end of the earth could have just been him trying to be poetic and flowery with language. He could have just sent me to find that letter so I would know that he's loved me forever. It could be closure for him—thinking about the beginning in the end. Sending me back to the beginning, to collect the one last buried relic of our lives together.

All of this could be in my head. Nevada could just be me grasping at straws. If something snapped in Brittany Brown, and she decided to start killing—why would she fail? She killed Annabelle.

Cole could be dead.

"He's not dead," I whisper to myself, putting the car in gear. "He's not dead. He's not dead."

I press my foot down on the gas pedal and take off down the highway with my heart in my throat. I find myself staring at the horizon, praying for a smoke signal or skywriting, or emergency flares to indicate that I might be right.

Or maybe I'm just a crazy girl, driving off into the desert for no damned reason at all.

Chapter Twenty-Eight

sophie shields, 2016

Fighting with all my willpower to keep my eyes open, I clutch a cup of coffee tightly in my hand as I drive the last few miles. The few drops of coffee remaining have gone cold since I picked it up from a gas station hours ago, along with a paper map. Cell service is unreliable out here, and I have taken a few wrong turns. I regret drinking my coffee too quickly, but I am still holding the empty cup in my hand, inhaling the fumes of the last sip, as if to convince myself that I have more of the stuff in my veins, fueling me, than I actually do.

When my phone's GPS starts working again, I

am grateful to see that it says I'm almost there. I feel like I have been staring at the same empty landscape for hours, with the sun rising over the desert. Even the most beautiful surroundings can quickly get old when you haven't slept in over twenty-four hours, and the last time you slept was an unsatisfying, quick nap right where you're sitting, in a cramped vehicle.

Also, sports cars aren't the most comfortable vehicles to take on a long drive. I really wish I had something roomier, like a suburban housewife's minivan, or a rapper's tricked out Escalade. My legs are going numb, and I feel like my butt is bruised from my bones pushing against this not-very-cushiony seat.

When the GPS informs me that my destination is up ahead, my eyes have been closing and they are reduced to tiny slits. I force them open and stare forward hard, trying to see a house, or cottage, or cabin—any type of dwelling. I'm not sure what to expect. There is a slight bend in the road, and finally I see it in the distance. A gorgeous house, situated on a beautiful forested, mountainside. It's tucked away and out of sight, and perfectly picturesque, like a fairy tale.

I immediately want to just move in and live here forever and never go back to the real world.

And I'm going to tell Cole that in about five minutes.

I hope.

Peering closer, I feel suddenly very awake, and my heartbeat quickens. I don't see a car in the driveway, but that's okay. There's a three-car garage in this mountain mansion, and I am sure that Cole's car is safely parked inside. Does he still drive the same old Lexus truck that he had years ago? That car was beat up beyond imagination, and it was always filthy from construction sites. But it was reliable, and it suited him.

Parking in the driveway, I feel a little odd as I turn off my vehicle. I finish off the last sip of my coffee before placing the empty container in the cup holder and reaching for my purse. As I step out of the car, I study the windows of the house, looking for signs of life. Walking closer, I feel a familiar fluttering in my stomach, like I would every time I saw Cole after a long absence. Like that time I broke him out of prison. I felt like my heart would burst at seeing him again, although I always managed to play it cool.

He always played it cool, too. Many of the hours of my drive were spent processing the words of his letter. They shouldn't have been so surprising, but they were. I knew it all along, how much he cared, but at the same time, I really didn't.

Everything is going to be different now, when I see him again. It's going to be a little awkward, perhaps, and we're going to have a lot to talk about.

And I'm going to have to punch him in his stupid face.

This is the thought that pushes me forward and gives me the courage to march up to the door and ring the doorbell. I can hear the loud sound echoing throughout the house.

"Cole!" I shout loudly, pressing my face up

against the frosted glass doors. "It's me. I know you're in there! Let me in."

There is only silence. I listen for the rush of footsteps on the stairs, coming to greet me, but there is nothing. I swallow.

"Come on, Cole! I followed your little Easter egg hunt. You have some serious explaining to do! I don't care how many bullet wounds you've got, we're going to sit down and have a long conversation."

Still nothing. I press the doorbell again. Once, twice, three times.

"Cole!" I scream at the house. I beat both of my fists against the door violently, until my wrist bone catches one of the molding designs and I wince in pain. Holding it, I kick the door with my knee. "Cole Hunter, you let me in this very minute. I don't care how exciting the anime you're watching is, or how much fun the video game is, or how epic the dream is, or how tasty the meal is—you need to let me in right now and show me that you're alive, because I'm freaking out here."

I place both of my palms against the cool glass door, and allow my forehead to fall forward against it. "Cole," I whisper tiredly. "Cole, please be here. I drove all night to find you, and if you're not here, I don't know where the hell on earth you could be. And it will be hell on earth, if I have to be here without you. I refuse to be here without you."

Turning around and putting my back to the door, I feel my breath coming in short gasps. I let my body slide down the door until my rump hits the floor with a little thud. I stare out at the scenery, shaking my head in disbelief. "He's not here," I say softly. "I read all the signs wrong. He's not here. There never was a sign. It was all in my head."

Pressing my hands into my hair, I knead my scalp as if to coax ideas into my brain. "Think, Sophie," I beg myself. "Is there anything you missed? Is there any way?" I am hyperventilating now, and tears are pricking the backs of my eyes. "He has to be here, right? God, I'm so tired."

Glancing down at my purse, I see the handle of my gun sticking out. I look at it thoughtfully before grabbing it and taking the safety off. I stand up and aim it at the glass window of the door, and I pull the trigger.

The sound is deafening, and my ears ring for a second. The kickback of the gun also hurts my wrist a little. Rubbing the back of my hand across my tired, teary eyes, I reach through the glass and unlock the door before stepping into the house.

"Cole," I say softly, looking around. There is no security system on this house, and that surprises me. Cole loves security systems. "Cole!" I scream out louder, moving through the house. I go to the kitchen first and check the cabinets. With how far this house is away from civilization, I expect it to be well stocked up. To my surprise, there is nothing. I open the fridge, and it is completely empty.

My heart rate is exploding now, until it pains my chest. I am starting to realize that there is a large probability that I am wrong about all of this, and he's really gone.

Moving toward the stairs, I grasp the railing to

drag my tired body up the steps. "Cole!" I call out desperately, as tears begin sliding down my cheeks. "Come on, Cole! This isn't funny. If you're waiting in a closet to jump out and scream 'boo' then I regret to inform you that we are not fifteen anymore, and my heart can't take any more of this. I'm afraid, Cole! Is that what you want me to say? I'm scared out of my mind! I am trying to keep you alive by just saying that you are. But I need you to work with me on this. I can't just make things happen by saying them. I need you to also do your part, and be alive. Just be alive! Is that too much to ask?"

I have been ripping doors open and searching for clothes, wrinkled beds, showers with droplets of water on the doors, or any sign of life. There is nothing. The house is spotless. It hasn't been lived in for years, but it seems like it has been regularly maintained by a groundskeeper.

"Cole!" I scream out again, and my throat is hoarse. My voice breaks as it echoes in the empty house. "Cole!"

Stumbling forward tiredly, I use both hands to hold onto the banister to keep myself standing. I lean forward, and my hair tumbles over my shoulder, hanging limply over the stairs.

It looks like this house has eighteen-foot ceilings on the main floor. I learned to estimate that sort of thing after working with Cole on many houses. I briefly wonder if I would die if I just let myself fall from this height. I briefly regret that I didn't go through with it at the gravesite. I was forced to live another day, and try, and be heartbroken all over again. I was forced to be heartbroken even worse, because I found that letter and saw a glimpse of the life we could have had. The life we should have had.

I have to give up. I have to admit it.

The earthquake was a lie.

Chapter Twenty-Nine

sophie shields, 2016

I am staring blankly, tiredly at the gunshot wound in the front door when my phone rings. I already know who it is, and I don't really want to answer. But my body moves anyway, in the rehearsed rhythm of a grown ass adult who does things she needs to do, even when she doesn't know why she should do anything at all.

The caller ID says that it's the hotel, meaning that it's Zack. As I expected. He's called a few times while I was driving, to check up on me, and I answered once to reassure him that I was fine. I decline the call, unwilling to show anyone how destroyed I am right now. But as I place the phone back in my bag, my hand brushes the letter. I pull it out, and stare at the last few sentences again. *Nothing can keep us apart for too long. Not hell or high water, meteor showers, the rapture, or the goddamned apocalypse. You can look for me at the end of the earth, if it ever comes to that. I'll always be there, waiting for you.*

"What does that mean?" I ask out loud as I tuck the letter back into my purse. "If this isn't the end of the earth, where is? Where are you, Cole? I'm so tired. Did I mess up? Am I in the right place? Do you want me to keep looking for you forever? I'm not that strong. It hurts."

Pulling out my GPS app, I look at my location on the map. I place my thumb and forefinger on the screen to spin the map, and zoom out a little, dragging the map around to survey the property. I see patches of green, patches of rock, and a little… water.

The hairs on the back of my neck stand up, and I pull my fingers apart to zoom in.

"Come hell or high water," I say suddenly. "High water from hell. A geyser."

The pieces of the letter fall from my fingers like leaves, and I shrug my shoulder to let my purse fall to the floor and set me free. I virtually run down the stairs, only stumbling once or twice as I stare hard at my phone. Once I am outside, I begin running in the direction of the water. How far is it? There is no road. It's hard to estimate. I don't think I can take the Bugatti, because it is too low to the ground and will definitely get stuck in some embarrassing situation.

Sports cars are like high heels. Pretty, but often impractical. Thank god I am not wearing my high heels as I race down a rocky path, using my phone to navigate.

Am I making this up again? Is it really all in my head? Am I really just missing a few screws?

"Where the earth boils," I murmur to myself. "Where giants used to make soup, and left their recipe for little boys when they're sick. The place that reminds him most of his mother."

I am surprised to see that my location marker is actually moving on the map. Somehow, these imperfect pieces of technology called legs do actually work to cover some distance, even in a short amount of time. My body is tired, and my form is sloppy as I push forward, but at least I'm wearing running shoes. My feet are still sore from walking all the fuck over L.A. yesterday, but I don't care. Pain can eat me.

I'm a woman on a mission. And I'll give anything, and suffer anything, as long as he can be alive.

The sun is rising high into the sky, and it's starting to go from very hot to excruciating. I ignore the heat and press on, although I need to slow from a run to a jog as my body starts to cramp up. The heat is unbearable, and it makes me want to peel all my clothes off, but I know that I'm going to need the protection from the sun as midday approaches. It could be worse. I could be walking through fire to find him. If he's actually dead, I still might end up doing that.

When I am about a quarter of the way to the

water on the map, I lose my footing on some uneven ground and trip and fall flat on my face. I groan and push myself up, ignoring the fact that the palms of my hands are skinned raw, and there is a new bruise on my face. I pick up my phone to reorient myself, but the screen is smashed and the signal has been lost. "No," I say, tapping the screen violently. "Not now, please." A shard of glass from the smashed screen slides into my finger, and I wince.

Now, I'm alone in the middle of nowhere, hours from humanity, and my phone is messed up. You would think the CIA would provide a durable fucking phone case to take along on my secret mission. I scream and kick the nearest tree, and immediately regret doing so as I clutch my ankle and moan.

So, I have two options. Do the safe thing and head back to my car, or keep wandering in the direction of the water, and possibly find nothing, and be too tired and injured to get back to the house and car. My body is already moving in the direction of the water, so it turns out that I never really had a choice to make.

I continue walking for what feels like hours, until my whole body feels like lead. My knees are buckling under me with every step, and I am thirsty, hungry, and half asleep. I never knew that you could fall asleep while walking, but apparently, it is possible. At least it's a lot safer than falling asleep in a Bugatti while driving 150 miles an hour. (Of course, I slowed down a little once I realized my eyes were closing. I only really tried driving so fast to use the excitement to keep them open.) When I stumble on a path that runs along a steep cliff with many, many rocks at the bottom, I rethink my previous thought about sleep-walking.

Unless my bra has airbags I don't know about, sleeping while walking is definitely more dangerous than sleeping while driving.

I giggle at this imagery and keep walking, if it can even be called walking anymore. I am half delirious, half mad, entirely miserable, thirsty, sore, and a small percentage hopeful.

But hope will only take you so far.

Eventually, I need to sit down. If it can even be called sitting down. At some point, I try to take steps, and my legs just won't work. My muscles feel like jelly. My boss was right about me needing some field experience. You can't just go from a desk job on the East Coast to being a mountaineer on the West Coast overnight. True story.

I don't know how far I am from the water. I still have no signal. The sun is directly overhead, and I am baking like a potato out here. My brain has turned to mash, and my arms are crispy, golden brown French fries. If only my legs were that crispy, I might be able to stand and walk, but I think they have turned into noodles.

"Come on, legs," I tell them, in a weak effort at a pep talk. "Don't be noodles. Be French fries. We can do this. We can keep moving while getting cooked alive. Getting baked isn't so bad. Well, not that kind of baked. Although, that would be nice right now. For medical reasons."

I push my skinned palm down on the ground to

lift my body up, and I force my legs to stand. They shakily propel me forward for a brief expanse of time, while my eyes drift closed and I see all kinds of pretty colors around me. I see Cole's buildings emerging from the mountain landscape, and this seems odd. I know all these buildings so well. And there's the hospital he died in.

There are people walking around these buildings, and I try to call out to them. Maybe they can help me. Am I thirsty enough to need a hospital? I am a little embarrassed to go to a hospital and ask for water. Maybe just a vending machine. But I left my purse back at the house, so I don't have any money. How will I manage to get water?

As I approach the hospital, I see that the people standing around are Zack, Professor Brown, and Benjamin. I turn around and start walking in the opposite direction, deciding that I will find another vending machine. Maybe in a skyscraper, or a shopping mall, or a church in New Jersey. But I see a cemetery, and Annabelle is standing there. Fake Annabelle—Brittany.

"Hey!" I shout at her, and my throat is dry. I should probably ask her for water, but all of a sudden, I can only think about semen. "Why'd you ask for Cole's sperm? You can't kill a guy and also want his sperm at the same time. That doesn't make sense. Unless you're a spider."

Then my eyes widen as she begins to get taller, and slowly transforms into a very large black widow spider. This is very confusing to me, and somewhat frightening. I want to ask the spider if there is a vending machine nearby, but I am already backing up slowly. I begin walking briskly in another direction. Was Professor Brown cruel to me because his daughter was messed up? Or was she messed up because he was cruel to her? As soon as I find a vending machine, I'll go back and ask the spider some serious questions.

But I trip and fall again, this time into something soft. All the tombstones and the buildings disappear. Dammit.

I hate hallucinations. I hate deserts. I hate Nevada, and New Jersey.

I have no idea if I lay here for a second, a minute, or an hour, but my head is throbbing. My eyes beg to stay closed, but my fingers curiously extend and test the softness.

Grass.

And where there's grass, there's water.

I roll my body over, and immediately cry out in pain as the sun stabs into my tired eyes. My arms lift defensively, but the damage has already been done, and I am temporarily blinded. "Solar flare," I mutter with frustration as I drag my tired body off the ground, remembering the effective attack from Cole's favorite anime. It was always used at the most opportune and unexpected moments, and it always hurt like a bitch.

Rubbing my eyes angrily, I continue moving forward, until I pause. It occurs to me that I have no idea which direction I came from. I have been stumbling around and sleepwalking and… there was a hospital…

I blink and look around, surveying the landscape. There are big, glowing dots in my vision, everywhere I look, precisely the shape of the murderous sun, who likes to kick a girl when she's down. I am wishing that the buildings would come back, even if they were hallucinations, when I am startled to see one up ahead.

My eyes squint and falter. I don't recognize the building. All of the previous ones were structures that I had helped Cole design. This one must have come from my imagination.

It's a gingerbread house, covered in candy.

Okay, it's really not, but I wish it were, because if you're hallucinating architecture, it might as well be edible. It might as well be colorful and tasty.

I drag myself forward with the graceful motions of someone auditioning to be an extra on *The Walking Dead*. I take deep breaths, because when you don't have water or food or coffee or sleep, air conditioning, or logic, you might as well appreciate having oxygen.

My eyes are finally beginning to focus better, and I see that the house is very small, but very beautifully designed. The roof is covered in solar panels that extend upward. It looks like the house... is also a car. I squint to make sure I'm not imagining things.

A house on wheels? Who's ever heard of anything like that! It's preposterous.

But also kind of cool. I wonder if Cole ever built a house on wheels. Or a house with wings. Or a house on the water. Or a house underground. Or a house shaped like a toilet. Or a house that is also a shoe, that a woman lives in, with her eight kids.

Wow, these are really good ideas. I'm so smart when I'm drunk.

But I haven't had anything to drink. If there is something to drink in that house on wheels, I could potentially get even smarter. That's mind blowing. Can you imagine if there's some gingerbread? I'll be the new Albert Einstein. I just need some gingerbread and beer. I don't even like beer. But I think it goes well with ginger.

Maybe I'll just go to sleep now.

Sitting down on the grass abruptly, I am grateful for the softness under my bottom. It's like a blanket from Mother Earth. I've never known any other kind. Of mother, that is. I've known other blankets. My body slumps to the side, and I smile as my cheek hits the cool grass. Even in all this heat, the grass is cool to the touch. It's like a soothing caress.

The moon is still just barely visible on the horizon, a faint wisp of a faded cosmic object, dwarfed and overshadowed by the sunlight. If the sun weren't here, she'd take care of me. But she can't do much about the brutal way he's beating down on me now. She has to look away. He's too strong.

I stare at the moon until she's no longer visible, and as she disappears, I see something else.

A spray of water into the air.

At first I think I'm imagining it, so I just close my eyes and let myself drift to sleep for a few seconds. But then I feel a sprinkle of water on my cheeks. My eyelids jerk open, and I lift my head off the grass.

Come hell or high water. It's the geyser at the end of the earth.

And there's a mobile home here—yes, that's a thing that's been invented. I remember now. A state of the art, newfangled mobile home like nothing I've ever seen before. It's a beautiful, sleek, silver bullet-style house that looks like it's from the future. From the year 2047, at least. There's only one person on this planet who could have designed such a beautiful piece of art that appears to be highly functional as well. Only one person—and I happen to be married to him.

And if he's inside that mobile home, there's a chance that he could live to see 2047. With me.

Because this world is all so breathtakingly beautiful that I can't bear to lose it. And there simply is no world for me, without him.

I don't bother trying to stand, because I've failed that too many times in the past few hours. I simply crawl forward, putting my raw palms in the grass to drag my upper body forward. Crawling is awesome. It's a great backup plan for when other things fail. When I am a few feet away from the house, I push myself back and sit on my knees. I stare at the house, praying that it isn't another hallucination, and won't just disappear if I try to touch it.

I've come too far, and tried too hard, to lose any more hope.

It would crush me.

I want to reach out and ring the doorbell or something, but I don't even know if it has a doorbell.

What are doorbells like in 2047? And what if no one answers? What if the wrong person answers? Did Cole build a time machine? Is this how he time traveled to give me that letter, and make it look old, but it really wasn't old? What if someone else built the time machine, and Cole isn't here at all? He's not a physicist. Oh god, what if there's a physicist in there? I put my head in my hands, and try to keep myself from crying, but there are no tears anyway. I am too dehydrated.

I guess I could just knock.

Staring at the door, I decide that I'm going to knock. But I can't seem to force myself to move.

"Knock, knock," I whisper. Nothing happens. I slam my fists into the ground, crying without tears. "Knock, knock!" I shout again, hysterically. "Knock, knock, *knock!*"

I stare at the door for several seconds, and I have almost given up when the handle turns. I shut my eyes. I can't look. What if it's not him? What if it's a physicist?

I take a quick peek. Oh my god. I saw a leg. It was wearing pants. I think it was his leg.

I think those were his pants.

I don't want to look up. I don't want to see his beautiful, ugly face, and muscles, and his hair blowing in the wind like a hero from a storybook in a trailer park in outer space. I can't take it.

All I can do is sit here with my head in my hands and cry.

"Scarlett?" says a man's voice. It washes over me, tender and warm.

It also cuts me to the bone.

I shake my head in refusal; *no*. I adamantly refuse the torrent of emotions that threatens to drown me. But in another instant, his arms are around me, and he is kneeling in the grass before me, and I am sobbing like a child against his chest.

"Oh, honey," he whispers, holding me so tightly that it hurts. "I never thought I'd see you again."

"Why," I whisper, my words coming out in short gasps between sobs. "Why would you do this to me? Why would you do this to me?"

"Scar," he says in amazement, cupping my face in his hands. "I didn't think you cared anymore."

I rip his hands off my face, and I hit him. I hit him hard, with all the strength I have remaining. I don't care if it kills me, I would happily die beating the shit out of him for this. And at least I'd die close to him.

"Hey! Ouch, ow, ow, ow. Scar, take it easy. I was really shot, you know." He easily grabs my wrists and restrains me, tackling me to the ground and straddling my body like when we were children.

"I hate you," I tell him, turning my face to the side so he can't see my emotions. "I hate you so much for doing this to me. How could you? You made me think you were gone."

He releases my wrists and lets his head fall forward so that his nose and lips rest against my cheek. It is only then that I notice a wetness on his face, and realize that he is also crying. "I never thought you'd find me."

Reaching up, my hand tentatively searches for

his shoulder. I am scared to make contact, lest he disappear, having been an illusion all this time. But when my shaking fingers touch his shoulders, he is hard flesh and blood and bone. I sink my fingers into his shirt and skin, and grip him tightly, for dear life. I can't stop crying. "Cole, you didn't have to be so goddamned convincing. I tried to die."

"No," he says suddenly, grabbing me by the shoulders and forcing me to look at him with a little shake. "You promised. You said you'd never…"

"What was I supposed to do?!" I scream into his face. "You were gone! There was a casket! There was a fucking casket and the morgue, and the will, and the detective, and Miranda was crying."

Cole does not respond, but he slides his fingertips under the top of my blouse and pulls out the crescent moon necklace. "You found my letter?" he asks me, with shock written all over his features.

"Yes. That's what led me here. To the end of the earth. Nice clues."

"Scarlett—I didn't think that you'd find that letter. And I didn't know it contained any clues or hints to my location."

"You're lying. I know you can travel through time, like Future Trunks. Your time machine is right over there."

He shakes his head. "I think you've been working for the CIA for too long."

"Shut up. I know you left me that stupid letter just to mess with my head! Was it all some game to you?"

"No," he says slowly. "It was goodbye. It was

closure. I'm just… I had no idea you still cared."

"Remind me to hit you again after I've slept," I tell him, lifting my body off the ground so that I can push him. I feel my second wind coming, and all my muscles are suddenly filled with power as I crawl over him to glare in his face. "What the fuck is wrong with you?" I ask, grasping handfuls of his shirt threateningly. "Love other people? I didn't want to love other people! I didn't need any other people! I just needed you, and you were never ready. Over and over, with this 'we're not ready' bullshit. When will we be ready, Cole? When we're both dead? When you get shot in the head, and buried in front of me, and I have to climb over a fucking mountain for you in the boiling hot Nevada sun, and hallucinate that you have a spaceship from 2047, will we be ready then?"

He slides a hand around my neck, crushing his lips against mine and kissing me soundly. His other hand wraps around my lower back, and his legs somehow get tangled up with mine. He kisses all the fight out of me until my whole body rests limply against his, and I feel like I no longer exist. Maybe I did die at the gravesite, and I am just a decomposing corpse, and this is all just a dream. Maybe this is all just heaven, and that's why I was able to find Cole here. I don't even care, as long as he never stops kissing me like this.

I no longer need water or sleep.

I just drink him in, kissing hungrily, tasting him, stealing his saliva.

"Jesus, you're so dehydrated," Cole says, pulling away. He rolls me off him and heads into his spaceship to retrieve a bottle of water. He tosses it at me, and it just hits me in the stomach. I am way too tired to be catching water bottles, and still reeling from that kiss. My body is here, but my mind is catapulted somewhere out into the cosmos.

Cole moves to my side with concern, opening the water bottle for me and lifting my head with one hand so he can put it to my lips. "When is the last time you slept?" he asks me. "Your face looks like death."

After drinking two thirds of the water bottle in about two gulps, I glare at him. "Your face looks like butt. Of course I look like death; I barely slept since I found out you were dead. I'm never going to forgive you for this. Never."

He smiles. "You really think my house looks like a spaceship?"

I can't resist him. I smile, too. He looks like a little boy, all proud of his accomplishment and seeking approval. I reach up to grasp the water bottle and polish off the rest before leaning my head against his leg contentedly. "Go to hell," I whisper. "In your cool spaceship." My eyes flutter closed, and I feel happy. I feel happy for the first time in years. I clutch his leg tightly, like he is my favorite teddy bear. "But then, after you go to hell, come back to me."

"Always," he says, sliding his hands underneath me to lift me against his chest. He rises to his feet and begins walking toward the shiny bullet house.

"Cole?" I murmur sleepily.

"Yes, my love?"

"Can you design a special house for me?"

"Anything."

"It needs to be made from gingerbread and candy. Because I'm really hungry."

He laughs, and I can feel the rumble of his chest against my body. It's the most precious feeling in the world, and I feel my heart swell with gratitude. He is alive, and I made him laugh. I get to hear him laugh, again and again, for as long as he remains alive.

I'd walk a million miles across the desert just to hear him laugh, every single day.

But not tomorrow, because my feet hurt.

"I will build you a gingerbread house," he promises as he carries me over the threshold of his spaceship. "Does that make us Hansel and Gretel?"

"Maybe," I say thoughtfully. "Their mother abandoned them. Like my mother."

"Did Zack tell you that I found your family?"

"What?" I say, my eyes snapping open wide.

"Yes. I told him a few days ago when he called, that I wanted you to call me back and discuss it. The DNA tests we did years ago—there finally was a match. Someone from your family was seeking information about his DNA, and it entered the database. It turns out you have a real brother living in New York."

This news sends me reeling, almost as much as his kiss, but not in such a good way. Mixed emotions cause my face to contort, with alarm, fear, and disbelief. Do I even want to know? After all this time...

"You're my real brother," I say dumbly.

"No, I'm not," he says with a laugh. "We were

just pretending. And let's face it, love, we never did a very good job. Your biological brother's name is Liam, and both of your parents are alive."

"Cole," I whisper, gripping his shirt. "I want to meet them. Tell me where…"

"Not today, sweetheart," he says, placing me down on a tiny bed in his spaceship. "You need to rest before anything else, because you are rambling like a lunatic."

"You're just upset because when I'm drunk, I'm smarter than you," I tell him stubbornly. What did I drink again? I remember a vodka bottle. It doesn't matter. "Come here," I demand, reaching up to grab Cole's wrist with both of my hands. I tug him down onto the tiny bed beside me.

He immediately moves to my side and wraps his arms around my waist, placing his head down beside mine on the pillow. I turn to look at him, and feel a deep sense of fulfilment and bliss spread through my body. The strange thing is that I didn't even need to walk twenty miles in order to earn this feeling. I've always felt happy and complete when Cole was lying next to me.

I reach out and place my fingers on his cheek, where I only just notice that there is a huge gash and several stitches. Grasping his hand, I interlace my fingers with his and squeeze tightly. "Are you really alive?" I ask him.

"Yes," he answers with a grin. "Don't I seem alive?"

"Maybe. There was a spider, before. I was hallucinating." I feel like there is something important

I need to say, but I can't quite remember. *Death.*
Someone is dead. My forehead creases with the effort
it takes to access my memory. "Also, I think Hansel
died in that story. The evil witch killed him. In her
oven."

"No," he assures me softly. "She meant to, but
they shoved the witch into the oven instead. The witch
burned."

A sleepy smile touches my lips.

"I guess she wasn't fireproof."

Chapter Thirty

sophie shields, 2016

I wake up, and my head is throbbing something fierce.

My throat is very dry and my tongue feels like sandpaper. I groan as I try to move, but every muscle in my body is incredibly sore and stiff. It takes a great effort to pry my eyelids open, and the little curtains of skin scrape over my dry eyeballs painfully.

I am lying on my side, facing a wall. There is a ledge running along that wall, and two pre-opened bottles of water sitting directly in my line of sight. There is also a chocolate bar. Oh, thank god for chocolate.

Reaching out to grasp one of the bottles, I find that I cannot move. I am imprisoned by a cocoon of blankets and a large arm wrapped tightly around my body. Looking down at the arm in surprise, my groggy brain wonders when Zack got such a deep California tan. It's kind of sexy.

And he's so warm. His entire body is pressed against mine like a man-shaped electric heating pad, with a velvety plush cover. I snuggle closer, sighing blissfully. There's something different about the way he holds me, something more intense than before. I can't quite put my finger on the difference. I am very thirsty, but I am so perfectly comfortable that I might consider dying of thirst to remain here like this.

I close my eyes and let sleep drift over me again.

But then an aroma tickles my nostrils.

My stomach growls in response. Is there real food nearby? I hadn't realized how hungry I am. It's a ravenous, ripping-meat-off-the-bone-with-my-teeth kind of hungry. Prying one eye open, I look at the chocolate bar again. I am startled to see that it isn't just any chocolate bar. It is my favorite chocolate bar.

So I can't die just yet, obviously.

Shrugging Zack's arm away, I reach out with determination, clenching my fist around the water bottle for starters. My throat is so dry that I don't think I could manage to swallow chocolate, meat, or anything else without some lubrication. But when I do this, I am startled by the sound of a man grunting behind me. And it isn't Zack's voice.

I release the water bottle and slowly turn back to look at the human-shaped object lying beside me. And I freeze. There is dark hair where I am expecting sandy blond. There is a wild and shaggy cut where I am expecting a fairly neat ex-military trim. There is sun-browned skin from long hours at construction sites, staring at buildings being made. There is a familiar bone structure, familiar skin sitting on top of those bones, and a familiar touch of stubble painted on last, like the garnish on a gourmet dish.

It's Cole.

Cole is here.

Cole is alive.

The events of the previous few days slowly come back to me as I rub my forehead and eyes. I reach for the water again and put it to my lips, but before I can drink, I hear a noise. My head turns to the right, where I see the door to Cole's trailer. Is there someone outside?

I place a hand on Cole's arm and silently shake him to alert him to the sounds. "Hey," I whisper. "Does anyone else know our location?"

He stirs in his sleep, but he doesn't wake up. There are more sounds from outside, like footsteps and the noise of something banging against metal.

"Cole," I say more urgently. "I think someone's here." My eyes dart toward the small gap beneath the door, where I see the shadow of shoes appear. I can almost swear that I recognize the particular shape of those shoes. There is a sharp knock at the door, which causes me to sit up a little straighter. Squinting, I can barely make out a third shadow beside the shoes—a slender shadow. Like a stick, or a… cane.

All the muscles in my body instantly grow tense, and my hand clenches around Cole's arm so tightly that my nails dig into his flesh. Could I have been followed? No. I was careful. I must have been tracked. The GPS locator in my car, or my phone? Does Cole have any electronics in this house? Of course he does. It's a stupid question. These days, there's always a way to find people, if you really want to find them.

"Cole!" I hiss softly. "Do you have a gun? Or a knife? Anything?"

But he won't wake up.

I can only stare in horror as the handle of the door opens to reveal a glare of sunlight. A person steps forward, the light glowing like a halo surrounding his head—and he is the last person who deserves to be wearing a halo. Before his face is even visible, I am sure of his identity. I see his hand move forward, clamped around the cane.

"Serena…" he says with a slow smile.

I scream. I throw my water bottle at him before rising to my feet and jumping over Cole to tackle the senator to the ground. He catches me and wrestles with me for a minute before pinning me to the grass. His slender build is surprisingly wiry and tough. When I catch sight of his face, I see something puzzling.

He looks younger. He looks the same as he did when I was twelve. Then, before my eyes, his youth begins to disappear. Deep wrinkles begin to crease his cheeks as his skin loses elasticity and sags, all while he is smiling at me. My hands falter in surprise, allowing his face to move closer to mine.

"Darling, I've been searching for you," he whispers, "for a very long time. See how old I've gotten?"

His skin withers into ash and falls all around me like dust, leaving only a skeleton. The skeleton wraps his bony hands around my neck and begins to choke me. I gasp and cry out, trying to pry his hands away from my neck, but they are too strong.

"Haven't you heard?" the skeleton asks, speaking clearly with no lips or tongue. "Death isn't death anymore. You will never escape me, no matter how hard you try."

When his bony hands begin to crush my windpipe, I claw at them madly as my whole body writhes to break free. I throw my head back, screaming at the top of my lungs.

"Scar!" Cole is shouting, clutching my shoulders tightly. "Wake up. It's just a dream."

My eyes snap open and I see that Cole is standing over me. I am still in bed, in the trailer. With my heart pounding out of control, I take several ragged breaths through my hoarse throat. It really does feel like I was just being strangled. Blinking several times, I allow my head to move around so I can orient myself with my surroundings. There is a delicious smell in the mobile home, like he's been cooking. And I've definitely been dreaming. *Or have I?*

"The door," I gasp, rubbing my neck. "I saw a shadow of Benjamin's shoes under the door."

Cole shakes his head, not even turning to look. "There is no gap under the door, Scar. This mobile home is watertight and airtight. It can actually float, if required, to survive floods, and even operate as a boat for brief periods of time."

It takes me a moment to process this, and I study the door for confirmation before looking back up to Cole. "Your spaceship is a submarine?"

"Not exactly a submarine…"

"An ark," I muse. "You built an ark."

He chuckles, reaching across me to retrieve a bottle of water. "You need to drink this," he says, offering me the plastic container.

As thirsty as I am, I ignore the bottle. "What if he finds us?" I ask. "Do you have anything that's transmitting a signal…"

"No way, Scar. Don't you think I know better? Look how hard it was for you to find me. If there was anything at all, you would have tracked my location almost instantly. We are completely off the grid here."

I take several deep breaths before putting the water to my lips and drinking. "Fine. I trust you." Then I look up and glower at him. "But you have to explain what you expected to accomplish by working with Benjamin. You have to explain a hell of a lot."

"Why don't you have something to eat first?" Cole asks. "I cooked for you. My specialty—and your favorite comfort food."

"Mac and cheese?" I ask in surprise, looking around in search of a kitchen.

"Not just any mac and cheese. Truffled mac and cheese."

I find myself frowning. "Where did you get the ingredients to make that? You asshole! You just came out here to the desert to enjoy sunsets and mac and cheese by yourself, forever? Forget everybody else? I don't understand. Why would you fake your own death? My head hurts, Cole."

"Shhh," he says, retrieving the empty water bottle. He sits and places his palm against my forehead to check my temperature. "I will answer all your questions soon, but I don't really feel up to discussing it right now."

"Do you have any way I can communicate with L.A.? I should probably send word to the detective, and tell Zack that I'm okay."

Cole abruptly stands up and moves away. He paces slightly, his body tense. Finally, he reaches for a glass of wine that is sitting on a desk, and lifts it gently, swirling the liquid. I think he is about to take a sip, but he turns and smashes it against the trailer wall instead, causing me to flinch. "You want to communicate with *them?* When you couldn't communicate with me? Why are you even here?"

He advances on me, a flash of anger in his dark eyes. "Why don't you just leave, Scarlett? Just run away like you always do. Take some water and head back to your car, and get the hell out of my life."

I stare at him for a second, in shock. His words are like daggers in my gut, and I can see the pain I've caused him, naked on his face. Images of the long trek over here dance through my mind as my pride forces me to shakily rise to my feet and move to the door. But when my hand is on the doorknob, my face softens. I turn back to look at him, feeling very vulnerable. "Cole…"

"I'm sorry," he says instantly, moving to wrap his arms around me. "I'm so sorry."

We stand there for a moment, embracing each

other. There is a heavy silence in the cabin now, containing years of unspoken words, longing, and oppressed emotions. The weight of it is so heavy that it's hard to stand. And he's right. Every time I've felt this way before, I have run away. He deserves to be upset.

"I'm broken, Scar," he says quietly, letting the words fall against my hair. "That's why I did this. I'm broken."

Pulling away slightly, I study his face.

"It wasn't the bullets," he tells me, "but they certainly didn't help. With all I've done, and how hard I tried—I just wasn't prepared to be shot at this point in my career. It made me feel like nothing mattered anymore. I just felt… alone. But I was broken long before this. I was trying to get better, going to therapy…"

"With Annabelle." I suddenly remember. "Cole, there's something I need to tell you."

"No, let me finish. You deserve an explanation. I worked so hard, Scarlett. I worked so hard that I just broke. And I couldn't even remember what I was working for anymore."

"So you take a vacation, Cole. A long sabbatical. Retire."

"Where?" he demands. "With who?"

"It doesn't matter. Anywhere. With anyone."

"You were gone. The only thing I could do to make it tolerable was to work ten times harder, all day, every day."

"Are you blaming this all on me?"

"No. I'm just stating the facts."

"It doesn't make sense, Cole. You have a thriving business. You have great friends and devoted employees. You can't just fake your own death and lie to everyone. You can't scare the shit out of the people who love you."

He pauses. "I didn't. I didn't lie to the people who I believed still loved me. They all know I'm fine."

"Cole. Do not make me hit you in the face again."

"Where were you, Scar? Where were you? I needed you. I always needed you."

I cannot respond. I shut my eyes and try to find the words. "Maybe this isn't enough. But I'm here now. And it wasn't easy getting here."

"I know. But it shouldn't have taken this—" he gestures around in frustration, "for us to be in the same room. In fact, I don't think I want to be in the same room if you're just going to disappear again. If you're just going to shut down and freak out and become someone else the moment I make a mistake. If you're just going to disappear the moment things get hard, and abandon me if there's a chance you might be pregnant. I'm not Benjamin!"

I feel suddenly drained. The world spins and I shut my eyes, trying to block out these memories. My first inclination is to turn to the door and grasp the handle and race back out into the desert. But when I try, I find both palms splayed against the wall and my mind going black. And red. And black. And red.

"Scar? Jesus, Scar. I didn't mean to bring it up. I'm sorry. Come back to me, please. Are you here?"

It takes me a moment. I breathe shakily.

"I need to lie down."

Cole guides me back to the small bed and kneels beside me, placing his forehead on my stomach and wrapping an arm around my hips. After I take several deep breaths to steady my own mind, I glance down at him. My heart aches to see him like this, on his knees. He looks almost prayerful in this position, and I can't resist running my fingers through his thick, dark hair.

"So maybe I did build an ark," he says suddenly, lifting his head to meet my gaze. "I was drowning in L.A., Scar. I just needed to pretend that the whole damn world got washed away, and it was just me and my little house. I just needed things to be simple."

"Things are simple," I tell him softly, brushing my thumb over the stitches on his cheek.

"It didn't feel simple. I was drowning in work. I was drowning without you. No matter what I did, I couldn't keep my head above water. When I got shot… it was just the final straw. It was my way out." He grasps my hand as it examines his injury and squeezes my fingers. "Wounds of the flesh never really bothered me, Scarlett. I'm just like you that way. You can get burned, beaten, raped—and you don't even notice. I'm the same. You know that about me. I've been starved, stabbed, shot, and lately, sued a whole lot, but I always got out of it alive. But you know what I couldn't take? Being away from you. It wore me down."

Only then do I notice how weary he looks. He has lost some weight. After Cole's experience in prison, he always made sure to work out regularly and keep himself in shape, but he's a little leaner than I remember. I reach out and touch his shoulder, where I know there's a tattoo under his shirt that matches the necklace he gave me. I sigh.

"Did you really make truffled mac and cheese?"

"Is that so hard to believe?" He scoffs. "I've been watching a lot of cooking shows lately. But I only have a few 'luxury' ingredients here; I mostly packed MREs for the road."

"Do you remember," I ask him softly, "when you couldn't even make Kraft Dinner?"

He smiles. "I was bad at a lot of things when we were in college. Cut me some slack."

I run my fingers through his hair idly. "You were never bad at anything. Those were good days." After a few seconds of reminiscence, my fingers pause and I swallow. "Cole? I'm sorry. I'm sorry that I was so scared. I'm sorry that I ran away."

His face displays a host of conflicting emotions, and he buries his forehead in my stomach to hide them. Wrapping his arms around my body, he draws a deep breath. "Just don't do it again. Just stay."

I let my fingers drift over his back, and I discover a lumpiness that can only be another bandage under his clothes. "Stay here?" I ask.

"Why not? I have everything we could need for years."

I hesitate. "We're going to have to go back to civilization to sort out a few things…"

"I don't want to think about that now, Scar. I can't think about that now. Just promise you'll stay with me, no matter where I go. Desert, city, forest, mountain, ocean. You came all this way, and I'm not going to let you walk away again. Promise me."

"Cole... I would love nothing more. But life gets in the way, sometimes."

"No. It doesn't. We won't let it," he says firmly, looking up at me with blazing eyes. "Life is *not* stronger than we are. Come on. Can you stop being difficult for five minutes? Can you just hold me and say nice things? You can go back to being realistic tomorrow. You can punch me in the face tomorrow. For this moment, I just want it to be you and me again, like it used to be. The whole world can burn for all I care. Everything else can disappear."

I don't know what to say. Reaching out to grasp his shoulders, I weakly pull him up onto the bed beside me. He wraps his arms around me and kisses each of my eyelids before resting his chin on top of my head.

Everything is a mess. My brain is a mess, my body is a mess, and my life is a mess. My thoughts are swirling in a chaotic jumble, and I can't make sense of what I'm supposed to do next. Between nightmares of Benjamin and worry over Annabelle, I feel like I'm failing everything. But I do know that Cole's touch is calming, and the warmth of his body slowly erodes my fears and anxieties. I try to hold onto my concerns, to keep me sane, but his closeness makes me forget about all the noise and drama outside of this little trailer. Nothing matters outside of us.

Maybe I needed to escape and hide away out here with him, too. For a little.

"Scar?" he asks, tightening his grip on me. "Whatever happens now, promise me we'll face it together. I never want you to leave my side again."

"We've been apart for a long time," I tell him softly, resting my cheek against his shirt. "We've both changed, and we should take some time to get to know each other again before making any crazy declarations."

"That's stupid, Scar. I've always known you— better than I know myself."

"I'm not even Scarlett anymore. I'm Sophie now."

He laughs lightly, and I can feel the low rumble in his chest. "Whatever you call yourself, my love, wherever you go, whoever you become—it doesn't matter. There's something unchangeable at your core, something that calls out to me. And I recognize you."

"What do you recognize?" I ask him stubbornly.

"We were always meant to be together. You can fight it all you want, or run away, or roll your eyes. But I know how this ends: on the last day of your life, you're going to be lying right here beside me, a wrinkly old woman with silver hair, and you're going to have to finally admit that some things are real. Some things last forever. And I'm going to say 'I told you so.'"

I pull away to check if he is serious—but of course, he always is. "No way," I argue. "Bet you fifty bucks."

Cole's eyebrows lift slightly as a grin settles on his lips.

"You're on."

The End

Now available:

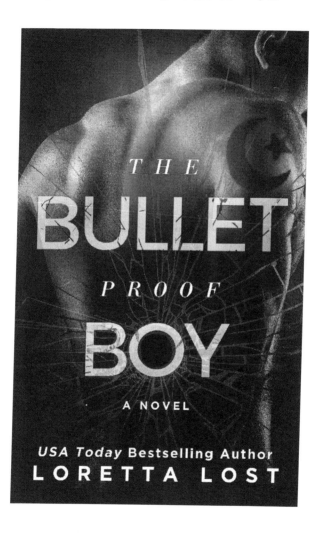

THE
BULLET
PROOF
BOY

A NOVEL

USA Today Bestselling Author
LORETTA LOST

The Bulletproof Boy

Sophie is given an opportunity to meet her biological family for the first time, but she is hesitant. Cole learns about Annabelle's death, and has to decide whether to go back to society and risk revealing that he is alive. More is discovered about the woman who shot Cole, and Benjamin resurfaces, on the hunt for his missing daughter.

Sophie would love nothing more than to hide away with Cole in their remote location in the desert forever. But she has unfinished business with Zack and Detective Rodriguez back in L.A., not to mention her job in Washington D.C. where she promised her boss she'd return for after-work cocktails.

For the first time, Sophie is feeling torn between her separate lives and identities. But when Benjamin starts becoming more aggressive in his attempts to find her, no identity or location might be safe any longer…

Visit Loretta's website for information about the new release! You can also subscribe to her email to be notified about new books.

www.LorettaLost.com

Thanks for reading!
Join Loretta's mailing list to be
notified of new books.
You will receive a free book
for signing up!
www.LorettaLost.com

Acknowledgments

For my mother. Thank you for teaching me what it feels like to be alone.

Nicolas, you always complained that my male characters were assholes. I just thought they were realistic. But you were right; we need at least one hero with no crippling flaws. Thanks for always challenging me to be better, and always being there.

Cecilia, thanks for joining my late night writing sessions at Denny's, and for always bugging me to email you the next chapter. I'm glad that you are back in my life. Now, please stop smoking so you can stay that way.

Gary, thanks for always checking up on my progress, and encouraging me. You always brighten my day with your kindness and jokes.

Ada, I am so sorry for how difficult this last year has been. I know that you will use all that pain as jet fuel to accomplish great things. Thanks for all your help with this book, and I really hope to be reading some of your new work soon!

Electra, thanks for the insight into the academic life of a genius fifteen-year-old, because it's been a while since I was one. Hit me up anytime for help with your papers; compared to writing books, they are just easy-peasy-lemon-squeezy!

Alex, thank you for spending so many hours working with me. I really enjoyed your company—until you got overwhelmed and gave up on your own book. Someday, I hope you get to the finish line.

Tommy, we met when I was twelve, and you were much older. We've been talking a lot lately, because this story takes me back to those years. I often wonder why I bother to keep in touch with someone like you. Thank you for showing me how cruel people can be to a young girl, and what an impact it causes when she has no one else.

Conner, you made things so much harder, when you really didn't have to. Things were already hard. I know that sometimes you tried your best, but most of the time, you didn't try at all. Then, there were those moments we'll never forget when you tried your worst. It will always be a part of my writing.

Thank you for going away, and setting me free.

Other books by
Loretta Lost

The Clarity Series:

Clarity
Clarity 2
Clarity 3
Clarity 4: After the Storm
Clarity 5: Loving Liam

*Note: The hero of the Clarity series is Sophie's
biological brother Liam Larson. However, he does
not discover Sophie's existence until book 5 of
Clarity, where Sophie makes her first appearance.*

The End of Eternity Series:

End of Eternity
End of Eternity 2
End of Eternity 3
End of Eternity 4

The Clarity Series

clarity

book one

loretta lost

Her world has always been dark, but he might be able to change everything...

Fiercely independent Helen Winters was born completely blind, but she vowed never to let her disability keep her down. She did not expect a traumatic event to devastate her life and force her to drop out of college. Disillusioned by the cruelty of people, Helen retreated from society to live by herself as a reclusive writer in the woods--where no one could ever hurt her again.

When a brilliant young doctor shows up on her doorstep, promising her that his new research can give her the ability to see for the first time, Helen stubbornly refuses. She has learned not to trust anyone, and to rely only on herself. But Dr. Liam Larson will not take no for an answer. He makes it his personal mission to rescue Helen from her loneliness, and bring joy into her world once more--the joy she has denied herself for so long.

When Helen's demons come racing back into her life, threatening to rip her apart and destroy the strength she has carefully rebuilt, Liam is the only one who might be able to save her. Can he reach the broken girl in time, helping her to heal and see the world in a different light? Or will Helen's grief send her spiraling out of control, lost to him forever?

End of Eternity Series

She lost
her husband.
Did she also
lose her mind?

end of
ETERNITY
book one

USA Today Bestselling Author
LORETTA LOST

*You never really know the person you've married...
until it's too late.*

Pregnant heiress Carmen Winters goes into shock when
she comes home to find her husband hanging from a
chandelier. Her immediate thoughts concern whether
she should snap a photo for social media.

As she gathers her wits, she begins to question the
events surrounding her husband's death, and suspect
that her estranged sister was the last person to see him
alive. Carmen's quest to understand the suicide is
complicated by her difficult pregnancy and aggressive
advances from her late husband's best friend.

Determined to soldier through the tragedy, Carmen
soon discovers information about her husband that
makes her realize her entire life was a lie...

USA Today bestselling author Loretta Lost writes to experience all the love and excitement that can often be lacking from real life. She finds it therapeutic to explore her issues through the eyes of a different person. She hopes to have a family someday, but until then her characters will do nicely.

Loretta has recently discovered Instagram, and she is now obsessed. Follow @loretta.lost for cute photos of her cat reading books. He refuses to cooperate unless they are really good books.

You can also subscribe to Loretta's mailing list for updates: www.eepurl.com/O0WTL

Connect with the author:

Facebook: facebook.com/LorettaLost
Instagram: @Loretta.Lost
Twitter: @LorettaLost
Website: www.LorettaLost.com
Email: Loretta.Lost@hotmail.com

Made in the USA
Charleston, SC
14 March 2017